Nigel Watts

Nigel Watts was born in Winchester in 1957. He spent two years in Japan where he wrote a large part of THE LIFE GAME, his first novel. This was awarded the Betty Trask Award in 1989 and was followed by BILLY BAYSWATER in 1990, which was shortlisted for the *Mail on Sunday*–John Llewellyn Rhys Prize, and WE ALL LIVE IN A HOUSE CALLED INNOCENCE in 1992. Nigel Watts has a PhD in Creative Writing from the University of East Anglia. He is married and divides his time between Dorset and Richmond.

SCEPTRE

Also by Nigel Watts and published by Sceptre

Billy Bayswater
The Life Game
We All Live in a House Called Innocence

Twenty Twenty

NIGEL WATTS

SCEPTRE

Extract from 'The Heart of the World'
© Alan Ereira, published by Jonathan Cape

Copyright © Nigel Watts 1995

First published in 1995 by Hodder and Stoughton
First published in paperback in 1995 by Hodder and Stoughton
A division of Hodder Headline PLC
A Sceptre Paperback

British Library Cataloguing in Publication Data

Watts, Nigels
  Twenty Twenty
  I. Title
  823.914 [F]

ISBN 0 340 64028 6

Printed and bound in Great Britain by
Cox and Wyman Ltd, Reading, Berkshire

Hodder and Stoughton
A division of Hodder Headline PLC
338 Euston Road
London NW1 3BH

Acknowledgements ∫

I am indebted to the monographs of Gerardo Reichel-Dolmatoff and to Alan Ereira, author of *The Heart of The World* (published by Jonathan Cape) and director of the television documentary of the same name, for information about the Kogi. The italicised discourse of the Kogi within the novel is taken verbatim from these sources. Mama Francisco is fictional, as is the UN Circuitry Database's use of the map stone, but other than these I have embellished or invented nothing about the Kogi: as far as I know, this is an accurate picture of their society and philosophy.

At the time of writing, the Kogi are thought to number eleven thousand. The Tairona Heritage Trust was established in 1990 as a response to Alan Ereira's book and film. The aims of the Tairona Heritage Trust are:

(a) to publicise the Kogi message

(b) to buy back ancestral land within the Sierra

(c) to allow all the surviving peoples of the Tairona civilisation the opportunity to benefit directly from world-wide interest in them.

The UK address of the Trust is: Chisholme House
Roberton nr Hawick
Rox
Scotland TD9 7PH

I am grateful for the financial support of The Oppenheim-John Downes Memorial Trust, the K Blundell Trust, and Joane Watts in writing this book.

For editorial input, ideas and support, I thank: Jon Cook and Malcolm Bradbury of the University of East Anglia, Bryan Keniry of IBM and the world, Ken Fegradoe (author of *Quantum Man*), my friends David Templer and Sara Marks, and of course, Sahera, my wife.

1

This is it. Seven hours of bone-shaking, freezing ride through almost total white-out, and here I am. Tulkina. I can hardly believe I've made it. From a distance I wasn't sure; the blankness has been playing tricks on my eyes and at first the village winked in and out of sight like a mirage, white roofs and walls appearing and disappearing against the backdrop of snow. But now I'm closer I can see its familiar ugliness is real: power lines criss-crossing the sky, squat bungalows like the shanty towns I had flown over the day before. Civilisation.

I drive past a triangular sign stuck into an oil drum and weighted down with rocks. Tulkina, pop.143 it says. The number clicks over in my mind as I drive past: 144. Into the village and I'm in the street's embrace, looking left and right at the buildings. The settlement is low and flat and desolate, but I don't think I've ever been so pleased to see the handiwork of an architect. I hate myself for my irresolution. Here I am, the first day of my new life and I face the very thing I'm running from with the idiot grin of a junkie.

Telegraph poles line the road like crucifixes, black against the snow, their lines slack and swaying in the wind. From where I am, I can see that the town consists of two streets, laid out in a giant cross. Pausing at the junction, I kill the engine and open the cab door to listen, but my ears are ringing. It's too cold to keep the door open for more than a moment, so I slam it and then realise I was warned against switching off the engine. I pump the gas pedal and then press the ignition button. The halftrack roars into life, starting up its rattling again. It's so cold up here, people keep their motors running for six months rather than face the task of unthawing a frozen engine.

The street is almost as wide as it is long. The snow is unmarked, no sign of the other one hundred and forty-three residents. Jack said a lot of folk had left; more polar bears than people, he told me. Should suit you fine.

I drive down the street, steering with my elbows, my fingertips in my mouth. The cold is slowing down my thoughts. The most extraordinary landscape I've ever seen, and my mind is as blank as the snow. Every building looks the same: flimsy white-walled things that look like retirement bungalows. I pause in front of one and look through its window, but it seems empty. What sort of people live here? This is supposed to be Canada, the year 2020, and I could be on the moon for all I recognise.

You can't miss the factory, he said. A two-storey white building on the end. I pass boarded-up shop fronts, snow drifts half way up their windows, metal shutters padlocked against God knows what. A movement catches my eye, a length of detached clapboard swinging in the wind.

I'm out of my depth and I know it. I'm a speck on a map, a hundred and sixty miles from the nearest town. Seven hours into the Arctic, and scared out of my mind. Nobody told me it would be like this. I lost the road from Inuvik three times, only aware I was driving over the tundra because my compass said so. I had to retrace my tracks, inching along with the headlights on, not daring to think about what would happen if I lost them. Three times I found my way back to the road, sweating in spite of the cold. Perspiration cooled down the inside of my shirt and though I stuffed a hand towel against my skin, my back is still clammy. The warmth of the air heater doesn't get past my ankles.

But at least I've arrived. This is what I was looking for, the huge horizon, the scraped clean landscape. I want to take my mask off and breathe the air, but the cab is full of diesel fumes and I'd probably throw up. Gasoline: another thing I'm reacting to.

The end of the street opens into a snowfield. This is as far as I can go. Any further north and I'll be off the map. But there it is on the end, unbelievable – Berry Lofgren's Twine Works. How many thousand miles have I come? A miracle I have found it.

I stop the halftrack and rub the fog off the windscreen with the back of my hand. It's a factory, just as he said. Square as a sugar cube, big as a castle; two storeys. And the last building on the block, nothing between me and the north pole but snow. A sudden gust rocks the vehicle, gritty snow thrown against the windscreen.

The ice rink in front of me is the Beaufort Sea, nothing to mark where the land ends and salt water begins. It's beautiful, in a frightening way. This was here all the time, this frozen backdrop, more space than I've ever seen. Why didn't I come here before? Why wait until I was suffocated by the city? The snow is baby blue, like the sky on a spring day. In the distance it edges into white, the only marks in its uniformity caused by the shadows of pressure ridges off shore, mounds of ice forced upwards like waves. Animals live in this desert, I realise, human beings as well. And I thought the hothouse I have come from was everything.

There's a kind of covered docking area to the side of the factory, so I park in it and leave the engine running. I check the outside temperature: minus 28. They told me at the airport that the weather should be getting warmer from now on. But don't blink they said, or you'll miss summer. I study the walls before I get out, waiting for the exhaust fumes to disperse. Concrete blocks, smeary hand marks over the whitewash, a painted sign: ALL VISITORS TO REPORT TO OFFICE. A stack of tyres is in the corner, a red oil-can perched on top. I struggle into my down-filled jacket. The price tag is still attached to the sleeve and I snap it off. They cheated me in Inuvik, charging me ten per cent surtax because I couldn't pay hard cash, but I couldn't care less. That is the last time I will ever be cheated. I am free now, free from ambition and automobiles and money and talking. I have washed my hands of society. From now on, it's me. Nothing will break my silence. I pull my lumberjack hat on, take a deep breath and open the van door. Here I go.

The cement floor is icy, and the first foot I place on the ground slips from under me. I twist and catch myself against the door handle, tearing an L-shaped rip in the arm of the jacket. Shit. I steady myself and then the cold hits me like a body-tackle. I cling onto the door, but the skin of my fingers is sticking to the metal and I have to let go.

I put on my gloves and pull the hat tighter onto my head. An image comes to me: freezing to death, mummified like a mammoth in a glacier. They'd find me in ten thousand years time, after all this is over, alien scientists defrosting my corpse: *homo nonsapiens*. Good luck to them, they are welcome to every last frozen corpuscle.

Steadying myself against the walls, I gingerly explore the ground floor. It feels as though somebody is pressing a line of ice cubes to my belly, but it's just where I haven't buttoned the wind flap over the zip. The cold is pinching my face and my vision is sparkling with tears. Through a doorway I can see a drive-in loading bay. Ice has drifted against one wall, melted and then refrozen, looking rotten like the insides of a defrosting freezer. Wooden pallets and a mound of unidentifiable vegetable matter are piled against the wall of an office. It looks as though it has been deserted for years. I can feel the cold coming through the soles of my boots, so I stamp my feet.

The silence after the constant row of the halftrack seems complete. I feel like the last man on earth, so cold I could be naked. I was warned against the wind, but I didn't imagine anything like this. There's nothing to stop it blowing as hard as it likes – no hills, no trees, no buildings. I hurry round to the back, almost losing my footing on the corner, and find the generator where Jack said it would be, in a lean-to by the back door. The doors have been painted green and pink, and are held together by a frayed length of nylon string. I have to take off my gloves to unknot the string, and within seconds my fingers refuse to bend, useless as frozen sausages. I scrabble at the knot, and then yank at it until the string frays into nothingness. I open both doors wide and shelter behind one of them. Even with my gloves back on, my hands have lost all their feeling. I've never felt so cold in my life.

The generator looks like a giant cockroach dipped in treacle. Jack was worried that I wouldn't be able to get it started, and I can see why now. If I can't get this thing working, it's going to be candlepower and seal fat lanterns.

I wipe the grime off the fuel gauge – half full. Jack made me bring a ten-gallon drum of gasoline, but it looks like I won't need it for a while. My calf muscles are so tight with the cold they hurt. I jog on the spot, looking for its start button. I feel as though I'm in the grip of a huge animal, squeezing the life out of me.

I turn the fuel on and press what looks like a button, but nothing happens. Forcing myself to concentrate, I try to work out how the thing functions. There's a mystery here I don't understand. I trace the fuel line from the tank to the body of the beast, but the only thing I recognise is a spark plug. I wipe it with a rag and replace the cap, but it makes no difference. I'm tired and cold and it's time a miracle happened.

Suddenly I can feel fear snapping at my heels. I can remember being a child, cliff scrambling at the seaside, climbing up to a ledge and getting stuck. Can't go up, can't go down. It's a long drop and I'm praying to God to get me out of this mess, vowing never to do anything so stupid again.

Now what have I gotten myself into? I could be at home, in a warm bubble, watching the end of civilisation on TV, but here I am fumbling with numb fingers in a shed in the middle of nowhere.

Not even two weeks ago, I was living my life according to plan. A year or two from compulsory retirement, pension fund at the ready, comfortable home. And then I started sneezing.

I straighten up and smear the tears of cold from my eyes. I'm not used to physical threat. I can't believe that if I don't get this generator working, my life could be in danger. I laugh in spite of myself. My life *is* in danger – guaranteed.

Then I spot the crank handle. It's like an old Model T. It doesn't want to turn at first, but I push against it until it moves, and then jerk it into action. Two more turns on the handle and it coughs into life.

I hurry out of the shed while the machine disappears in a cloud of acrid smoke. I make sure I'm upwind of it, and watch until the smoke clears and I'm sure that the shed hasn't caught fire. The generator is chugging erratically, pausing to clear its throat, but after a minute it settles down to a steady hum. I kick the doors shut and then hurry round to the front of the building. My exposed skin – an inch between the bridge of my nose and my eyebrows – is burning, my eyes watering so badly I have to blink almost constantly.

Jack said a service elevator would take me to the second floor. I find it in the corner and the door opens when I press the button. Bravo – electricity! The lattice gate is fixed with a padlock, and I try the most likely looking key from the bunch Jack gave me. The steel padlock is too cold to hold for long, even with my gloves, and I have to jiggle the key into place. It opens easily, and I push the gate back. I can smell diesel even through the mask, so I stay on the threshold. The elevator is like a small room, its metal sides scored with marks from a forklift. Only one way: up. My toes are curling under the grip of the cold, so I go back to the truck and start unloading.

I would have come with nothing, but Jack insisted on compiling a list for me. He's done a good job. There's something we're bound to have forgotten, but I haven't discovered it yet. I was reluctant to buy more stuff. The tyranny of shopping is one of the things I was glad to escape, but I guess it was sensible: food and water, solar still, pneumatic mattress, hollowfibre quilt, silk underclothes. Medication. Together with the hire of the halftrack, it has cost me an arm and a leg, but what price Custer's last stand?

A little bit of exercise and I'm warmer already. I pause from unloading the van and take off my mask. The air is sparkling with tiny ice crystals, and it's too cold to inhale, so I take nips of air, trying to smell what's on offer. Nothing – just coldness. I pause to listen, but there is no sound other than the muffled drone of the generator.

Calculating food intake on a calorie per day basis, I have enough canned and dried food for one month. I was assured that there would be a local store, but it's nearly thirty years since Jack was last here, and things look quieter than he described. A month is enough, anyway.

I put my mask back on, and go up in the elevator. The machine wheezes and judders, but it gets me to the second floor. I pause before I press the button to open the doors. I've come fifteen hundred miles on the strength of a childhood memory, so let's hope Jack remembers well. He had inherited the factory from Uncle Berry – dead five years, but out of business twice that long. Jack used to play here as a kid, helping the machine operators load the twine, being teased by Eskimo women with unpronouncable names, scared to death of the black rats that used to live in the bales of hemp. The keys had been sent with a bundle of letters and a collection of mildly pornographic nineteenth century postcards via a lawyer. Jack was a good friend, he wasn't about to refuse my request, but I could see he wasn't too happy. We went through the motions of agreeing how long I would stay, but nobody was fooled. I wanted to reassure him that when the time came I would leave it tidy, but how do you form the words in your mouth?

I jab the button to open the door and slide open the gate. The first impression is one of size. The room is probably sixty feet long, twenty feet wide. Windows line two sides; the street and the snow field. The lift doors want to shut, so I wedge them open with a heavy box of canned food, and step into the room.

I can't believe I'm going to live here for the rest of my life. It's a factory, for Christ's sake, fifteen foot ceiling, half an acre of wooden floorboards. The floor is grey with dirt and littered with spools of twine. Some kind of dusty machinery is jumbled at both ends of the room. Empty tea chests, cardboard boxes bulging with ledgers and files, burlap bags – doubtless home to the famous black rats. It's going to take me weeks to make it habitable. And there are probably twenty things I'm allergic to here.

I walk to the windows at the far end and look out. They were designed for illumination, not the view. This is north-facing, looking over the bay. It's like being on a ship on a misty day, the join of the horizon invisible; just a pale grey void. I could be facing a whitewashed wall for all the difference it makes.

Carla tried to persuade me to see the medics, but I dismissed the sneezing as a summer cold. I wasn't about to admit anything. When the rash appeared I kept it a secret from her and made an appointment for the Test.

It was a day like any other. It was dry so I cycled to work, a couple of tutorials in the afternoon, and then an appointment with the university doctor. The Test takes thirty seconds; half a minute to turn a life around. The results were no surprise. I was issued with a mask, given an appointment with a counsellor and a prescription for the pharmacy. The doctor declined to shake my hand when I thanked him for his time. My card would be amended as soon as I was out of the room: INFECTED.

In the corridor I pocketed the mask. Illegal, I know, but I wasn't ready to advertise my health status. I strolled outside, calm as ever. It was when I found my bike had been stolen that something tore inside me. It wasn't as though it hadn't happened before. The third time, in fact. I didn't bother to report its loss, instead I went to the bus stop, caught the bus and sat at the back. When we passed my road I didn't move. By that time some part of me had already decided I would never go home again. I turned to watch the bus stop receding as we drove off, and then I just sat and looked out of the window. The sun was shining, it was just another day. We drove through the suburbs, an area I knew well enough, but it was as though I was seeing it for the first time. The roads, the neat houses, the gardens.

I had no idea how long the journey would last. I wasn't really thinking. We drove for a couple of hours, people getting on and getting off. The suburbs seemed to go on for ever, a gradual degradation until it was one ghetto after another. The road became so bumpy with the pot-holes I had to hold onto my seat. I wondered how I could have lived in a city for twenty-five years and never seen this side of it.

Some Hispanic kids got on and started making threatening noises, swinging from the straps in front of me, calling me names, but I was too tired to take much notice. I thought of showing them my mask to frighten them off, but they were probably infected themselves.

Some time in there my phone rang, but I didn't answer. Carla, I expect, checking where I was. I just let it ring, meeting the annoyed stare of an old woman who turned in her seat to look at me.

At the last stop, the driver switched off the engine and told me I had to get off. I was the only remaining passenger and the driver waited impatiently as I walked the length of the bus. I was in no hurry. I neither knew where I was nor where I was going. I paused to have a word with him, but he'd switched his intercom off and only stared at me, just as the old woman had done. For a moment I wondered if there was something about my appearance I was unaware of – perhaps my infection was visible to everybody? I asked him where I was, but he couldn't hear me, and made no effort to switch on his intercom. Presumably all he heard was the muffled voice of an old man mouthing something through half inch glass.

I went to a cheap hotel and checked in. I had only the clothes I stood up in, a briefcase with my students' assignment cards and a reader. Hotel Belleview, room 306: the belle view was of a football field, which I sat and stared at until it was dark. I phoned Carla and told her the news. She cried. I refused to tell her where I was.

I smashed my phone to pieces on the mock fireplace of my room and considered ways to kill myself. I suppose I slept that night. On the second night it rained. It was years since I had walked in the rain, but now there was nothing to stop me. I walked round the football field, my head tilted back, my mouth open, tasting the bitterness of the rain. Crossing the road back to the hotel, a car swerved to try and run me over.

When the hotel owner saw how wet I was he took a pistol from under the counter and told me to leave. He kept the gun on me while a bellboy fetched my case from the room. It was the first time I experienced the power the plague gives its victims.

My reactions had been getting so bad I had to leave the hotel anyway. Weals had appeared under the skin on my legs. They itched like hell, and as I stood dripping in the foyer, scratching one leg against another, the discomfort was all that mattered. I couldn't think about the future.

And then I remembered Jack and his uncle's factory. I got in touch with him and explained I needed a holiday. No point in scaring him over the phone. He knew the sound of a man in trouble, and didn't ask me about it. When I collected the keys from him that night, he could see the state I was in. I did him the courtesy of wearing my mask, and waiting on his porch. He did me the courtesy of not asking how long I'd been infected. He compiled a list of things I would need, explained how to find the factory and then drove me to the airport. Brave man.

I managed to book a flight for the next morning. My datafile had already been changed. Nobody said anything, but I was allocated a seat in the secluded zone of the airplane. Another advantage of my changed status, I had the place to myself.

I ate nothing on the plane. I was beginning to discover the extent of my reactions. Milk was out. Flour products. Coffee. I drank bottled water and stared through the window, imagining myself a tiny person flying over a beach at low tide. It went on and on and on. Sometimes we passed over settlements like elaborate sandcastles, and then it went white. The first sight of snow was like surf. And here I am.

My skin is already tingling with all the dust in the air. The dust is penetrating my mask, making the base of my nose itch. I haven't seen so much filth for years.

In the corner is a door. It's unlocked, and I open it. It's supposed to lead to a fire escape, but the metal staircase has come adrift from the wall and is hanging uselessly in space. The drop to the snowy ground is twenty-five feet. This snow is as hard as cement, enough of a fall to break a leg. I shut the door and turn to face the room.

'Perfect.'

2

Judging from the angle, you are lying on your back, staring upwards. It's so dark, you could be outside, but you know the walls of the hut surround you. So easy to get lost in here. You count seven concentric rings of reed woven into the thatched roof, circles within circles. You guess there are more, but the conical roof disappears in smoke and darkness. The murmuring of conversation from the shadows is like an erratic engine running. No good focusing on the sound, it's dipping in and out of auditory threshold level. A rooster crows outside. It must be morning. Letting your eye drift upwards with the smoke from the four fires, you slip past the cross-beams of the roof and through the gap at the apex. You can't be more than six inches across to make it through the chimney vent. The smoke is plausible, but no unpleasant stinging in the eyes. Out in the open, you breathe deeply, smelling the morning: a fresh lettuce thrust into your face.

Nice one, Jarnier.

You see your words print out as you speak them – blue subtitles across the bottom of your vision.

Up.

You let yourself go higher and higher, floating twenty, fifty, a hundred feet above the hut. Looking down, you assess the regularity of the compound: a wheel of thatched huts, the larger meeting house as their hub, a streamer of smoke being pulled from its pronged chimney vent. Beaten earth, a black pig nuzzling in a heap of vegetable compost. Two palominos tied to a post. It's cooler up here. You rise further still, the ground becoming hazy as you glide above the jungle flanks of the mountain. A macaw screeches below you and to your left. Layers of mist hang like cobwebs between the trees. Higher still, and you're in low cloud, your skin prickling with the cold damp.

Stop.

You roll onto your back, tempted to close your eyes and sleep here. But it's uncomfortably fresh, almost burning your lungs as you breathe in.

The two operators hadn't seen Dr Beecham come in, and when he spoke, they looked up in surprise.

'What's going on?' Beecham said, referring to the screen.

'He's lost in cloud.'

The project director watched the high resolution screen for a moment. Glimpses of trees were visible through the mist, but there was no telling where he was. 'How long has he been in?'

'Forty-seven hours, fourteen minutes.'

'And sleep?'

'Just under eight hours in three periods.'

Beecham wished he had that sort of energy. He was sleeping more and more recently, afternoon naps as well. Old age was catching up on him. He pushed back his old-fashioned spectacles and nodded at the screen. 'How long has this been going on?'

'A couple of minutes. He's tiring. Getting clumsy.'

Something had gone wrong with the air-conditioning. This was the third time in as many weeks that maintenance had had to be called out. If only they were allowed to open the windows, at least some of the desert breeze would stir the stuffy air, but until the air-con was fixed everyone would just have to sweat in their one-piece, disposable suits.

The temperature was nothing compared to what William had gone through over the last two days. Jarnier had ruled out ambient temperature control. This was to be as authentic as they could get, and if he was in a South American rain forest, he would have to stew. No tourist comforts here; the only parameters in the program were those of Jarnier's imagination. There was a control override. They weren't going to risk losing a valuable test pilot through stupidity, but the haptic feedback mechanism could snap a human arm as easily as a twig. But it wasn't the exoskeleton which posed the problem, the danger was in such extended immersion. Nearly forty-eight hours, Beecham knew he was pushing his luck, but there was no secret about his remit: iron out the kinks in the system and see how much their best pilot could take. If they stood any chance of selling this on the open market, they would have to convince the HSE it was safe. Any more civilian casualties and Omnisens could be litigated out of business.

The director walked to the data bank and ran his eyes over the read-outs. Temperature, heart beat, brain waves, blood sugar level. William's core temperature was 35 degrees and dropping. With bodily activity lowered, even the best test pilot's metabolism turned sluggish. If this ever made it as a commercial program, they would have to do something about that. A visual display, probably. Likewise nutrient and liquid levels. William had lost 250 grams of body fluids in the heat of the hut, and though he may have thought he was sucking up moisture from the cloud, the vapour existed only as minute electrical impulses. The sweat in his suit had vacuum-dried as soon as it had left his body; if his salt level dropped any further, he'd have to be signalled to take a drink. It hadn't taken them long to learn that the body would forget itself once lost in a synthetic reality.

The monitor above their heads showed a mass of swirling grey and white clouds. William was supine at an altitude of seventy-two metres, and rising again. Much longer, and he'd be off the program.

The pilot was young and in good shape, no sign yet of dislocation. He could probably endure a lot more of this, but it was too early to be reckless. He pulled the microphone towards himself. 'William. This is Dr Beecham. Respond, please.'

He glanced at the screen, watching the sentence appearing as surtitles above the swirling cloud. Damn this computer, it could never spell his name right: it had come out as 'Beechum' again.

Confirmation took a few seconds to come. The longest Beecham had tried deep immersion was a couple of hours. He couldn't imagine how disorientating it must be for these youngsters. A couple of days in a make-believe universe, it was a wonder more of them didn't crack up. The test pilot's reaction time was slowing, but he was still on his toes.

Beecham had flown simulators in the early days, worked on the early reality engines, but his first deep immersion in virtuality shocked him. When the face mask was pulled off, he felt as though he'd been suddenly awakened from a dream. He'd pretended to recover quickly, but it was seconds before he could function, minutes before he could shake free from the experience. If a couple of hours could do that, he could see how extended immersion could unloosen the tiny screws that hold our reality together.

Ready.

'Get out of that cloud, and stop clowning around.'

Yes, sir.

Beecham watched a second screen. It showed the figure of a man strapped into a complex harness. William Morrison, twenty-seven years old, graduate of Washington University and the Institute advanced training program. A lot of these young pilots were screwballs, computer addicts whose idea of fun was to spend the day in cyberspace, but those who made it to the top were frighteningly normal. There was no room in psychological endurance testing for anyone less than a complete package. Any cracks and they would fragment under the assault course that had been invented for them. Beecham disliked these elite pilots – mostly women – not just because of their absence of humour and imagination, but because of his guilt. These people were neural cannon fodder. It was only a matter of time before they were invalided out of the company.

William had been floating there for nearly two days, his body ignored by the programmers. That was just the wetware. It was the large monitor they were interested in, computer graphics so distinct it was like looking out of a window. Eighty million polygons per second, a degree of resolution too sophisticated for the human eye. It would take an eagle with eyeglasses to appreciate the detail it was capable of offering.

Down.

The view on the monitor slid so quickly before their eyes, it was hard to see what was happening. The spinning image of a wooden hut flashed by. Digits in the upper left corner of the screen indicated he was dropping at a virtual altitude of ten metres a second. The screen suddenly filled with fluorescent green hexagons.

'He's off the program, sir.'

'Pull him out.'

The operator tapped a couple of digits on the keyboard in front of him. 'We're going to unhook you now, William.'

There was a moment's delay before the pilot's words came from the speakers beside the screen.

Okay.

'You ready?'

Ready.

Beecham nodded for the man to go ahead. The huge monitor went blank, and their eyes turned to the second screen. Two technicians entered the test room and began detaching William from the girdle. The body suit had been designed by NASA, and it looked like it. It was an astronaut's suit, cumbersome on the ground, but in the exoskeleton you could swim like an eel, fly like a humming bird.

'Get Dr Kinderling on the phone for me,' Beecham said. The director watched the catheter being unscrewed as he waited for Kinderling to answer his phone. He remembered the early days when teledildonics was the craze. Things had changed now. Porno had been left way behind; the new puritanism had made sure of that. Sex was for kids and deviants; the serious money was in reality holidays. And in litigation against software companies. Omnisens was surviving only because its lawyers were keeping one step ahead of the pack.

The technician handed Beecham the phone. 'Kinderling? We've taken him out. You'll be needed soon.'

'I'll be right over.'

The camera zoomed onto William's face as the helmet was eased off. He looked dazed, his face still pale from the chill of a South American cloud forest.

'Welcome back, William,' Beecham said. A two-day trip down Jarnier's brain machine; he didn't look too bad.

The young man looked round for the camera, and then gave a half-hearted company salute. 'Thank you, sir.'

The guy was perfect for a test pilot, but Beecham wouldn't want him for a drinking partner. He watched the technicians help him out of the suit. William couldn't stand without help, and even supported by the technicians, his legs buckled.

'He looks tired.'

Beecham turned to see Dr Kinderling, the project psychologist, watching the same screen.

'Time for you to do your bit. Let's see if it's scrambled his brains yet.'

3

I cover myself as best I can – polymer jumpsuit, mask, goggles – but fifteen minutes of sweeping is enough to get my eyes streaming and skin itching. As I thought, I have a dust allergy to add to the list. I have to take the mask off to have a sneezing fit, but with each breath I'm inhaling more dust, so I go to the window and sneeze into the street. When it passes I put my mask back on and lie down on the mattress, suddenly exhausted. I make myself breathe slow and steady. I'm suffocating with snot and stale air inside my mask, but this room is so toxic my bronchioles will constrict into pinpoints if I try and breathe without it.

I survey the tilted room from the floor and resist the temptation to scratch my skin. What I need to do is dampen the floorboards and give them a good scrub, but I'm too tired. I wish I had a dust extractor or something. I'd gladly exchange cold air for dust.

A nap seems a good idea, but unless I keep on the move my limbs start to ache with cold, so I get to my feet and look out of the window. The ice is so bright it makes my eyes sting. On the map this area is called the Frigid Zone. When I read that I knew I was going to the right place. A picture of a huge ice woman came to me, cold and beautiful and unresponsive. I remember being in love with the Snow Queen as a child. Wrapped in her furs, speeding along in her sleigh, an irresistible mix of disdain and sex; this woman would crush you to death. A small price to pay to spend a moment against her bare flesh.

I've decided to use only the far end of the room for living quarters. It has everything I need: a sink and a toilet, electrical power points, natural light. Jack told me there would be no mains water, a water truck would come round twice a week to fill the tank. Just put an orange card in your window, he said. It seems pretty unlikely. I tried the faucet, but it didn't even make a gasping noise, so I guess I'll have to put my order in at the local store.

The more I get used to the size of the room, the more I like it. I've always lived in cluttered places, forever tripping over furniture, having to jam clothes into already full drawers. Even when the kids left home, there was no visible emptying of the house. Somehow Carla managed to fill their absence with more of our bits and pieces. But sixty foot by twenty: this is the sort of scale I always wanted. Big, open, simple. A whitewashed wall with not one painting on it. It's as soothing to my sight as an eyebath.

The cold is descending on me again, so I go back to work. The machinery is bolted to the floor, impossible to move, so I wipe the dust off with a wet rag. It's some kind of winding device, long wires strung the length of it like an enormous fret. I try twanging one of them, but the tension is too slack to make anything other than a slapping sound.

Half an hour is all I can work before I have to stop for food. Not that I'm hungry, but I can feel my sugar level dipping out of sight. I don't know if it's an overactive imagination, but since I was confirmed as infected, I can hardly keep any food down. One thing I've discovered that doesn't make me throw up is home-made rye bread. I came across it in Inuvik, Hi-Lyphe bread it's called, a smiling woman on the packet telling me how nutritious it is. Though I believe her, I very nearly didn't buy any because of that lamb-to-the-slaughter smile. Common sense got the better of me in the end and I bought five boxes of the stuff, a little cooker to go with it. I stir water into one of the packets and pour the mixture into the toaster.

I remember my medication, and take one of the capsules, holding it in the well of my tongue until I have enough saliva to swallow. I have a month's supply: fifteen hundred dollars' worth. The pharmacist said it might take a few days before I saw any improvement.

While I'm waiting for the bread to cook, I take one of my

student's cards and slot it into the reader. Marnie Blackwater, one of my better students, a chance that one day somebody will want to read what she has written. Not this though. I take off my gloves and scroll through the story quickly. The assignment was to invent two characters in conflict; here we have a man and a woman arguing in a stalled elevator. It's all too obvious, no subtext beneath the words they're saying. I switch the screen off. I've been reading this crap for years, no need to make a virtue out of a habit. I'm on my own now, no need to play the game. The virus has kicked me into touch.

The sound is so sudden and sharp I'm on my feet and tensed for action before I know what it is. A high-pitched electronic screaming is trying to burst my eardrums. I'm stunned by the noise, grappling with the list of possibilities: alarm clock, telephone, car alarm, rape alarm. It seems to be coming from everywhere. And then it starts raining, and I realise what it is. The smoke alarm.

At five-yard intervals, little metal umbrellas in the ceiling are showering me with orange water. I press myself against the wall and watch the downpour. What the hell started that? I look around the room for a clue, and then spot the toaster, a little funnel of smoke issuing from my burning bread. I adjust my mask and dash for the power point and switch it off. No sparks or anything, so I guess nothing has fused.

The downpour continues unabated, a thunderstorm of rust-coloured rain. Where is it coming from? I thought there was no water. I watch for a moment, grudgingly impressed by the efficiency of the sprinklers: no part of the room is exempt. I guess the stopcock for the sprinkler system is under the sink, so I get down on my knees and turn off every valve I can find. The shower eases to a drizzle, and then stops.

The alarm is continuing its shrieking, so I open a few windows to get some air circulating, and throw the blackened bread out. I can see the smoke detector winking its red light at me, but it's fifteen feet up on the ceiling, out of reach even if I stand on a chair. I cover my ears with my hands and wait for the noise to stop. It does so, as abruptly as it began, leaving a ringing silence in its wake.

The floorboards have done a good job of absorbing most of the water, but shallow puddles have formed on every non-absorbent flat surface. My clothes are still in the rucksack, but my quilt has taken on a dark sheen. The winding machine is a long trough now, two inches of water in the bottom. Perhaps I could keep goldfish.

I go to the window and look down. Two black postage stamps lie twenty-five feet below me in the snow. My lunch.

Then the skin on my face starts to tingle. I take my mask off and rub my face with my hands, but that just makes it worse. My face is burning like acid. Whatever has caused it is on the back of my hands as well. I run to the trough and splash water over my face. There's a moment's relief as the freezing water cools my skin, and then I feel as though somebody has slapped my face, hard. There's something in the water. My eyes are stinging so badly, I can hardly keep them open. Whatever is in the water, I've got to get it off – quick. I grope towards my bags and search out some face cream. I can't see what I'm doing, and squirt some of it onto the floor. I can hear my breath coming in pants as I smear the cream over my face, careful not to get it in my eyes.

What was in that water? I can smell something synthetic, like gasoline. Then I realise that it must be antifreeze, goddamit.

The cream is helping a bit, but I realise I have to wash my face in clean water. I hurry to the elevator and pull the gates shut and jab the button.

Outside, I kneel in the road and scoop snow over my face. It hurts like hell – it's more ice than snow – but I keep patting it onto my skin until my face is clean. My skin is still burning, but with cold now. My eyes are watering so badly I'm blind. I push myself to my feet and lean against the wall to get out of the wind, hot tears jiggering down my cheeks.

Even though I'm wearing insulated gloves, my fingers are numb. I rub them as briskly as I can and shove them deep into my jacket pockets. It's a couple of minutes before I can see anything except diamonds of light through my stinging eyes. My face is taut with the cold, the fillings in my teeth aching.

The sidewalks are solid ice, but a light powdering of snow on the surface keeps me from slipping. I walk to the end of the road and turn to look at my erratic trail of footprints. I stamp the snow off my boots, slapping my arms against my sides for heat. It's supposed to be spring, and it's so cold my eyeballs hurt. My lips have cracked so much they're bleeding.

There's another set of footprints on the main street. I feel like Robinson Crusoe as I follow them, trying to guess who left them here. They lead me past shuttered houses and piles of rubbish. Most of the buildings are prefab ramblers, cheap and just waiting to fall apart. One of the windows of the school house is smashed, and I peer through it. Empty, no chairs or tables, just a few children's paintings on the wall.

A crow, bigger than I've ever seen, watches me from its perch on a telegraph pole, black against the white sky. When I'm underneath it, I realise it isn't a bird at all, but a plastic bag, caught on the wire.

I measure my pace by the footprints, putting my feet into their depression. The paces are short, the feet small; either a short old man, I guess, or a woman.

They lead me to a provision store. At first I think I'm hallucinating. On the pavement I see plastic buckets, snowshoes, lengths of lumber tied together with string and a fishing pole. A skidoo, its fuel tank dented, has been parked in front, almost blocking the doorway. In the window, beside a dusty crate of bottled water, is a precarious pyramid of boxes of soap powder, cans of paint, clothes pins, and a fluorescent orange, children's ray gun. There is a careless display of Eskimo knives and seal skin boots. A cat is sleeping on top of a flickering old-fashioned television set. According to the faded sign above the window, this is *Harry's Store and Post Office*, established 1998.

I wander past the store to the other end of the street. Nothing. No sign of life, just empty buildings and snow. It's getting too cold to stay out for much longer, so I hurry back the way I came.

I don't want to go into the store, but my eyes are drawn to the television set, so I watch it for a moment. I can't hear the sound, but it's a documentary of some sort: what looks like a mid-West food distribution centre, dusty sacks of grain being hefted off the back of a truck by a skinny teenager in a wool sweater and running pants. There's something familiar about him and I squint at the screen to see what it is. I don't recognise the face – it's something else. And then I realise. He's wearing my sweater.

It's more ragged than when I saw it last, and far too big for him, but without a doubt, it's the sweater that Carla bought me. I stare at the screen. My sweater. It's been years since I've seen it, but it must be mine. I recognise the spilt paint down one arm. That's why I gave it away – it was only good for decorating, and when we moved house, it was bagged up with a lot of other clothes and taken to a Goodwill.

The picture changes – back to the newsroom – and I stare at the mouthing of a handsome young newsreader. Weird. I want them to rerun the film, but it's the weather now. The cat wakes up and watches me through one eye. I notice it has no ears.

I put my mask on and check my reflection in the plate glass window. Face covered with mask and UV goggles, I look like the Invisible Man.

I'm still hesitating about going in when I notice a portable typewriter under the television. It's an antique, heavy and black, the sort of machine Hemingway would have written on. I study it closely. It looks industrial, an implausible gateway for anything as soft and useless as literature. One of the first reality machines, I suppose. Ink into emotion.

I step round the skidoo and push against the door. It's jammed tight and I have to shove it with my shoulder. When it finally opens I almost fall into the warm interior of the shop. A bell jangles above my head and I reach up to still it in a reflex action.

Most of the shop's stock is in the window display. High shelves, presumably once burdened with goods, are mainly empty now. A few wooden brooms hang from the ceiling, a shovel and a pickaxe are propped against a sack of what looks like bird seed. Rope, cans of powdered milk, stainless steel cutlery, everything looks so old, so depressingly dated. Standing behind a counter as though he's waiting for me is a small man in a hat – presumably Harry. It's impossible to browse under such relentless scrutiny, so I walk up to him.

He's the first to speak. 'Morning,' he says. I see that he's a Native American – Inuit presumably. He's about my age.

'Hello, there.' God, how English I sound, even muffled by my mask.

He reaches a hand over the counter for me to shake. I keep

my glove on, and clumsily squeeze the end of his fingers. 'Harry Homme,' he says. 'With an "H".'

Homme? French Canadian? I'd expected something more ethnic, like Harry Running Water, Harry Blackfoot.

'You come here for hunting?' he adds.

'No. I've moved here.'

He considers my comment for a moment. 'You won't find a tracker.'

I shake my head. 'I don't want a tracker. I've moved here,' I repeat.

My insistence is clearly absurd to him, so he decides to ignore it. 'You're passing through, then.'

Passing through? From where to where, I want to ask him. 'No. I've moved into the old twine factory.'

His eyes narrow for a moment. 'Berry Lofgren's place?'

I nod.

'You're staying with Berry?'

'He's dead.' Suddenly I have my doubts. 'Isn't he?'

He makes a sucking noise by puckering his cheeks. 'That's right.'

'I'm a friend of his nephew's. Jack.'

'I know Jack Lofgren. Nice kid.'

Hmm. Jack has lived nearly two thousand miles away for the last thirty years. He's a hundred pounds overweight, alcoholic and twice divorced. There are many things you can call Jack, but 'nice kid' isn't one of them.

'You an anthropologist?' he asks.

'No.'

'Sociologist? Archaeologist?'

I shake my head twice.

He studies me for a moment. 'Can I sell you anything?'

I scan the shelves behind him. 'You got an electric heater?'

He bends down and unplugs one by his feet. 'Yup.' He lifts the still glowing two-bar heater onto the counter. I'm tempted to take my mask off to feel the heat on my face, but I resist it. This place is a dust bowl. Instead I hold my blotchy hands out, warming them on the heater.

'You want something for your cold?' he says.

'Cold?' I realise he's referring to my mask. 'No, thanks.'

There's nothing more to say so we decide a price for the heater. He doesn't want dollar credits, but after listing all the things I can give him in exchange, he settles for cash. I'm about to leave when I remember the water truck. I expect him not to know what I'm talking about, but he nods when I mention it.

'There ain't been a water truck for a couple of years now.'

'What do you do for water?'

'Fill a bucket with snow.'

'What about the plumbing? How does that work?'

'You want some honey bags?' He bends under the counter again and brings out a bundle of orange plastic sacks.

'Honey bags?'

'For your shit.'

I want to laugh, but he's serious. 'What do you do when it's full?'

'Chuck it out.'

'And someone will come and collect it?'

He pushes the bundle towards me. 'Ninety-five dollars.'

'That's a bit steep.'

'You can pay me next time.'

On an impulse I ask to see the typewriter and Harry disentangles it from the window display. The cat complains about being disturbed but Harry ignores it.

'How did she lose her ears?' I ask.

'Frostbite.'

The typewriter keys are well oiled and respond easily to my fingers, though they need to be struck harder than I'm used to. The ribbon, half black and half red, looks stretched and dry.

'Can I try it?'

He rips a piece of wrapping paper off a box and hands it to me. I wind it into the machine.

It's forty years since I've used one of these things. I take my gloves off and type slowly:

To be or not to be, that is the qwsetion

'Two hundred dollars and it could be yours.'

I shake my head. I haven't written anything for years, just

corrected other people's mistakes. I wouldn't know what to do with a blank sheet of paper.

On the way back to the factory I pull off my face mask and smell the air. The wind gets under my hat, making my ears burn. I can't believe how quiet it is; nothing except the sound of wind.

Why have I come here to die? Why come to this clean, white nothingness, this *tabula rasa* of civilisation? I can't say.

I see a polar bear pawing through the contents of a garbage tip. I didn't realise how big they are. This one is the size of a car, its fur yellowed as though someone has pissed over it. The animal doesn't have that cute look they're supposed to have; it bares its teeth in a snarl as it rips open a plastic bag of empty tin cans. I recognise the bright orange of a honey bag. The plastic has been torn and I can see its contents have frozen into a block.

I give the animal a wide berth, hoping that it's not going to see me. I assumed Jack was joking when he mentioned polar bears. I wish I'd asked him how dangerous they are.

4

Julia had found the coolest room in the compound. Cork-lined and windowless, it was little more than a closet, but it suited her needs. Administration was reluctant to let her use it, but a desk, a chair and a table lamp was all she needed to make it an office. They informed her she would have to add a potted plant to meet health and safety requirements, and she told them she would arrange it herself. Illuminated only by the flickering of the video player and the daylight from the half open door, she realised she liked the room because it reminded her of the carrel she had used at university. There was something safe in its privacy.

The video player on the desk in front of her was only a little larger than the notebook in which she was writing. The screen showed a dark-skinned man, dressed in a white cotton tunic and pointed cotton hat. The costume was exactly as she'd described it to them, the lined face of the man as real as the photographs she had sent the Institute. It took an effort to remember that this was a computer generated image; that Mama Francisco, as they called him, did not really exist. Likewise the forest, the animals, the birds – all coloured dots on a video screen.

Julia had been looking forward to viewing this tape ever since she'd been on the project. Although she had a doctorate in South American shamanism, the Tairona had never been more than two or three monographs to her. The society had been documented on and off since the 1940s, but there was almost no source material, and nothing approaching an anthropological expert on the group. She told the Institute this, made it clear that the best she could do as project advisor was to give them a sketch of an extinct society, but they seemed satisfied with that. The request had taken her by surprise, and her first reaction had been to decline. It was six years since Julia had worked, and she told them so, but once again it made no difference. They wanted her and nobody else.

The Tairona civilisation had lasted at least a thousand years, probably more. As far as anyone knew there had been four distinct groups: Ika, Sanha, Kanuamake and Kogi. The Kanuamake had been the first to go, then the Ika and Sanha devolved into just another alcohol-ruined indigenous group dressed in football shorts and tee-shirts. Anthropological interest had always focused on the Kogi, the purest strand of pre-Columban society to make it through the twentieth century. Julia knew of no other indigenous group that had so successfully sidestepped the assault of the new world, and she had not been alone in championing their continued isolation. The Kogi had accepted no innovations from the outside since their retreat into the Sierra. They had spades, sugar presses, they grew maize, but there were no wrist watches, no mirrors, no written language. It was a culture frozen in time, the year 1600. Since then only a handful of ethnologists had penetrated their veil of silence, and what they brought back was like nothing else Julia had known.

The Kogi had learnt to avoid the conquistadors and their hunting dogs by melting into the forest and keeping their distance from outsiders. This tradition had served them well. Their cities may have been given over to the jungle and the tomb robbers, but the ethos remained unchanged. There was a time at the end of the twentieth century when their numbers were growing, and it looked like they would survive, but when the Japanese built a cable car to the top of the paramo in 2004, their fragile isolation was over. The combined pressure of settlers and tourists proved too much. Flu devastated the population, villages were fractured and their fragments absorbed into mainstream Colombian life. Pockets of Kogi were rumoured to still live in the high Sierras, but their society was extinct. After five hundred years Christopher Columbus had won the last piece of America.

Julia had finally taken the job because, spurious reason though it might have been, the program gave her a chance to see something that no anthropologist of her generation had witnessed – the enactment of Kogi culture. It was a fake, but at least it was a good fake.

She ran the tape at half speed. She didn't care how much computing power this program demanded, the scene before her wasn't a product of science. It was magic. Last night she'd glanced at some of the technical literature they'd left in her room, but details of gigaflops and BIPS meant nothing to her. Billions of instructions per second? How much was a billion?

There were fifteen characters in the program: six women, five men and four children. She had expected caricatures, but the sophistication of their responses astonished her. They looked real, they moved realistically, they had distinct personalities. Just half an hour into the tape, and she was already getting to know them.

And the forest was perfect; the sunlight dicing through foliage, the monkeys chattering in the tree tops. Even ants. It was unbelievable what the programmers had achieved. She recognised the amount of effort that had gone into it. Her input had been just three months' work; the zoologists and botanists had been engaged on the project for years.

One of the acoustic engineers had tried to explain the process of sound synthesis they had used, but she had been deaf to his words. The scratchings and rustlings were all she needed to hear. She had visited Colombia in the days when it was still possible to travel, and she knew the country as well as any foreigner could. Not just the outside, the cocaine money and unending shanty towns and sticky heat, but the inside as well. She knew the rain forest, the mountains, the jungle. And the programmers had got it exactly right. Apparently the flight suit filled in all the rest, the temperature, the smells; but this was enough for her. Watching the video run, she was there, in the wood smoke of the *nuhue*, the ceremonial house. She noted with satisfaction the accuracy of its reproduction: the four fires, the long benches on either side, the hammocks hanging from the supporting pillars.

A hand came into view on the screen. Seeing the world through another person's eyes had disconcerted Julia at first, but she was getting used to it now. She watched the hand point to the stripe running down the side of the native's tunic. Even before the question was asked, she realised she hadn't given them the information.

What is this stripe called?

Data not available.

The Tairona language hadn't been replicated. There was no point in trying to write a language that no outsider, not even the ethnologists, knew. The project managers weren't interested in linguistics. They wanted a good story, something they could sell to Disney. And in American English.

Julia paused the tape. There was a lot she didn't know about the Kogi. They had given the world only what they thought the world needed, and it didn't include details of the stripe running down the side of their clothing. They had never welcomed prying questions, and a lot of Julia's input to the project had been based on her understanding of other indigenous groups. She made a note on the pad, and started the tape again.

What does it signify?

Data not available.

She paused the tape again. It was probably something to do with status, but she didn't know precisely what. She wondered if she should invent something, or just admit she didn't know. Three months of intensive work, and there were still huge gaps in the program.

It remained a mystery why Omnisens were so keen to have her on the project. She was no more of an expert than a handful of others she could name, and her brain had had six years of motherhood in which to go soft. And then there was her nationality. It was far easier to find an American anthropologist than go through the hassle of hiring a Brit. Foreign work permits were almost impossible to get, so somebody must have really wanted her on the project. But they insisted it was her they wanted, and so she said yes. She read everything she could, taking notes on a paper pad at the kitchen table, glorying in her sudden change of status. An earner after all these years, she was the envy of all her friends.

After a couple of months the Institute insisted she come to them in person. This was another matter entirely. She was happy to do the work, but leave home? Go to the States? She couldn't see the point of a flesh-to-flesh with the American team, but as Paul pointed out, this was a two billion dollar project. Teleconference security was too easily breached with that kind of money at stake.

The British Embassy advised her against it. The plague was far more widespread in North American cities than anywhere in Britain. The secession of Southern California had made no difference – a water-borne virus was no respecter of state lines. Omnisens was persuasive, however. The Institute was in the desert, a security zone 6, she would work within a defended building. She would be met at the airport and flown by helicopter to the base. Health insurance would be provided, and the fee for her consultancy would be twelve thousand ecus. A week.

Somebody must have pulled strings somewhere, for it had taken only a week to get her visa clearance. Ten thousand dollar credits had been deposited in her account: spending money, she had been told. Julia felt important and not a little afraid. Even after she had packed, she was still on the verge of turning them down; in six years she had never been away from the twins for longer than a weekend. She tried to persuade herself that being cooped up in a research institute in the middle of the desert with a bunch of strangers would be hell. But real travel, to real destinations, intellectual company – it was too tempting to resist. Before she knew it, she was checking into her room and anxiously wondering if they weren't expecting too much from her.

Julia was leaning back in her chair when a shadow fell across the wall in front of her. She spun the chair round and saw someone silhouetted in the doorway. She recognised William immediately. 'Hi,' she said with a smile. She hated how propitiatory the monosyllable sounded, but his surprise appearance had unnerved her. It was only a matter of time before someone on the project spotted her as a fraud and sacked her.

'You must be the famous anthropologist.'

'I'm hardly famous.'

She could see from his smile that he had intended his remark facetiously. She winced inwardly. 'And you're the cybernaut.'

His laugh surprised her. 'Pilot, please.' He held his hand out for her to shake. She automatically took it.

'William Morrison, United States citizen.' She noted the lilt of teasing in his voice. He was dressed in a blue serge suit, with silver buttons. It was only the open neck of his shirt that belied the impression that he was wearing a uniform.

'Julia O'Brien.' She wondered if she should have used her title, but 'doctor' sounded like a medic, and she dreaded being misunderstood.

'Are you settling in okay?'

'I keep getting lost.'

He invited himself into the tiny room, and sat on the edge of the desk. 'I'll show you around later.' He picked up the video player, and tapped the image of the native. She noticed he bit his fingernails. 'Bernardo, right?'

Julia nodded, not wanting to correct him. She was uneasy about the names. The Kogi had only ever used Spanish names when in contact with outsiders, and this was all she had to go on. These Europeans names, the very same as their sixteenth century persecutors', must have been mouthed with a peculiar irony by the Kogi.

He pointed at the stick and gourd that Mama Francisco was holding. 'What do they call this thing again?' The gourd was about six inches long with a thick deposit of bright green quicklime around its neck.

'Anthropologists call it a *poporo*. It's not uncommon among Latin American indigenous groups.' She could hear the pomposity in her voice, but he was making her nervous.

He eased the tape forward so that the hands of Mama Francisco moved in slow motion. 'What's the point of it? I never got it.'

He was settling in for a chat, and Julia gave up trying to resist him. 'Don't you know anything about them?'

'They keep me in the dark so they can blind test the program.'

'Should I tell you, then?' She wasn't very good at this sort of thing; should she be talking to this man at all? Almost the first thing she'd done on the project was to sign an industrial secrets agreement. She guessed that even before being offered the post, her background had been checked out. A European national with a suspect lineage, she wondered what Omnisens would have made of the fact that her father was ex-IRA. Did it make any difference that he had died before she was born?

'If you don't tell me, this little guy will,' William said, indicating the image of the Mama. The volume was down, but she could see the man on the screen talking to the unseen figure of William, slotting the whittled stick in and out of the hollowed gourd, transferring the powdered lime from its centre and building up a hard calc around its neck. When Julia had first seen a *poporo*, its narrow base and bulbous head had reminded her of an ice cream cone filled with peppermint ice cream. She watched the image of Mama Francisco licking the tip of the stick and then slotting it back into the neck of the gourd. It was only the wad of coca leaves in his cheek that stopped his mouth burning with the quicklime.

'The *poporo* is at the heart of Kogi ritual. The gourd represents the womb, while the stick is the penis. The lime powder inside represents the essence of fertility – semen, if you like. By constantly impregnating the womb with the stick, the cycle of life is maintained.' She had been reluctant to explain, but once she started it was hard to stop. 'Have you heard of the lingham-yoni of Hindu iconography? Same thing – masculine and feminine principles in constant interplay.' She slid two fingers in and out of an open fist to demonstrate.

'Kinky, huh?'

She was glad it was too dark for him to see the prickly rash that suddenly flooded up from her collarbones. She felt angry and intimidated at the same time, cursing herself for allowing him into the room. She took the video from him and turned it off. 'All this is in the program, anyway.'

'And they really carried these ice creams around?'

She smiled in spite of herself. 'Just the adult males.'

'Weird, if you ask me.'

Every word this man said was a slap in the face. 'They've got a lot going for them,' she said defensively.

'No, not just these guys – the whole program. How they decided to run with this idea beats me. A bunch of spaced-out Indians high on coke – pretty subversive if you ask me.'

He had touched a nerve and her response was immediate. 'Coca leaves are *not* the same as cocaine. And they're not spaced out.' She made no attempt to disguise her contempt. 'This culture was an incredibly sophisticated theocracy – its foundation was meditation and spiritual practice, not getting "spaced out" as you call it.' The inverted commas were etched in acid.

Judging by the expression on his face these distinctions were lost on him. All he saw was men and women with long black hair and an obsession with a gourd and a stick.

'Look – I've got to get on with my work. Do you mind?' She could hear the vibrato of anger in her own voice, but William smiled and got up.

'Guided tour in thirty?' he asked, glancing at his wristwatch.

She didn't want to forgive him so readily, but it was too early to make enemies. 'Okay.'

He left and she returned to the screen, but her concentration had gone. It *was* strange. What had the Kogi got to do with reality holidays? The glossy brochure had said a lot about replicating the rain forests and protected habitats of the world, but why not just invent an indigenous group of their own? The Kogi were one of the least documented groups in the world, and Jarnier had wanted to know *everything* about them. She hadn't met the chief programmer yet, but there had been no shortage of mail from him. Every time she checked with her monitor she found another couple of packets from him. She had scanned his public biofile before she came over but found nothing she didn't already know. Rising quickly through the ranks of minor companies, he had become the chief programmer of Omnisens at the age of twenty-four. Asking around, the opinion was that he was either a major whackjack or a genius.

A strange project or not, if Omnisens was going to spend billions on reproducing a hidden culture of Colombia, it suited her fine.

5

By the time I get back to the factory I'm too tired to do anything but plug the heater in and lie on the mattress wrapped in a sleeping bag. The shower from the sprinkler system has kept the dust down, but I continue to wear my mask to keep my face warm.

From where I'm lying I count four radiators lining the back wall – oil-fired, I guess. Even with fuel, it would probably take an engineer to get the system running. My fingers are burning with cold so I roll over to toast them on the heater.

People worked here, Eskimo women with lined faces and fur boots. I try and imagine the clatter of machinery, the heat of activity, and for a moment the place is alive. They've all gone now, but they have left something of themselves behind.

I catch the whiff of melting plastic as my gloves scorch, and whip my hands away from the fire. It's years since I've been so cold. The last time was as a child in England, playing in snow, plastic bags over my shoes. Now with two pairs of thermal socks, snow boots, and a hollowfibre sleeping bag my toes are still so numb they've disappeared. I will have to do something if I'm to survive. Heating 20,000 cubic feet of refrigerated air is going to take more than a two-bar electric heater. I'll try and partition the room with plastic sheeting or something, live in just one section.

I get up and make some herbal tea. I drink it at the window, holding my hands round the mug and inhaling the steam. Sunlight is leeching out of the day, the sun slipping under the horizon. I feel as though I am on the bow of a ship, looking north, the churned up waters of civilisation behind me, all our mistakes, all the mess in the past. This is the last frontier, the only wilderness left. But even here I know there is hidden poison: oil in the water, fug from southern factories. The Eskimos have long gone. This isn't wilderness; it's waste land.

It doesn't get dark for hours. I lie on my back, my arms crossed over my chest, the echo of the morning's journey vibrating inside me, but though I'm tired, sleep evades me. For the first two days of my new life in the Hotel Belleview, I did nothing but sleep. I want to hibernate now, but I'm too on edge to sleep. The mattress is comfortable enough, and even the cold is bearable. It's the silence that keeps me awake. I'm reminded of a time when I camped in a desert, nothing between myself and a fathomless blanket of stars but a two-mile envelope of air. It was so clear I could see a satellite going overhead.

I try not to think about Carla and the mess I've left behind. The Taoists say that the sage passes through life leaving no footprints. My path is strewn with honey bags, and here I am facing my future and I can't even flush the toilet.

What am I doing here? Asked to account for myself, what could I say? Why did I abandon a comfortable life for this? A plague death is not so unpleasant. I could have spent my declining years in warm, well-fed isolation, taken the easy way out if it got too much. Carla was shocked, of course, to hear that I was infected, but she wouldn't have abandoned me. The woman loved me. Finally, after the preoccupation of parenthood, we were ready to settle down to companionable old age, and suddenly I take off, not telling her where I'm going.

I have been on automatic these last few days, out of control, my mind curiously blank. I don't want to think too much. Carla agreed not to tell the university I was infected, so they'll probably think I've had a breakdown or something. They may be right.

I've always wanted to do this. Go mad, throw over the demands of propriety, rationality. And now I've done it. After years of carping I've sloughed off the itchy skin of a compromised life, just as I said I'd do. The missed tutorials, my lecture on characterisation – unchanged for twenty years – the garden fence I promised to replace, dinner at André and Jayne's, I don't have to do any of it now. Here I am on the moon, a viral gun to my head, finally free of the trivia of a junk life. I don't know if I'm frightened or excited.

I watch the slow dawn light pick out details on the ceiling. But why not tell Carla where I am? She must be frantic with worry now. Am I really so selfish?

Telling Carla I was infected was the most difficult act of my life. I know there should be no guilt attached. I am an innocent victim, it could have happened to anyone, but I felt as though I was admitting something grotesque and shameful. To be so out of control of my body, to be buzzing with a viral infection, the nuclei of my cells multiplying their distorted disease. *Ecce homo*, I wanted to say, maggot-ridden man. My intellect tells me there is nothing I could have done to prevent it, but the bigger part tells me I should have done something. I should have single-handedly steered the ship of culture round, prevented this collision of nature. The plague was the inevitable iceberg towards which we were heading, and here it is, breaking through my bows, my guilt manifest.

I want to be on my own for my last days. I am going to keep my contamination to myself. Nobody, least of all my wife, is going to be infected by me. I will be the last maggot man.

I get up as soon as it's light and tip all the sacks and piles of paper out of the fire escape onto the street. Any portable bits of machinery are sent down in the elevator, and by eight-fifteen the room is empty apart from two trestle tables and the long winding gear bolted to the floor. No books, no television, no conversation, no demands, no nothing. I stand in the middle of the room, itchy under my face mask, unaccommodated man, pink and new and naked.

I strain to pick up any sound, but apart from the hum of the generator, it's so quiet I could be deaf. In a perfectly silent anechoic chamber, you can hear two sounds: a deep rumble and a high-pitched whizz. Your blood system and your nervous system. Listen for that enough and you'll unravel yourself.

So, this is it. I have arrived. From now on there is nowhere to go, nothing to do except wait for the end. This is as good as it gets: the long, empty room, the mattress by the heater, two trestle tables and a makeshift pantry.

I make breakfast – rolled oats soaked in apple juice – and sit at one of the tables. I don't know if I'm imagining it, but I think I can feel the virus taking hold of me. Nausea, waves of fatigue, dizziness. I didn't realise it would be so quick.

My scalp is itching; I'm becoming allergic to my own hair. I'm going to have to buy some scissors.

I'm aware of the pace of my thoughts, but though I try to slow down there's a gerbil on a treadmill inside my head. Hurry, hurry, hurry. Trivial nonsense scampering on a journey with no destination and no arrival. I want to stop, but I can't.

I take a box of matches down and gather all the debris I dropped from the fire escape into a bonfire. I finally get it lit, and warm my hands on the blaze. It's a windless day, and the plume of smoke rises straight up. I imagine it is visible for miles. I'm calmed somehow by the smoke, the gerbil slowing its pace.

I walk down the deserted street to the shop, slapping my arms against my sides. Tulkina is a ghost town. I can see the footprints in the snow from yesterday. Nothing has changed. I walk steadily along the street, aware of the silence above my head like a marble slab, waiting to fall should I make any sudden movement. I glance through the windows of the bungalows I pass. Some contain furniture and pictures on the wall, others are as empty as packing cases. There are no cats or dogs.

The same display is spilling onto the pavement in front of Harry's store. The TV is on, and my eyes are automatically drawn to it. I can't hear the sound, but I recognise the logo of the programme which is just starting. It's the talk show that Carla fronts. I wince as though I have been punched in the belly. I turn away before her face can appear on the screen. Pushing open the door, I go into the store.

I recognise my wife's voice, asking a studio guest questions in her charming and flirtatious way. I say hello to Harry and then find myself talking so I don't have to hear her. The network loved her English accent so much she took elocution lessons to refine it. Twenty-five years of gradual Americanisation had dulled the edge, but now her vowels are as polished as steel blades.

'Why did you think I was a sociologist?' I ask.

Harry is leaning against the counter. He looks at me from under the brim of his cowboy hat, his expression as neutral as you can get. 'Everyone who comes up here is either a hunter or some goddam-ologist.'

I pretend interest in the fishing reel on the counter. I'm aware Harry is watching me, Carla's voice in the background.

'Where *is* everyone?' I say at last.

'Gone south.'

'Why?'

'The Eskimo bent over while the white man fucked him up the ass.'

I'm not sure how this answers my question, but I leave it. I wander round the store, selecting things I don't want from the dusty shelves. Harry's making me nervous. My nerves are shot.

He tries to sell me the television, but I shake my head. Instead I buy two thermo pads, a pair of nail scissors and a carton of coconut milk. A paraffin heater has replaced the electric heater he sold me.

He doesn't say anything more, so I pay and leave. I glance at the typewriter in the window on my way out. The sheet of paper is still in the machine: *to be or not to be, that is the qwsetion.*

When I get back to the factory I clip my hair as short as I can with the nail scissors and then shave off what's left. I also do my beard and eyebrows and then cover my skin with face cream.

A couple of hours later I find myself reading through the student assignments for the second time, adding one or two fresh comments. All that passion and imagination; it can so easily be ridiculed. I keep thinking back to the typewriter in Harry's store. For years I had thought about writing a final novel, a last stab at having my say. But have I got anything worth saying, anything to add to two people arguing in a stalled elevator?

I've been a bad father to my books. For years now I have disowned them as the progeny of an irresponsibly fertile younger person, somebody so removed in time and experience from myself that, apart from the name, nothing remains of the writer. I don't even have any copies of my novels, and the scrapbooks of reviews have long since been lost. Writing was too much of a commitment for me, it required too much of a belief in myself, more than I could muster in the end. The older I became, the less sure of anything I was. For the last thirty years I have been a probation officer for other writers' offspring, occasionally approving, mostly proscriptive.

But I find myself lacing my snow boots again and tying a scarf round my neck. I have no excuses now. Harry Homme has a typewriter for sale, and I have till the end of the world. I'll buy it. I'll go into Harry's and buy that bloody machine, type my postscript, if that's what it turns out to be.

Together with a ream of unbleached paper, Harry wants five hundred dollars cash. I offer him a hundred and fifty dollars, and he accepts it. He is no more talkative than before, and I am in and out within two minutes. No polar bears, thankfully.

The typewriter stays in its case for the rest of the day. In the middle of the night, I can stand it no longer. I switch the lights on and drag a trestle table over to the heater. One thermo pad on my knees and the other on my feet, I arrange the typewriter and pile of paper in front of me. It looks just as it should, just as it does in the movies. I roll a sheet of paper into the typewriter and find myself facing it, hands together as though I'm a concert pianist about to play the opening chord of a piano concerto. I lay my hands on the keys, lower my gaze until it rests on the white paper.

6

William returned to her room exactly thirty minutes later. Julia wanted to continue with her work, but she let him in.

'Have you had lunch yet?'

'Yes,' she lied.

'Let me show you the test room, then. I don't suppose they gave you a tour yesterday.'

She put the tape into her briefcase, and stood up. Why not? She was going to be here for a couple of weeks; she might as well make friends. 'Okay.' Gesturing for William to leave, she followed him out, closing the door behind her. It locked automatically, and she wondered for a second if her card would open it again.

'How was your trip? Wasn't it some kind of record?' In the daylight of the corridor, she could see he was younger than she had thought.

'For the west. The Chinese have gone a couple more days inside.'

'Is it hard work?'

'Work? It's like playing a cyberdrome game all day.'

'And it's safe?'

'Of course.'

They passed some oil paintings which Julia wanted to stop and look at, but William didn't notice her hesitate. She skipped to catch up with him. The corridor ended in a sealed door, marked Restricted Zone.

'Am I allowed in here?' she asked doubtfully.

'With me you are.' He slid his key card in the lock, and glanced at the retinal recognition system. The door swung open and they went in. Julia was aware of the camera processing her image as she passed. She braced herself for the sound of a siren, but nothing happened.

Two technicians – a man and a woman – were in the test room. They were drinking coffee, and Julia could see their entrance had interrupted something. William ignored them and walked to the girdle.

It dominated the room. Two chrome loops, one within the other, contained what looked like the metal skeleton of a person. She looked from the machine to William. His look said one word: *impressed?*

'It's actually very simple,' William said. 'Fiddly engineering, but the design is pure Newton.'

He was right: it looked like a seventeenth century astrolabe or gyroscope or something. She circled the machine, gazing at its chrome arms and legs. It was a nightmare.

The system had been named MAYA, and its logo was embossed on each leg of the machine. When she had first heard the name she assumed somebody must have confused the Kogi with the Mayas, but now she realised where it had come from. *Maya* was the Sanskrit word most laymen translated as 'illusion'; presumably its meaning in this context too. Julia wished she had told Jarnier before it was too late; she was fussy with her definitions and intolerant of those who used important words loosely. To translate the word as 'illusion' was to miss the point: *maya*, in its Buddhist context, was the creative power which brings the phenomenal world into existence. The deluded mind, not the product of delusion.

'This is the cutting edge of simulators,' William said proudly. 'Nobody has matched these specifications.'

She looked from the machine to William. So this was it, then, the rock face of virtuality. What a different world they lived in. While she'd been spending her working life in a library charting the extinction of cultural heterogeneity, this man had been playing with a video game. 'I haven't tried a simulator since I was a child,' was all she could think of saying.

'You've never tried a body suit?' He was astonished. 'You don't know what you're missing.'

'I can imagine.'

'No, you can't.' His contradiction was final. 'This system can transmogrify you into anything the human mind can conceive.'

She looked doubtfully at the contraption. 'Is it very disorientating?'

'Not really. It takes some people a minute or so to get back to CR.'

'CR?'

'Consensus Reality.'

She hated this sort of jargon. 'What other sort of reality is there?'

He nodded at the girdle. 'I'll show you.'

She thought he was joking till she saw his face. 'Strap me into that machine? No, thanks.'

'You're turning down a ride on a two billion dollar machine?'

There was something charming in his incredulity. He was looking younger by the moment.

'What do I have to do?'

'Get changed, and I'll tell you.'

The technicians were polite enough to leave the room with William while she changed into the white body stocking. She ran her hands over her legs, unhooking the snags, aware of the video camera hanging from the ceiling. The fabric seemed to be designed to accentuate the bulges in all the wrong places. She sucked her belly in, wishing there was a mirror in the room. Four children had sagged all the important bits; she thought she must look like a bag of suet.

When William came back in with the technicians, she felt naked and ridiculous. They measured her and weighed her, and then selected a flight suit. She was relieved to slip into its padded anonymity; anyone would look fat in this. The female technician zipped her up.

'We can do without the catheter, I think,' William said to her.

Julia looked down at her groin to see a nylon nozzle waiting for a pipe to be attached.

'For peeing in?'

'You don't think I hold on for forty-eight hours, do you?'

She shrugged. She'd never thought about it. 'Do you eat when you're inside?'

He picked up a transparent plastic pouch filled with reddish brown liquid. 'It's designed to be as bland as possible. All extraneous sensory input is kept to a minimum.'

The woman slid the gloves over Julia's hands. 'We'll just have a few simple digital commands. Point your hand up—' she demonstrated, holding her index finger towards the ceiling, 'to ascend. Down to descend. You'll see your virtual hand, so there won't be any confusion. Palm out to go faster, palm towards you to slow. We'll control your size. Got that?'

Julia repeated the instructions. Her heart was pounding inside her padded suit.

'We're giving you the twenty dollar ride,' William said. 'The full works need security clearance, but you'll have haptic feedback and tactile sensors.'

They helped her step into the girdle, fastening her feet, and then snapped the corset around her torso. They calibrated the machine to fit her, and she allowed the limbs of the suit to be slotted into armatures, corresponding to arm and leg joints.

'Just relax,' the female technician murmured. Julia felt as helpless as if she was undergoing a gynaecological examination.

'Try some movement,' the technician said.

Julia moved her arms tentatively. She felt extraordinarily fluid, the machine did not hinder her movements at all.

'Now legs.'

She flexed her knees. She felt as though she was in the grip of a powerful and sensitive robot. It was hard to tell where her body ended and the machine began.

'This feels wonderful!'

'Try this.' William took the outer ring and flipped it upwards, tipping her onto her back. She cried out, expecting to crash onto the floor, but the machine held her. Her arms, her legs, even her head were held in place. She twisted her torso experimentally, turning onto her front. She was horizontal, moving her arms in front of her. 'It's like swimming in air!'

This was a toy they had all enjoyed, and the technicians smiled at each other. She hadn't seen anything yet.

'Now the face sucker.' William tilted her upright and then held the helmet above her as though it were a crown.

'Ready?' He lowered it onto her head. The head-mounted

display was not much heavier than a cyclist's helmet. The eye pads cut out all the light, and for a moment, she panicked.

She heard William's voice, muffled. 'It'll take you a while to find your feet.'

At first she thought he meant it literally, and she instinctively looked down. She wanted to be unhooked from the machine, but it had taken so long to set up, she was afraid to say so.

She felt hands adjusting the earpieces so the speakers fitted snugly into her ear.

Deaf and blind, she waited for something to happen.

Can you hear me, Julia?

The words sounded inside her head.

'Yes.'

Her vision exploded in light: a deep marine blue.

Have fun.

You are underwater. No, floating through a pale blue universe. You hold your right hand out and see a hand. It is perfectly formed, slim fingers tapering to perfect nails. But not yours. You feel your body lift upwards as though bobbing to the surface of a swimming pool. Remembering the instructions, you point down, and feel yourself descend.

This is great.

Your words are printed at the bottom of your vision.

You didn't tell me this —

You can't finish your sentence. Seeing your words in front of you as soon as they leave your mouth is as disconcerting as listening to an instant playback of yourself.

William?

Yes?

It is his voice, the word hanging for a second in front of your eyes before dissolving into the blue background.

Just checking.

Points of light are visible in front of you, and you hold your hands out to touch them. They grow into coloured discs, tiny at first and then expanding rapidly. You realise they are balls flying towards you. A roaring sound fills your head. Planets, not balls.

They tear past you at an extraordinary speed. You feel

the heat on that side of your body, the buffeting of their wake.

I'm scared. I want to slow down.

Palms facing yourself.

You do as instructed, and the planets slow to a stop until they hang like exotic beach balls around you. You mouth the word *beautiful*. You don't want the scene interrupted by your words.

Suddenly the landscape changes. You are standing on a field of orange grass under a yellow sky. A house stands on your right: blue walls, opaque green windows, white picket fence. It is a cartoon house.

Horrible colour.

The sky turns turquoise.

That's better.

Try walking, Julia.

You tentatively take a step. You can feel the cool grass on your feet. You look down to see somebody else's bare feet. Wiggling your toes, you see the virtual toes respond. It's odd; enough time spent here, and you could believe these toes are yours. Your eyes travel up your body, and you realise with a shock that you are naked. Your eyes freeze when you reach your groin. They have made you a man. You can hear faint laughter, but you're not sure if it is coming from inside or outside.

You take another step, and another. Judging from the change in perspective, you are either thirty feet tall, or it is a doll's house next to you. You walk past the house, and then begin jogging. Remembering your speed controls, you hold your palm in front of you. You are loping towards the horizon, the landscape slipping beneath your feet. You vault hedges and cartoon streams, travelling faster than you have run in your life. It is exhilarating, like a flying dream. The horizon unfolds, a perfect, flawless sphere as you race across the orange landscape.

Visible in the distance is another house, and as you near it, you see it is where you began. You have circled this make-believe planet. Nearing the house, you can see it is a pastel version of the original, in fact everything beyond it is frosted as though seen through a mist. Then you realise you are separated from it by a translucent barrier. Turning left and right, you see that it stretches out of sight. You slow to a walk until you reach it.

Pushing your hand against it, you realise it is some kind of elastic membrane. It is as though you are inside a vast, white balloon.

Push it.

The words appear in blue at the bottom of your field of vision. As you nudge the membrane, the sound of a violin bow being drawn across two strings fills your head. The sound is so appropriate to the movement that you laugh aloud. You knead the membrane experimentally. It has exactly the quality of resistance of stretched rubber.

Push harder.

You do as William says. The bow is being jerked across the strings now. You hesitate, fearing the membrane will break.

Push.

Who does he think he is, a midwife? You take a deep breath and shove harder. Something snaps, an orchestra of sound compressed into a fraction of a second, and you are plunged into darkness.

You shriek, the sound transliterated across the bottom of your vision, the same two letters as though somebody is holding a couple of fingers on a keyboard key. You can feel yourself spinning head over heels, your hands flailing to catch your balance. You shut your eyes, trying to picture the girdle spinning aimlessly in the test room. William's voice comes to you as though he is standing just behind you.

Keep your hands still if you want to stop.

Of course. Immediately you do so, the spinning stops, and you open your eyes.

You don't know what you are expecting, but the sight of the serpent's tail of coloured light makes you gasp. It is a fractal, suspended in the air in front of you against a pitch black background. You point your index finger at it, and feel your body jerk forward. Though the shape grows until it fills your field of vision, you aren't nearing it. No more detail is visible, just a further unfolding of these fragments of colours. It is like being in a kaleidoscope, geometric patterns of light infinitely repeating around you. You turn round, looking above you. You are in a galaxy of lights, complex and breathtaking. You realise your breath is coming shallow and fast.

Get me out of here, William.

*   *   *

There was only one thing that approached the thrill of flying a machine this smart, and that was turning somebody on for the first time. William looked from the screen to the girdle, watching her tumbling in space like a fairground ride. She had been a bit snooty with her anthropological stuff, but this would take her down a notch or two.

This had been the most exciting time of his life and few people could understand the kick of flying these machines. It was better than dreaming, better than reality enhancers; this was near total environmental control. This was like playing God. And safe, too. Sure, they had built parameters into it, but even those didn't extend beyond discomfort. You could throw yourself from the top of a skyscraper and bounce like a rubber ball. You could breathe under water, make yourself as small as a molecule. He remembered the motto he'd read stuck onto one of the programmer's terminals: *Whoever said the sky was the limit showed a serious lack of imagination.*

William was proud of the project, proud to be a member of the team, proud to be a flier. The most difficult part of the job was the confidentiality agreement. He wanted to tell everybody about it. A couple of months, though, and this package would get Federal approval and travel agents would be queuing up for copyright clearance.

'Give her the fractals,' he'd said to the technician. 'She'll like that.'

He had sat down and watched the screen. It was amazing how computerphobic some people were. He'd seen people go to pieces in cyberspace, others so cautious they might as well have stayed on the outside. But this woman was getting the hang of it, moving her body well, remembering the digital commands. She was right into the fractal now, looking round like a star gazer on a cloudless night. He knew she'd like this; she was just the arty sort who'd appreciate it. He'd give her a bit longer and then he'd feed in music.

It *was* safe, he had few genuine doubts any more. There were reports of post immersion psychotic episodes from some of the Chinese pilots, but he put that down to inferior technology more than anything else. They hadn't come close to the Omnisens specifications; they were two years behind, at least. William knew plenty of test pilots, and apart from a few of them preferring virtuality to the real thing, they were no crazier than before they went in.

Kinderling had debriefed him thoroughly after each sortie, checking on him every day. Apart from sleeping badly at night, there was nothing to report. Sure, he'd lost any sense of CR after being inside a while, but that was the whole point. He had no trouble distinguishing real from false when he was unhooked.

He looked up in surprise when he heard Julia's call for help.

'Program end,' he called out.

The screen went blank, and he stood to take her helmet off. Perhaps they'd overdone it for a first go. 'Don't struggle. Let me unhook you first.'

He slid the helmet off, and she shook her hair free. She was breathing deeply, her face flushed.

'Thank God for that,' she gasped.

Her pupils were dilated. It had been quite a ride, and she'd only been in two minutes.

The technicians unhooked her from the armatures and helped her out of the girdle. Her hair was stuck to her forehead with sweat. She was unsteady on her feet, and William guided her to the chair.

'Well?'

'I never knew it could be so . . . *realistic*,' she said, unzipping the suit.

'That's about the degree of sophistication of a good cyberdrome game. We reached that level five years ago.'

'It was as though I was in another world.'

'You were. A virtual world.'

She held a gloved hand in front of her. 'I could touch those colours. I could *feel* them.'

William waited in the corridor while she changed into her day clothes. He was glad she was impressed; hopefully, she could see it was more than just fancy television. Biocomputing had got a bad name amongst academics, and Omnisens funding this project hardly helped the matter. Though the big bucks were in mass market entertainment, fantasy holidays were nothing compared to what was possible.

Jarnier had hinted as much when William was being briefed for the project. He wasn't giving much away, but it was clear this was no ordinary endurance project. 'We've invented a game for you,' he had told William. 'A quest.'

'And what do I have to find?'

'Knowledge,' he had said. Knowledge of what, he didn't say.

7

William allowed his arms to be guided into the sleeves of the flight suit and then shrugged himself into position so the front could be fastened. He always got a thrill at this stage, being suited up. It must have been like this in the old days of air combat, the paraphernalia of padded clothes and helmets, the adrenalin rush of venturing into the unknown.

He stepped onto the platform, and let a technician strap his ankles into the girdle. The armatures were slotted into place, calves and thighs first, then arms. He automatically ran through the test routine, starting at the feet, flexing and extending every limb in turn. He realised he was still tired from his last flight. He'd just had twenty hours of CR since last time, and seven of those he'd been asleep. The corset had rubbed a raw patch on his ribs, and though gauze had been stuck over it, he could feel the sting as the padded suit grazed it.

The helmet was eased onto his head, the eye and ear pieces adjusted by invisible hands. A minute pop indicated that the line to control had been activated.

Welcome back, William.

It was Jarnier. William made himself relax, waiting for the visuals to come on. A hissing noise was coming through one ear piece, and he told control. The sound cut out immediately, and he was in perfect silent blackness.

He always thought that if there was one moment he would panic, it would be now. Waiting for something to happen, he was locked into a machine from which he could never escape alone. If the technicians wanted to, they could leave him and he would die still strapped into this girdle. Though his fingers had the apparent dexterity to thread a virtual needle, in fact with the padded gloves, he wouldn't even be able to unfasten his helmet, let alone unhook himself from the armatures.

As William waited he thought about Mama Francisco. Since Julia had told him about the training of the priests, William had felt grudging admiration for the man, virtual though he was. The Mamas were the priests, she had told him, elected by divination at birth, who spent the first nine years of their lives in a cave or a hut. Food and drink would be carefully controlled; white food only, nothing to drink other than warm water. The child – usually a boy – would be taken outside only at night, and then shaded with a hat so he could see nothing. All sensory input was kept to a minimum; the world was to be known firstly as an idea, and only after childhood would it be revealed in its fullness. Day and night the apprentice would be taught by the mamas. Taught about the great Mother, the nature of reality, taught how to meditate. After an initial cycle of nine years – a year in a second womb for each interuterine month – a decision would be made. If the child could stand the rigour and had the aptitude, the training continued for a further nine years. If not, the child was returned to its family. Ideally, the successful candidate would complete his training when he was eighteen, when he would be returned to the outside world to begin his work as a Mama.

And that wasn't work? William had said. Not even eighteen years of back pay? He had wanted to lighten the woman up, but Julia wasn't playing. These people had been for real, she had said, working for the benefit of the planet. They were due our respect. William had kept his mouth shut, watching the way her lips shaped each word. He didn't know whether to try and seduce this woman or not.

There were beings known as *moro*, she had continued, Mamas who had trained in the dark for thirty-six years. No outsider had ever met one: they were the oracles who lived high in the Sierra, seeing nobody other than Mamas. Anthropologists considered their deeds mythical: stories of flying, of travelling through spirit worlds, making huge rocks fly through the air, miraculous healings. This was standard indigenous fare, but Julia believed every word about them. She also believed there must still be isolated pockets of these people in the mountains – such power could not so easily be erased.

Weird, William thought, arching his back in the girdle, feeling a bone in his neck click. They sounded too sci-fi to be true, but apparently they weren't alone. Druids and Tibetan monks likewise trained for such periods in the dark. The first cybernauts, explorers of inner space.

What *was* the work of the Mamas? They obviously had a social function. The Kogi were a feudal and theocratic society with the Mama at the top, but their fundamental role was their work in *aluna*, the dimension of thought. Julia had looked as though she really believed it: the world must be balanced in the *noumenon* otherwise the phenomenon would cease. It was the Mamas' job to do the balancing.

William shrugged his shoulders in his harness. He steadied his breathing to take his mind off his confinement. 'Hurry up and turn me on, boys and girls. I ain't got all day.'

No answer. He shared none of Julia's misgivings about using the Kogi for the project. He knew his defence of Omnisens was hard to refute. Tourism had been ruining what little there was left of natural habitats until reality holidays had taken hold. People had a right to recreation, and they had a right to know the world they lived in. What better way than creating an electronic replica, saving the real thing to recover? And anyway, the Kogi weren't such utopians; they were as antidemocratic as you could get. He had watched her as she had groped to define what was wrong. It was the exploitation of the Kogi that was bothering her. This was a group of people who saw themselves as the custodians of the planet: elder brother, they called themselves. By anyone's standards, theirs was a wise culture. The technological world was the younger brother, strangers to reverence, too clever by half, who in their short ascendancy had brought the planet to the edge of an abyss. And they knew plenty we didn't, she finished with. Average life expectancy? Ninety years.

There was a whole week's argument in there, but William had let it pass. She was so easily rattled there was no sport in teasing her.

Thirty years ago, she had told him, the Kogi had broken their customary silence to speak to the world. Their message was so simple that few people heard it: slow down, respect the planet, otherwise it will be too late. They had their say, and then they withdrew. But then the Japanese built their cable car, disease took hold and the last indigenous flame of the Americas was snuffed out.

Now we were turning the Kogi into caricatures of themselves. If we had screwed our world up, at least there were these noble savages in their prelapsarian utopia getting it right. The Kogi had always wanted to be left alone, she'd said at last, and here we are, digging up their graves, making them dance like performing monkeys.

But this is virtual reality William had said, unable to restrain himself any longer. Not real.

But it *is* real, she had said. Thoughts are real, intentions are real.

Visuals coming on.

A deep electronic blue flooded his vision. William drank the light as though it were water. He realised how tense he had been and let his muscles relax. He loved this colour. It had been tailored for him by the project neurophysicists, and it was as refreshing as swimming in a pool of cool water. He breathed the highly ionised, oxygen-enriched air through the face mask. He could stay like this for ever, leave the moral arguing to the politicians and bleeding hearts.

Jarnier again. Before we get going, I want to tell you about the map stone. Check it out. I've been designing it over the last couple of days – I think you'll like it.

'What is it?' He hated these last minute surprises that Jarnier kept springing on him.

A stone, about two metres tall. Check out the markings on it . . . Uh-oh, here comes the boss.

William shook his head in disbelief. How this guy was allowed access to a multi-billion dollar project, he would never know. Just one look at him was enough to see he was a subversive: all that frizzy hair and talk about freedom of information. And the clothes he wore; he looked like a college kid. Okay, so he might be a genius, but so was Dr Frankenstein.

You in good shape, William?

He felt his body come to attention. It was Dr Beecham.

'Yes, sir.'

We need more human interaction. So we're programming a meeting with . . .

William could hear the faint sound of shuffling paper as the director sought the name.

. . . Mama Francisco. Go with him, and hear what he has to say. We're not going to keep you in as long as last time.

He was worried to hear it. Did this mean they were winding him down? Though it hadn't been official, he knew they were displeased with his last trip inside. He mustn't lose it this time. If he wanted to keep his job he had better follow instructions and keep himself under control.

And, William?

'Yes, sir?'

No more cloud floating, please.

The first thing you see is the map stone. At least, that's what you assume it is. Taller than you, and as broad as your arm's span, it is made of some unidentifiable rock, criss-crossed with scratches. Looking closer, you see the lines have been etched into the rock, no more than a couple of millimetres deep, and in some places almost obscured by the lichen that grows across its surface.

Your run your fingers over the stone, feeling the granular surface beneath your fingers. It is warm, and curiously welcoming to the touch. You can see it is old, these chisel lines have been rounded through years of rain water.

Congratulations, Jarnier. It looks very authentic.

You feel something tap you on the shoulder, and you turn round. Mama Francisco is standing near you, his old brown face in repose. A wad of coca leaves is in his cheek, giving his face a swollen look. He holds a *poporo* in his hands.

He gestures for you to follow him. He treads through the undergrowth with no sound, and you wonder if this is a fault in the programming. Compared to him you are clumsy, stumbling against branches, the roots of plants catching your feet. It is uncomfortably hot, and already you're beginning to sweat.

You are led to the ceremonial house, the *nuhue*. Ducking through its low opening, you step into its dusk and pause to allow your eyes to get accustomed to the gloom. At first all you can see is a tall column of light through the smoky air. It must be a solstice date you realise, the only time they take the cap off the hut. And then you are aware the hut is full of people – men sitting on benches or lying in hammocks, working their *poporos*. One or two glance up at you before continuing, licking the end of their sticks and dipping it into the gourd, smearing the lime paste onto its neck. The only sound is the rattling of their sticks. You count the number of people: nine or ten. They must have doubled up the numbers without telling you.

Someone behind you nudges you forward, but you're reluctant to move further into the gloom. The corset is still rubbing against your raw patch and you find yourself twisting to reduce the pressure.

Control – can you do something about this?

You feel hands on your torso and the pain lessen as your suit is adjusted.

Thanks.

Again you are nudged from behind, Mama Francisco this time. You dare not hesitate any longer, so you allow yourself to be led between two open fires. He indicates for you to sit on the stone bench, facing the wall of the hut.

Here?

He nods.

You brush the dirt from the bench and do as he says. The wall in front of you is made of woven thatch, an overlapping of patterns which plays tricks with your eyes. You imagine it is full of insects and immediately your skin starts to itch.

What are you going to do?

There is no answer so you twist to look at the old man. He jerks his chin at the wall to indicate you should turn round again.

Come on – you can tell me.

You regret the words as soon as they are out of your mouth. Too much insubordination and you'll be off the project. The man takes your head in his hands and turns you to face the wall. You offer no resistance, and find yourself staring at the thatch again. It's times like this when you wonder who is in control, whether the program hasn't taken over. You can feel the familiar sensation of balancing between two worlds, each equally real – or unreal. If you shut your eyes and concentrate you can be back in the test room, suspended in the exoskeleton, a team of technicians monitoring your every function. But you can sense the presence of a man behind you. If you reach out and touch the wall in front of you, it will be as real as a wall ever was. *A man who dreamed he was a butterfly, or a butterfly dreaming he is a man?*

The voice of the Mama comes from behind you. His voice is low. 'A person's life should be given over to knowledge. You should learn, younger brother. Learn about the law of the Mother.'

There is a silence, so you take your cue. 'What should I learn?'

'Learn that every object, every action, every thought has a meaning and a spirit. Listen well.' The flickering shadows on the wall in front of you are like his words. As he continues, you fall into the shadow, hearing the words coming from inside yourself.

> *In the beginning, there was blackness.*
> *Only the sea.*
> *In the beginning there was no sun, no moon, no people.*
> *In the beginning there were no animals, no plants.*
> *Only the sea.*
>
> *The sea was the Mother.*
> *The Mother was not people, she was not anything.*
> *No thing at all.*
> *She was when she was, darkly.*
> *She was memory and potential.*
> *She was aluna.*

The Mama stops talking, and you turn to look at him. His skin is lined and leathery, a sheen on his cheekbones from the firelight. He is working his *poporo*, dipping the stick into the gourd and then building up the lime calc on its neck. He looks calm and sad.

His eyes are hooded, visible only as a twinkle in the half light. You find yourself staring into those eyes, travelling closer to him, shrinking in size. You are being pulled into his left eye, falling through the black iris into a maze of fluorescent green bars.

William, this is Dr Beecham. You're off the program. Take three retrograde steps.

You hear the words, but they mean nothing to you. You just rest in the maze of light, watching the colour, breathing oxygen-enriched air.

Acknowledge, please.

8

The writing is going better than I dared imagine. Turn on a tap, and out it comes. I forgot that it is possible to slip out of one world into another, spend an entire day in a fictional universe. I never questioned why I became a writer, why even after I'd stopped, I continued to read and teach. But a single day spent in front of the typewriter, and it's staring me in the face – I write to escape. On the page, I am God. Nothing except the limits of my imagination holds me back. I am in total control of events; I can make people die, I can make them fall in love, say ridiculous things. I can contradict myself, destroy planets, I can float so far out that nobody, not even myself, can decipher the meaning of my words.

And I'm surprising myself. I don't know if the writing is any good or not, but the pages are filling up. A thousand words a day snatched from the ether and pinned to paper. What was it Hemingway called blank paper – the white bull? Surprisingly, no such fears for me. After twenty-five years of talking about writing, I was apprehensive about any words being left for myself. But it seems I have an imagination still, something to say. I don't know if it's worth reading, but there's ink on the page. *Toro! Toro!*

I push the typewriter away and stretch my arms above my head. I'm frozen. My fingers have contracted into claws, bleached white from the knuckle to the fingertips. The thermo pad on my lap only accentuates how cold the rest of my body feels. I rub the outside of my arms and legs but it makes no difference.

A movement above my head catches my eye. One of the

fluorescent lights is swaying. I can see something green perched at the end – it looks like a bird. I stand up and duck my head so I can see better. A green parrot is sitting on one of the strip lights scratching its neck. Before I can register anything other than surprise, it straightens up, shuffles its feathers into place and then looks down at me.

What does one do when a green parrot comes uninvited into one's life? I make a cup of herbal tea and sip it through a straw. Where has it come from? Does the presence of this bird mean there are people in town – parrot-keeping people? I guess such a bird would swiftly perish outside in weather like this, but I've got to get rid of it. I'm sure to be allergic to parrot feathers.

I put on my mask and open a window. Then I stand under the light and clap my hands. The parrot twists its neck to look at me, but is not startled by the noise. I take a plastic cup from the corner and throw it at the bird. It misses by a few feet, but it is enough to get it airborne. The bird flies, not through the window as directed, but further down the room, to perch on the winding machine.

I spend five minutes throwing things at it. Most of the missiles are ducked if they come close enough, but even a bullseye with a pair of socks doesn't persuade the bird to leave. I give up when I smash a light tube with an ill-judged aim of a shoe. 'Bastard!' I end up shouting, wagging my finger like a schoolmaster.

I ignore the bird and do some half-hearted exercises to warm myself up. After a minute I'm so out of breath I have to lie down. My lungs are wheezing, something rattling inside my rib cage. This is new. Perhaps a screw inside my chest has come loose.

The mattress is more comfortable than I thought. As long as I don't freeze to death in the night, I should sleep as well as I did at home. *Home* – is that the way I still think of it?

My gaze ranges over my sleeping equipment. This is one area I came well prepared for: orthopaedic pillow for my neck, night cap for my head, bed socks for my feet, electro-acupuncture kit for insomnia. Sleep used to be a simple pleasure before I got ill, now it's an industry. Now I lay me down to sleep, a man old before his time. Sixty-three years old, for God's sake. Still young inside, but my body's packing up on me.

Strange. In some ways I couldn't care less about my illness;

all the symptoms so far have been bearable. It's the ignominy of passing on my contamination that bothers me. Three score years and three and what will I leave behind? Two sons, a handful of books and a trail of death.

It's time for my medication. With my gloves on I have trouble pressing the pills out of their plastic, so I take them off. My fingers are scarlet, with cold I hope. So far the capsules have made no difference, so I pop three of them. I almost choke on the third and have to slap my throat to dislodge it.

At what point can we say we've failed? Is there a critical mass of accumulated fuck-ups, when the verdict of our life is no longer conjecture, but as undeniable as oak apples on a diseased bough? Two boys, an averagely successful marriage, an averagely successful career at the university, and here I am, radioactive with infection, lying on an inflatable camping bed, staring up at a broken fluorescent tube on a factory ceiling in the middle of nowhere. Is that failure?

If not the tangible reality, then what about the missed opportunities, the cowardice and selfishness. The duplicity and hypocrisy. Is *that* failure? Have we all failed through nothing but greed and ignorance? I wish I didn't still care, but I do. Somebody must be punished for the mess we've made.

Of one thing there is no doubt: Carla was a far better wife to me than I was ever a husband to her. Unremittingly loyal, she didn't deserve being left in that way. Not one indication of where I am, what I'm finding myself doing. I hate myself for it, but I still can't bring myself to contact her. I want her to forget me. I want all trace of my life to be removed.

I have a lot to thank her for. She did a good job, kept my feet on the ground for thirty years, guided two boys around the fringes of delinquency, made a home with all the bits. But it was all a dream. None of it happened. I ceased to exist long ago. There is an imposter in this body, staring up at the roof, wearing a stranger's clothes, foreign coins in his pocket. If I stretch my imagination I can remember being a real person once, complete and unselfconscious. Now I'm a jigsaw person, still searching for the same missing pieces, no sense of history, fearful of the future.

Dusk is a slow affair this far north. I lie on the pneumatic mattress watching the light seep from the room, my thoughts slipping and sliding until it is almost dark. I enjoy this gradual descent into dusk; no street lights here to take the place of the sun, just the deepening grey of wilderness and the glow of the electric heater. I want to die here and never wake up.

I hear a rustling in the corner and turn just in time to see a rodent's tail disappear behind a radiator. Not only do I have a parrot for company, but it seems I have rats, too. Doubtless I'm allergic to them, but as long as they don't crawl over me, they're welcome to stay.

I suppose I should be hungry. I switch on the lights and open a can of fruit cocktail and eat the multicoloured pieces with my fingers. The label on the can says *Yum-yum Fruit*, but I guess it's mostly peaches and pears. I go to the window to eat, looking out over the slate-grey nothingness. The slices of fruit are so cold they have an edge of ice to them. I have to hold the fruit pieces in the well of my tongue until they defrost. I consider heating the juice, but I can't be bothered, so I drink it straight from the can.

Carla, I suppose, is blessed with an undeveloped imagination. Is that an unfair assessment? Possibly. Perhaps the lack is within myself: a lack of sense of integrity, an absence of glue to hold my pieces together. Certainly life was a far simpler proposition to Carla than to most people I know. Food, possessions, children, career; the ground she stood on was as solid as her self-assurance. For thirty years she observed the continental drift of my personality like a sightseer on dry land watching icebergs sliding past. Patient and tolerant – no small thing for a woman of her passion – I suppose it was love that pulled her through all those years. I *did* love her, I still do I expect. But not as well as I could.

I suddenly feel sick. My belly heaves, and I just make it to the sink before a spray of *Yum-yum Fruit* spouts from my mouth. I'm caught so much by surprise I can't even take a breath before the second mouthful gushes out. Red stars sparkle in my eyes as the food is ripped from inside me. Clearing my throat, I spit out a piece of diced cherry and then stand up. I lean against the sink, tears prickling behind my closed eyelids. One more go? The final eruption empties my stomach and I know I've finished. The plughole is blocked, the ceramic bowl half full of fruit salad and what appears to be condensed milk. I look for something to clear the blockage, but find nothing so I stuff my fingers into the bowl. I'm surprised by how warm the vomit is, pleasant to the touch. I look closely at the contents of the bowl; the fruit pieces look no different to how they were when I first ate them. It doesn't look as though I have gained much from their sojourn in my stomach.

Carla was an exemplary mother; the only responsibility at which she balked was clearing up vomit. That was always my job; one whiff of child's puke and she'd be sick too. When I started getting ill and I had trouble keeping food down, she would have to leave the room, her fingers in her ears to block out the sound of my retching.

The bowl isn't emptying, and I remember that the water I poured into it earlier didn't drain away either. I guess the waste pipe has frozen. There's only one thing for it. I unwrap a honey bag and scoop the vomit out with my hands.

I don't know what it was about *Yum-yum Fruit* that upset my stomach, but I hope this isn't going to be a pattern – I have twenty more cans of the stuff.

Carla was never a mild-mannered woman, but I could have told her where I was going, refused to guess when I'd be back. There would have been tears and shouting, but it has been years since it has made much difference to me.

She'll survive. Well shot of me, if the truth be told.

I tie up the honey bag and take it to the window. The hinge has frosted shut and I have to bang it open with the side of my fist. I notice a thin sheen of ice has formed on the inside of the glass. It's windy outside and the cold air snatches at my jacket like an animal. I quickly drop the bag into the darkness and then pour some water over my sticky hands.

9

He'd been having a nightmare. The details had gone now, but he was lost in the jungle, fighting to get out. Faces hiding in the shadows, and then falling through space. William lay in the tangle of damp sheets and stared at the ceiling, trying to piece together the fragments for the report. They'd ask him about the dream whether he mentioned it or not. There would be no denying the videotape of him thrashing around in his sleep.

He looked at the glowing numbers of the clock beside his bed: it wasn't even 11 p.m. He'd slept for just two and a half hours. Swinging his legs out of bed, he stood up, hitching his boxer shorts higher. He looked at the video camera hanging from the ceiling. Better get it over with. 'Disturbed sleep. Bad dream, something about the jungle,' he said in an unnecessarily loud voice. He closed his eyes to try and capture the fleeting images of swift movements in the foliage. 'Detail has gone now. Something about threat, being chased. Falling.'

He shrugged and turned his back on the camera. He didn't want them to see his face. There was nothing new in disturbed sleep patterns, and even nightmares had been common since he joined the project, but he didn't want them to see him like this. He switched the light on, and leant on the windowsill to look across the quadrangle of sand. Kinderling would no doubt pull the dream apart in the morning as though it were a cryptic crossword puzzle, delivering the solution to William in his crisp mid-Atlantic way.

He didn't like Kinderling. Their daily sessions unnerved him, all those unanswerable questions, digging for something that wasn't there. The project psychologist was a subversive, he was sure of it. Like Jarnier. People who pretended to support the project, but all the time were looking for faults and weaknesses. He had his doubts about the English anthropologist as well, all her whining about cultural integrity.

William thought back to his last trip inside. They had pulled him out immediately, ignoring his protests. He had been inside less than fifteen minutes, and still felt as fresh as when he started, but Beecham was adamant. William knew he had wandered off the edge, but oddly, Kinderling hasn't asked him why. Lucky, because William couldn't have given him an answer. He'd clocked hundreds of immersion hours, but he'd never fallen apart in this way. Okay, it was on the heels of an endurance record, but wandering off the program? He was behaving like a rookie. *You're off the program.* Any more cock-ups and he would be. Permanently.

He pulled on his slacks and jacket and then looked in his fridge, but he wanted real food, not orange juice and soya snacks. Meat, proper meat. Cow, that's what he wanted. When was the last time he had eaten any real meat? He couldn't remember.

He drank a Coke standing up, thinking about Julia, wondering if she was asleep. Strange, she wasn't his sort, but there was something about her he liked. She was hopelessly technophobic, but she wasn't stupid. He got fed up with the jocks on the test program, all their beer and small talk.

His eyes strayed to the watercolour he had pinned to the wall. It was a landscape he had recently copied from a magazine, but for a moment he was unable to focus his mind on it, and it appeared as abstract shapes, purple and grey blobs floating in a green medium.

He decided to see if Julia was still awake. He switched off his light and wandered down the corridor to her room. Light was coming from under her door so he tapped his knuckle on her plastic nameplate.

'Who is it?'

'William.'

There was a pause before she unlocked the door and let him in. She was still dressed, but her feet were bare. William could see by the depression in the bed that she had been lying down.

A face towel hung over the video camera, identically positioned to that in William's room.

'You don't have to worry about that,' he said. 'They won't be watching you.'

'How do I know?'

'A red light comes on when it's operating.' He pulled the towel off. 'See, no red light.'

She took the towel from him and folded it over the back of a chair. A baseball cap with the project logo across its rim – MAYA in red and gold letters – had been hooked over the chair arm.

'Work going okay?' he asked.

She made no effort to reply.

'I couldn't sleep.' He sat down and scanned the contents of her room. It was identical to his, but somehow she had made hers look smaller. A suitcase spewing clothes took up one corner, a holoplayer sat on the floor in the other. Messy, he noted. 'You neither?'

'I was reading.' She nodded at the paperback on the bedside table.

'Don't they have it on digiback?' William had never read a hard copy novel in his adult life. He sometimes bought manga, but even those he preferred to read on screen.

'I like the feel of paper.'

He nodded, not hearing her answer. 'You're married, aren't you?'

'Yes.'

She was genuinely old-fashioned, he decided. He wondered if all Brits were like this.

'Children?'

'Four.' She said the word almost apologetically.

'You must be a Catholic.'

She shook her head. 'It just happened that way.'

Irresponsible use of resources, he wanted to say, but he held himself in check. Zero growth in the first world was being screwed up by people like her. 'My father was a Catholic,' he said at last. 'And a Brit.'

'Was he an earner?'

He looked up at the ceiling, trying to remember. 'He was a librarian, I think. My parents split before I was born.' He looked at her. He didn't know why he was there, but it wasn't to talk about his family. And neither was he about to seduce this woman. He realised he wasn't interested in her, at least not sexually. A shame, he decided; a little diversion wouldn't be a bad thing.

He was aware of his attention flicking from one object to another, but he couldn't bring himself to settle.

'How was your last trip inside?' she said.

He looked blankly at her. She'd been there, hadn't she, watching him making a fool of himself.

'Or aren't you allowed to discuss it?'

He realised his knee was bouncing up and down. He rested his hands on his thigh to try and still it. 'I'm allowed to discuss it.' The 'but' hung in the air, until discomfort drove him forward to explain himself. 'It's hard to talk about,' he said at last. He didn't even know if he had words to describe what was happening. As he sat in the silence of the room, he could feel something slipping away from him. Something that nobody had ever mentioned. He glanced up at the video camera to make sure the light hadn't come on. 'It's getting to me, I think.' He was surprised to hear the words coming out of his mouth. Surprised to be saying them to a woman he hardly knew. 'I'm dreaming about them. The Kogi.'

This was why he had come to this woman's room. He had to talk to someone, a person, not a psychologist. But what was there to say? 'It's so real on the inside. When they take the digital display away, there's nothing to show it isn't CR.' He looked up at the camera again. 'And now I'm out, I've got no proof that I'm not inside.'

'They must have told you to expect this.'

He shrugged. They had, but he hadn't thought they'd meant it. Not like this. He had quietly despised the people who handled virtuality badly, the hallucinators and neurotics. But now he was joining their ranks. It was surprise he felt as much as anything else. He was a test pilot; psychological endurance was part of his training. He had spent days in solitary confinement, been dunked in sensory deprivation tanks, ate and slept in zero gravity. He knew the anticipated side effects of long-term exposure to the machine; the disorientation, the depression. He knew that some arcade kids were having breakdowns, but they were children, not trained, and the programs they flew were so basic they were almost bound to induce hallucinations.

'Do you know the Chinese story about the man who dreamt he was a butterfly?' she said.

'Tell me.'

'When he woke up, he wasn't sure what he was – a man who'd dreamt he was a butterfly, or a butterfly who was dreaming he was a man.'

'Thanks for the encouragement,' he said facetiously. He'd heard this recently, but couldn't remember where.

'You've just been shaken up,' she said. 'You'll get over it.'

He got to his feet, wondering why he'd even come to this woman's room at all. There was nothing anyone could say; words didn't stretch that far.

'How about a drink?' she said. 'I smuggled in a bottle of wine.'

'I'm not allowed.' He hesitated at the door. He was too restless to sleep. 'I'll have a juice.'

She asked him about himself while he sat in the chair sipping a carton of mango and pineapple. His responses were automatic, but they helped calm him down. He told her about his childhood in Virginia, his degree in computer science from Washington University.

She asked him when he joined the company.

'I always wanted to be a flier,' he said. 'Since I was a kid.'

'You didn't want to fly real planes?'

'No.'

'Just simulators?'

'Just?' he raised an eyebrow at her. 'It's the real thing.'

She watched him guzzle his drink. 'And what about your parents?'

'I never knew my dad. My mom brought me up alone. She ran a stud farm. Horses.'

'Have you got brothers and sisters?'

'No. Connie would rather breed horses than people.'

'What was her name again?' The tone in her voice made him look up. She was puzzled about something.

'Connie.'

She paused as if to compose herself before asking the next question. 'Tell me about her.'

'Nothing much to say. She met my dad in London.' He shrugged. 'She lives in Seattle.'

'What was your father's name?'

'James. Why the interest?'

'No reason.'

He finished his drink and lobbed the carton into the basket under her table. He didn't notice the look on her face.

There was a long pause. 'Do you read novels?' she asked.

'I haven't got the time.'

'You need a break. Why not read a good book?'

He shrugged. 'Maybe.'

'I've got one I think you'd like.' She went to the table and picked up the paperback. 'It's a bit ragged,' she said turning to face him. 'But it's worth reading.'

'Are you through with it?'

'Nearly. Here, you take it.'

He held his hand out to accept the book and slipped it into his pocket without glancing at it.

'What?'

She sat up in bed, forcing her eyes to open. It was still dark. Somebody was hammering at the door. 'Who is it?'

The hammering continued and she forced herself out of bed. 'Who is it?'

'It's William.'

'What do you want?'

'Let me in.'

'Hold on.' She groped her way to the sink and splashed water over her face. She dabbed herself dry with a towel and switched on the light. Its brightness dazzled her, and she had to dim it before she could look at her reflection in the mirror. She tied her robe and went to the door. He was rattling the handle in his impatience to get in.

William pushed past her without a word and sat down. 'I read that book.'

'Yes?'

'Where did you get it?'

'I found it a couple of days ago. What's wrong?'

'Something weird is happening.' He glanced round the room, his eyes flicking up to the video camera. He was nervous of something. 'Let's go for a walk.'

She looked at the clock. Four-fifteen. He must have read the book straight through. 'Why can't we talk here?'

He watched her in silence, and then stood up. 'I'll wait for you outside.'

She dressed quickly and joined him in the corridor. They walked the short distance to the outside door in silence. William checked the air monitor before they stepped out. The desert was as dry as a bone here, but it was only prudent to check. It was cold this early, and she wrapped her arms around herself to keep warm. In the east, the first silver-grey light of dawn showed.

Julia knew it was important that he gather himself, so she waited for him to speak first. They walked side by side in silence, the sand muffling their footsteps.

'You've read that book?' he said at last.

'Most of it.' She knew what was coming, but she waited for him to say more.

'Tell me the biographical data of the two main characters in the book.'

She took a deep breath. She could smell the faint sweat of his body from here. 'James Morrison is a librarian. He's British. He has an affair with Connie, who works with horses, and is American. From Virginia.'

William stopped, and she paused beside him. Julia could hear traffic from highway 54, three miles away.

'In fact, exactly the same as my parents,' he said quietly.

She made no reply.

'What's going on?' he said at last.

'I don't know. When you started talking last night about yourself, I realised that—' The sentence was too absurd to finish, and she looked at him. He was staring up at the pinpoints of stars above him. He addressed his next question to the dawn sky.

'Where did you get the book?'

'I found it on my bedside table when I arrived.'

'So, somebody set it up.'

'Can't it be a coincidence?'

'In the book James lives in a place called Shepherd's Bush – fact. My parents met at a party – fact. They had a crippled friend – fact. She left him to study at agricultural college – fact. Coincidence? Somebody has written a novel about my parents.'

She rubbed her arms to keep warm. 'Perhaps your parents knew a novelist.'

He took the book out of his pocket and flicked through its pages. 'It was published in 1992, a year after they met. That's pretty fast writing.'

'Could your father have written it? He was a writer in the book, wasn't he?'

'Yes.'

'And in real life?'

'I don't know. I never knew my dad. But his name was James Morrison, I know *that* much.'

'Maybe he wrote this book using a pen name?'

His eyes glittered in the first rays of sun as he studied her. '*Is* this a set up?'

'What do you mean?'

'Is this part of the project? Testing me to see what I'll do?'

'I'm an anthropologist, William. I'm not a psychologist.' She saw his look. 'Or security.'

She was wondering exactly that about William. When she had found the book on her bedside table she had barely glanced at it. But earlier this evening when she saw the name of the author, she started it immediately. At first she had assumed it was fiction, but now she realised it wasn't possible. Either that, or the man was lying.

William turned and they walked back towards the low-lying buildings.

'Why don't you ask your mother? She'll know who wrote it.'

He didn't answer. The walls of the base were orange with the dawn as though the buildings were on fire.

10

It takes you five sweaty minutes to reach the village. The bastards could have put you there in the first place, saved you a journey. Though you know the slime that has found its way into your boots is generated by electrodes in your sock, it is no less uncomfortable for that. You can smell woodsmoke, and then you see the conical roof of the *nuhue*. You realise the silhouette of the mountain is echoed in the profile of the pointed roofs of the huts, and you wonder if it is intentional. A tethered horse whinnies when it sees you.

The air is cooler here, pleasant to breathe. But they've made these Kogi a surly lot, not one of them greeting you as you enter the compound. The drive for verisimilitude may have been taken too far with this lot. Nobody would pay good money to spend a day with such a bunch of sour faces.

You have been given instructions to engage every anthropoid, so when you see a man weaving, you join him outside his hut. Propped against the mud wall of the house is a loom, four wooden poles lashed together and two thinner ones forming a cross in the middle. A square of coarsely woven white cloth is in the process of being made. The man is singing dully and off key.

> *I shall weave the fabric of my life;*
> *I shall weave it white as a cloud;*
> *I shall weave some black into it;*
> *I shall weave dark maize stalks into it;*
> *I shall weave maize stalks into the white cloth;*
> *Thus I shall obey divine law.*

He falls silent, concentrating on his task. A striped bag has been slung across his back, the stick of his *poporo* poking through its opening. As he brings the weaving sword down to batten the weft, so the stick nods forward.

'Why are you here?' he asks without turning round.

'Just watching.'

'You have come to steal knowledge from elder brother.'

It's a statement, delivered in a tone so assured that you don't bother to protest. 'What are you doing?'

'The great Mother taught men to weave. I have not forgotten.'

The shuttle is passed from one side to another, and the weaving sword brought down with a clack. 'In the beginning, only the great Mother knew the secret of weaving. She kept it a secret. Nobody knew how to weave, but Serankua watched his mother one night through a crack in the wall. The next day Serankua began to weave and his Mother was angry. But the secret had been learned, so she gave her son two balls of cotton yarn. Serankua and his wife began to weave. They forbade their children to watch, but everybody in the Sierra knew the secret of weaving by then. And we have still not forgotten.'

You don't try and make sense of any of this. Suddenly you want to get out of here. You close your eyes and fall backwards. A bearing in the exoskeleton has been playing up, and you can feel the resistance as your legs tip up.

'What do you want me to do with this?' you ask. You know they won't tell you, but you want to speak to someone. Someone real.

'Dr. Beecham. Give me a hand here. Do you really want me to learn about weaving?'

It's Jarnier's voice you hear, not the project director's.

It's knowledge we want, not information.

There's a difference? It's comfortable in this position, and so you allow yourself to doze for a while. When you open your eyes you're on your back, a pig nuzzling your sleeve. Bastards for waking you up like this. You shoo the animal away and get to your feet.

William, we want you to check out the rope bridge. Beecham, this time.

'Which way is it?'

Into the jungle – north-east from where you are.

You check the compass in the upper left of your vision, and set off. You realise how drowsy you still are. Not enough sleep last night, reading that crazy book. It *must* be part of the project – they're playing games with you.

You never knew jungles were so wet. Even the air is wet. And the greenness is overpowering – shades from lime to almost black, everywhere you look. The path disappears in places and you have to part waxy leaves, broad as dinner plates, to open up another few paces. Your hands are scratched, something acidic in the wetness of the fronds making them sting. One of your boots has been sucked off in the marsh, swallowed up and disappeared. No leeches, thank Christ.

A rotten tree trunk lies at an angle across the path, and you rest against it. You blow cool air on the back of your hands to ease the stinging, but it makes no difference.

'Hard work.'

You wait for the display, but nothing comes. So, they've switched off the language readout. The temperature gauge as well. You wonder when you last saw the time digits in the corner. No telling how long you've been here.

The volume of the hidden chirrupings and screechings increases as the jungle swallows up the disturbance of its first ever human intruder. Every sound is no doubt acoustically exact; extinct or not, these animals are very much alive here.

You come to a crevice, the ground falling away into a deep cut, foliage clinging to its rocky sides. It is too steep to negotiate without falling so you squat to catch your breath. You could try launching yourself off the side, but this is no plastic playscape, and you'd get no further than you would in CR. There must be a way out, they wouldn't expect you to try scaling this cliff. You strain your eyes to look through the leaves, but there could be anything in the green shadows of the undergrowth.

'Which way?'

You wait for an answer, but nothing comes.

'Give me a break, control.'

A fluorescent green arrow flashes in the corner of your eye.

You force your way through the undergrowth until you see a rope bridge to your left.

'Thanks.'

The rope bridge is rickety, but it doesn't look too unsafe, so you hurry across it. You're moving too fast and the bridge sways dangerously, threatening to tip you into the gorge. If the bridge is designed to snap you realise you can cling to the overhead branches of the trees which are within reach. Nice touch, that.

And then it all happens at once. A dark shape falls from above, showering raindrops on you before you are knocked to your knees. Your reflexes are fast, but the animal is faster, and you're on your back, your head over the side of the rope bridge. It's mauling your torso before you can even fight back. You see a black silken coat. It's a jaguar. Twisting round, you manage to wrench yourself from its jaws, and then you have your hands round its throat. One arm is burning, and you know its claw has torn open your garment, probably broken the skin. You're thrashing about together, the animal fighting like a domestic cat, using its back legs to scratch at your body. You can see right down the animal's throat, past its slimy fangs. It bellows into your face, half yowl, half roar. The bridge is swinging alarmingly and you find yourself lying crosswise, your legs dangling over the drop, your head over the other side. You can match the strength of the jaguar, but you're on your back, fighting in a losing position. You try and hook your feet round the liana that forms the side rails but your shins are being scored by the scrabbling claws of its back legs. You're tiring – it's going to win.

And then you have your hands round the throat of a man. You are so surprised you let go and fall backwards off the bridge. You are aware of performing a slow backwards somersault before you land face-down on some boulders. Your body bounces as though you have fallen onto a sprung mattress. No pain, just winded from the impact. You roll onto your back and stare up at the swaying rope bridge and the canopy of leaves above it. The man is looking down at you, laughing, a half-eaten pineapple in his hand.

'What the hell was that?'

No answer. You run your hands over your belly to check for damage, but the material is not even torn. They could have warned you there would be an assailant in the system. The man, a Kogi is guzzling the pineapple, thrusting his hips backward and forward like a mating dog.

'What's going on?'

Sorry, William. A prank of Jarnier's I think. Let's go back a bit.

Your shoe reappears and you find yourself standing up. The man has gone. When you move, you bang your head against a rock outcrop. It clangs incongruously, like a hollow metal pipe. Suddenly, you're angry. A tic has started in your left eye. You want to do damage to something.

They hadn't planned for you to be down here, and the route to the top looks difficult. You compose yourself for a moment and then start climbing. They should write in a couple of steps, a rope ladder or something. If a system offers too much of a challenge, the average punter gives in. Or panics. For a moment you conjure up the image of your body in the girdle, making climbing movements with your arms and legs, groping for a hand-hold in thin air. A sudden sense of humiliation comes over you. Fuck the bastards.

'Expand.'

The sides of the gorge slide before your eyes until your head is level with the rope bridge. You tear the bridge from its supports, as flimsy now as a cat's cradle, and throw it into the jungle as hard as you can.

'Expand.'

With a virtual height of twenty-five metres, you can see over the tops of trees to the compound in the distance. You step out of the gorge as though it's a ditch and stride towards the village.

Standing above the six huts and two larger ceremonial houses, you pause to decide which one to choose, and then you bend down and tear one of the smaller huts from the earth. Squeaky human voices protest, and you see two Kogi men the size of rats at your feet. You ignore them and shake the hut. A child falls out, tumbling head over heels towards the ground.

'Who the hell does he think he is?' the director scowled, watching the screen. 'King Kong?'

The programmers exchanged glances, but said nothing.

'Damn Jarnier,' the director muttered, watching the figure on the screen give the hut one more shake to make sure it was empty. 'Where the hell is he?'

'He's just left.'

Programming that assault was typical Jarnier. If he wasn't careful, he would push his luck too far one day and find himself off the project. He might be brilliant, but the company had limited patience with mavericks. 'Any problems?'

'Nothing technical, but he's getting a bit weird.'

'Give me digital display,' Beecham said, turning the mike on. 'William, this is Dr Beecham. Put that hut down.'

They waited, but there was no response. Beecham repeated the order. The hut fell, shattering at William's giant feet.

'And return to zero size.'

There was a delay of half a minute before the huts rose to meet William. Beecham watched the screen with increasing concern. William's slowness to respond was either rebelliousness, or the man was beginning to come unstuck. Either way, it didn't look good.

He noticed Julia at the back of the room with her notebook. It took him a moment to remember her name. 'Dr O'Brien, how's it going?'

The woman looked disconcerted, and he wondered if he'd got her name wrong.

'A few gaps, but nothing that can't be filled, I think.'

'All this information is right, is it?' he said, indicating the giant screen. William was sitting in the compound watching a couple of dusty chickens pecking at roots.

'The detail is mostly right, a few minor mistakes. You've compressed the habitat a lot though.'

He realised it was nervousness that was making her ill at ease. He remembered her at the tele-interview, she'd been so self-effacing, she'd almost talked herself out of a job. He sat beside her, hands on knees. 'The program is nine square kilometres. And in that we had to fit,' he counted them on his fingers, 'mountain, rain forest, jungle, cloud forest and sea shore.'

'You've done an excellent job.'

He turned to look at her. 'We have, haven't we?'

He could see she wanted to ask a question but was holding back. 'What is it, dear?'

'The animal attacking William – was it really necessary?'

He sighed and looked at the woman. This was probably his last project; in a year he would face compulsory retirement. Even if she was one of headquarters' spies, it would make little difference what he said.

'Not necessary at all.'

As soon as the virtual jaguar had turned into a man Julia realised what had been done. Jarnier had written Kasindukua, the mythical jaguar-mama, into the program. Julia remembered how interested he had been in the story, quizzing her several times about the details, her interpretation of it. The great Mother, the story went, had given Kasindukua two power objects: a jaguar mask and a blue pebble. Julia had told Jarnier that the jaguar was a symbol of shamanic power, the blue pebble presumably a hallucinogen. By wearing the mask and swallowing the pebble, Kasindukua was given the power to see beyond surface reality – disease was made visible as beetles, women turned into pineapples. The great Mother warned him to use his powers wisely, but he ignored her and began raping women, pretending to be eating pineapples. The first virtual rapist.

'What's it got to do with reality holidays?' she asked Beecham.

The older man shook his head. 'Maybe you should ask Jarnier.'

William had been inside just over sixty hours when Beecham called an end to it. Julia watched the monitor, relieved and worried, as William was unhooked from the girdle. Since the episode with the hut he had been acting strangely, sitting in the dust staring at nothing for two hours, sleeping fitfully. But strange as it was, it all seemed plausible to Julia. She had watched the screen, almost hypnotised by the slow scanning of his gaze, the focus on tiny detail: fingernails, the ragged ear of a pig, a sea shell. The man was disintegrating.

It was oddly intimate, watching this huge screen. Like eavesdropping on somebody's dream. Though she had felt uncomfortably like an intruder, she had forced herself to stay. While she sat drinking coffee and biting her fingernails, the body of a man was strapped into an iron maiden, lasers firing images onto his retinas, his employers adding pressure to see how much he could take before flipping out.

Four days on the base had done nothing to quell her disquiet. Reality holidays? She had been prepared to swallow some professional pride so she could see the Kogi in action, but Omnisens had turned her into a playscape attendant. She should have realised when they told her the fee they would pay her. It was suspiciously good for an academic. They were buying her. And now she was part of a team about to turn the Kogi into one more flavour of the month. She could see how it would evolve if the program was a success: fashion houses marketing white cotton tunics, funny little hats, gourd farms producing an assembly line of *poporos*, green wads of chewing gum to represent coca leaves. It had happened before with almost every successful virtuality system; television had nothing on multisensory playscapes as a generator of merchandising. She had seen it with her own kids. Music, clothes, language, every season a different fashion sweeping through school like the plague.

She was angry at them, angry at herself. The project had been presented as an educational reality holiday, and now it transpired that it was little more than a glorified hunt-and-destroy game. She cursed herself for her naivety. Omnisens, a company with the second largest slice of the entertainment pie in the world – what did she expect? And now they were pushing William to see how long it would take a human being to crack. Well, it looked like they'd found out.

If I sit with a thermo pad on my feet and my hands between my legs I can just about maintain sensation in my extremities. Fingers and toes, we are told, are the first parts to be abandoned as the body withdraws heat to its core. We can lose our digits, nature's reasoning goes, but heart, lungs and liver need their full quota of hot blood.

I once saw a man with frostbite, blackened toes as dead as frozen potato chips. I can't think where I could have seen him, I suppose it must have been on TV. I remember how cheerful he was, even though the necrotic stumps of his toes had been amputated, glad I suppose not to have lost more of his body. When they found him – I think he was a mountaineer who had fallen down a crevasse – he had white patches of frozen flesh on his face like a fungal bloom. He was as cold as if he had spent a day inside the ice compartment of a refrigerator.

I take my gloves off and rub my face. Perhaps I should have brought a mirror to check myself. If I'm to win the battle between frigid entropy and my dancing blood corpuscles, I'm going to have to keep an eye on myself. Keep moving. I waggle my fingers above the typewriter keys. Type to survive.

I stare at the piece of paper in front of me and then play with the steam of my breath, trying to blow smoke rings. I stop when I taste the snot which has dribbled into the corner of my mouth. Oops.

For a moment I have one of those insights, increasingly common, of seeing myself displayed for all to see, a pinned butterfly on a cork board. I'm an old man, a nose blue with cold, and snot dribbling down his face. Dribbling while Rome burns.

Sliding forward, I wedge the thermo pad between my thighs so that my upper legs can warm. Everything aches: my few remaining teeth, my elbows and knees, my hips. This isn't arthritis – it's cold. But I can't get any closer to the electric fire without my clothes singeing. My toes are so frozen they feel as though somebody is standing on them. I look around myself. Trying to heat a room this size is like warming a cave with a couple of candles. If I don't do something about it, my end is going to be swifter and more uncomfortable than I realised.

I could do it now, walk down to Harry's Store and spend the afternoon tacking some plastic sheets into place. I could make a nice little greenhouse for myself, but I'm suddenly too sleepy to move. Hypothermia, I remember, leads to a constriction of capillaries in the brain, inducing a state of vagueness, clumsiness, fatigue. Double oops.

There are no new footprints in the snow which lead me to Harry's Store. I follow the same route, crossing the road in the same place, turning at the crossroads to look back at the factory as I did on my first day. The sun is brilliant, the sky blue and clear. The ozone above my head is as thin as melting ice on a pond. I pull my hat down and keep my hands in my pockets. Skin cancer I don't need.

By the time I reach Harry's, the ache in my toes has numbed. I stamp the ice off my boots at the door, trying to get some feeling back into my feet. I'm glad to see the TV is turned off. Harry is on top of a rickety ladder stacking boxes on a high shelf when I come in. He looks down at me. 'Your missus just phoned.'

I'm too surprised to say anything.

'She said she'd ring back tomorrow at midday.'

'My *wife*? How did she get your number?'

The old Eskimo shrugs and returns his attention to his shelf stacking. 'When a woman wants a man, she can get awful creative.'

So, she has found me. Jack must have told Carla where I was going. Bastard – he promised not to. 'What else did she say?'

'She asked how you was.'

He gingerly descends the ladder and turns to face me. I'm glad

I still have my mask on, for a white sediment of powder – flour or cement dust – is clinging to his clothes.

I feel ridiculous dragging information out of him, but I have to ask. 'What did you say?'

'I says you was walking and talking.'

I can hardly believe this wrinkled Eskimo has actually spoken to my wife. Two worlds in collision. I want to ask Harry how she sounded, but I force the thought out of my head.

'Have you got any Visqueen sheets?' I made myself pace out the room, estimating the amount of plastic I'd need to seal myself into one end: about 300 square feet. Harry works out how many sheets I'll need. Four will give me plenty left over, so I buy them, along with some tacks and a ball-peen hammer.

I linger in the store, feeling my muscles relax in the warmth. Harry ignores me, his attention on a radio he's dismantling. What is he doing here? I'm his only customer, and even then he ignores me. The door has jammed shut and it clatters as I tug it open.

'See you tomorrow,' he calls.

'Hmm,' is all I can say. Tomorrow at midday. Am I in the same time zone as Vancouver? Is her midday my midday? I'm going to have to think about whether I want to speak to her or not. The telephone in the hands of the wrong person is a dangerous weapon. I feel hunted as I walk down the main street, adding one more set of tracks to the snow. Suddenly my world is smaller.

I know I don't want to speak to Carla but, goddamit, I *do* want to know what she's thinking. Damn her inquisitiveness; it's like a tyre iron threatening to break my carefully sealed solitude. She has always done this; poked and probed, partly through love, partly through some feminine urge to possess. I should have insisted Jack didn't tell her where I was going, it was asking too much of her not to contact me. And now she's got me wondering.

As I cross the street to the factory, something strikes me on the back of the head, just under the rim of my hat. I spin round, ready to defend myself from attack. A bleached bone, probably the thigh bone of a cow, is lying in the snow. I rub my head and look around, but there's nobody in sight.

I estimate the distance to the nearest building: forty feet at least. If somebody threw it from an upstairs window, they must either have a singularly good aim, or I must be singularly unlucky to have been thus struck. I get the feeling I'm being watched, but I don't know from which direction.

It takes me the rest of the day to get the sheeting in place. It means standing on a chair on one of the trestle tables in order to reach the ceiling, but I manage not to fall off. I hate heights, convinced the world is going to crumble under me and I'll break a hip or something absurd. It's hard work, and I seem to have less energy with each passing hour, but by the evening a plastic wall, floor to ceiling, is in place. It gives me a living space of about twenty feet by twenty – more than enough for what I need. The sheets overlap in the middle so I can get in and out. There's enough polythene left over to cover the windows if necessary. Basic, I must admit, but effective.

I keep finding myself at the desk, staring at the paper in the typewriter. I don't know what I have to say. The assumption is that the author is the one who knows, the one with authority, but all I seem to be able to do is raise questions. Questions I can't answer.

I look round the room for the parrot. I think it must be making friends with me. Although I keep finding its curled white slugs of shit, so far it hasn't scored a direct hit on me. It spends most of its time on the light fittings, asleep or meditating – it's hard to tell which. I've left a small window open just in case it wants to escape, but it doesn't seem interested in the great outdoors.

At first I resisted naming the parrot, which I realise now is probably some sort of parakeet, but from somewhere a name came to me, and it seems to have stuck: Toto. I cluck my tongue to draw its attention. It looks down at me, crouches for a moment and then launches off its perch. It swoops towards me, and I just have time to bring my mask up to my face. I don't know how much I'm allergic to it, but I'm not going to take any chances. The bird lands nimbly on the platen of the typewriter, tucking its wing tips neatly into place. It looks at me from over its fearsome bill.

'Well?' I ask.

Nothing.

'Shall I speak to Carla?'

Still nothing.

I suppose it's hungry. I go to the larder and bring back a packet of sunflower seeds. It tilts its head at the crackling sound of cellophane, and when I tip some seeds out onto my palm, it shuffles a little dance of excitement. It doesn't eat directly from my palm as a pigeon would, but takes a seed in its prehistoric claw and ducks its neck to nibble at it. Bending close to observe it eat, I can see its dry and swollen tongue, hardly a tongue at all, more like an oral digit.

'Can you speak?' I hold another seed out and as it bends to take it, I jerk it away. 'Say something,' I coax, teasing it with the seed. 'Toto, Toto,' I cajole.

The bird is shuffling along the platen and ruffling its feathers. I give it the seed and then try again. Its eyes are fixed on the food, and when I jerk it out of reach, it opens its bill, pauses as if thinking and then gives two piercing whistles. The sound is so loud it's like being struck on the side of the head with a heavy object. I offer Toto the seed, but it just bounces up and down on the spot, screeching again and again.

'Okay, okay.' I drop a handful of seeds on the table, but it has started something it's not ready to stop. The noise is so overpowering I have to walk to the end of the room with my hands over my ears. There is silence while the bird eats. When it has finished I walk back to it and sit in my chair.

I stare at Toto, and Toto stares back. Extraordinary thing, this close up. Its eyes are as inert as buttons, and even when it slowly winks at me, it just looks like a robot toy pretending to be alive. But it *is* alive; more than a machine, surely. The bird clicks its beak at me as though cracking an invisible seed. There *is* a brain of some sort in there. Not much of one perhaps, but there are presumably enough neural connections going on under its feathered skull to create critical mass. I try and imagine the process. Flash-bang! every nanosecond and a Bose-Einstein condensate is pulled out of nowhere like a rabbit out of a hat: parrot consciousness. A whole greater than the sum of its parts.

What does the world look like through the button eyes of a parrot? When it ducks its head to watch me, what is it seeing? A kaleidoscope? A mountain? Spirit bodies? God?

A brain the size of a pea, but still unfathomably more sophisticated than the best analogue computer system. And my brain, the most complex structure in the known universe, these rucks and folds of who I am, all tucked neatly into a shell. What do I see when I look at the world? What there is? Or just a version? Fact or fantasy? Fact, and then I'm just a biocomputer of cosmic complexity. Fantasy, and it's a reality machine behind my eyes.

'But really real?' I ask the parrot. 'Or subjectively real?'

That is the question. This dried chestnut inside my skull is either delirious with delusion, joining the dots between pixels on a screen and thinking there is something of substance out there. Or as cool and decisive as God, collapsing the wave function of the noumenal into this room, this table, this parrot.

The bird launches off the table, leaving a tiny green feather circling in its wake. I stare at the paper in the typewriter. Why am I bothering? Nobody is going to read this, and even if they do, it will change nothing. People will always be stupid. Let the world burn. Let's toast our toes on the heat of South America and Africa. We've got – oh, *weeks* left before the flames reach us.

Splat! A dollop of yellow bird shit lands on the paper. I look up to see the bird on the light fitting above my head. It opens its beak and squawks something. It is only when it repeats the call that I realise it has spoken. And what has it said? 'Fuck the bastards!'

12

It was only when the leaf came away from the stem that William realised the plant he'd been absently toying with was real. He dropped it into the pot and turned to face the psychologist. 'I don't know. What should I say?'

'There's no right or wrong answer. It's not a test.'

William glanced at the clock behind Kinderling. He'd been here nearly half an hour, and he still didn't know what they were talking about. He hated these debriefing sessions, the constant probing like a dentist looking for a cavity. He watched Kinderling watching him. But at least a dentist would have told you if something was wrong; this man in his snazzy jacket and pants seemed to think his conclusions were none of your business. And these obscure questions: what did you think about the Mama's reference to 'the Mother'? Freud was a hundred years old, for Christ's sake.

William forced himself to sit down. It's not a test? Of course it was; it wasn't just the psychological impact of the Kogi program that was being assessed. His every word and movement were being monitored, and for what reason if not to pass or fail his suitability to continue with the job? He was twenty-seven years old, hardly halfway through his working life, but he was one of the oldest test pilots he knew. If he came out of this project badly, it might be his last job – ever. He'd been warned against this at university: piloting new systems was a high profile job, but the chances were you'd be burnt out at thirty, and unqualified for anything else. Just a company pension to look forward to.

'I didn't see any significance in it at the time,' he said at last. 'Mother, father – it makes no difference to me.'

A professionally long pause, and then, 'I notice you refer to him as Francisco.'

'That's his name,' William said guardedly.

'*Mama* Francisco, is his name.'

William gave no response, duly noted by the psychologist on his electronic pad. This game playing was stupid: they knew he had freaked out twice, and they knew it wasn't because of his mother, but because for nearly five days out of seven he had been swimming in the goo of somebody else's imagination.

William knew Kinderling wanted to quiz him about his first abort – disappearing off the edge of the program, but he still hadn't asked a direct question about it.

'Tell me what happened when you fell into Mama Francisco's eyes.'

At last. William felt a tug in his belly as he remembered what had happened. Some moments of virtuality were more real than real, and this was one of them. It had been more than sensory stimulation that he had felt. He wanted to tell Kinderling that it was no illusion, his falling into the black hole of Francisco's eye, but he hesitated. It *was* an illusion. Everything seen and heard and felt was either externally generated, or the product of his own imagination. But.

'It was weird,' he said at last. 'Suddenly I was being funnelled towards the eye of the man.'

His hesitation was saying more than the words he used, and the psychologist waited, his face betraying no emotion.

'It was like a vortex I was being sucked into.' William closed his eyes to recapture the moment. 'I tried to resist, but—' He shrugged. The force was as irresistible as gravity. He fell, and nothing could stop him.

'Why did you give the command?'

'I gave no command.'

The psychologist frowned his contradiction across the desk at William.

'I didn't,' William protested. But even as the words left his mouth, he doubted himself. He could remember the falling, but nothing else. The episode had seemed so automatic that he assumed it had been programmed. He looked up at the video screens on the wall as Kinderling rewound the tape.

'Let me show you something.'

Engage digital command.

William grimaced as his voice came over the speakers, the words confirmed by the read-out along the top of the screen. He looked at the second monitor which provided a simultaneous record of the test room. The body in the girdle clearly brought finger and thumb of the right hand together as the digital command for size reduction, pointing a forefinger away from the body to indicate rapid forward movement. He looked back at the computer simulation to witness the falling into the left eye of the Kogi, bursting into a maze of green hexagons.

William stared at the screen. He had purposely flown off the program. He remembered nothing of this.

William, this is Dr Beecham. Take three retrograde steps.

Kinderling stopped the tape. 'They gave you thirty seconds, and when you made no reply, they pulled you out.'

It had never happened to William before. He had wandered off the program once or twice, but that was usually because of poor briefing. This was the first time he had ever failed to respond to instructions.

'Do you remember anything of this?'

There was no point in lying. He shook his head.

'What *do* you remember?'

'Just falling into that black space, and then being unhooked.'

'*The sea was the mother,*' Kinderling said, reading from a sheet of paper on his desk. '*She was memory and potential.* What does that mean to you?'

'Not much. Isn't it basic aboriginal stuff?'

'Perhaps. I'm interested why those words would make you want to fly off the program?'

William was aware he was chewing the inside of his cheek, and stopped. 'I can't help you, doc.'

Kinderling didn't respond to the sarcasm in William's voice. 'How much do you remember of the last trip?'

William shrugged. 'What do you want to know?'

'The last two hours. You just sat, and did nothing.'

'I was tired.'

'How did you feel after you had been jumped on by the jaguar?'

'Angry.'

'Is that why you destroyed the hut?'

'I guess so.'

The psychologist slid back in his chair and let his glance drift to the ceiling. 'Writing in my notes that you're being uncooperative is going to look worse than anything you tell me about your feelings.'

William said nothing.

'Your place on the project is under review. If you don't play ball with us, that'll be it. Grounded.'

William realised they were sitting in the same posture: legs straight out, fingers laced over the belly. He sat up straight. 'I was really mad,' he said slowly, emphasising each word. 'Nobody told me about the assailant.'

Kinderling was waiting for more.

'This is supposed to be a reality holiday, not a combat training tool.'

'And if it *was* a combat training tool, then . . . ?'

'For Christ's sake, you don't own me!' he shouted. 'What gives you the right to fuck with my head?' He could feel his anger returning, the urge to smash something up. He imagined how satisfying it would be to punch Kinderling on the nose.

'Anything else you want to tell me about?'

William knew he was teetering on the edge of trouble. 'No,' he said dully. He stood up to leave. It was tempting to tell Kinderling about the book, tell him he was onto them, but he held himself back. It probably was a set up, but he wanted to be sure before he said anything. If Omnisens had arranged a fake novel just to wrong-foot him then he'd be marked down as a paranoiac for not saying anything. But if it was nothing to do with the project, him telling them that he had found a book apparently based on his parents' lives would be interpreted as the ravings of a madman. Not his fault, he knew, but somehow it would cast doubts on his own sanity.

He watched the man in front of him running his finger down a sheet of paper on the desk, apparently checking points off. William didn't know what to think about the book now. Maybe his father *was* a novelist, maybe he wrote and published his story within a year. Or it could be a coincidence, the names, the details;

strange perhaps, but not incredible. But he distrusted serendipity; it had no part in a two billion dollar project. Chaos theory was all very well, but the hand of God was confined to mathematics. This project had been running for four years; the program was the most sophisticated ever. Fortuity had no part in it.

'Kinderling wants to keep an eye on me.'

William had been in Julia's room for nearly ten minutes, and he was only now coming to the point. When she saw him carried out of the test room on the stretcher, she knew he would come to her sooner or later.

Julia watched him fidgeting without saying anything. He needed to talk, but he had to find his own words. She could see he was trying to disguise his disappointment with bravado, but there was a wounded look in his eyes.

'They think I'm cracking up.'

It was taking a lot for him to say this. Pride and the need to tell were at odds inside him, their battle evident in his fiddling with the strap of his wrist watch. She wanted to take his hands and still them, but she thought her action might be misunderstood.

'You just need a rest,' she ventured. Julia couldn't help feeling protective towards him; there was such a child under that company uniform. She wasn't surprised he was curling at the edges. To be so completely scooped out of yourself for days on end, what did they expect? That he would come back to consensus reality as though he had been watching television? And then to find your parents' lives have been written about in a novel?

'I bet Denver will take over,' he said bitterly.

She'd met Denver: a loose-limbed young black woman who constantly chewed gum. Julia nodded vaguely, not understanding the rivalry between the two test pilots.

She could feel William's insecurity tugging at her mind like an insistent child. He was lost. But so was she. The question of the book had never left her since William had confirmed the similarity. It had been too strange – to find the book on her very first night, and then meet William within hours of starting it.

'Did you get in touch with your mother?' She tried to make

the question sound as innocuous as she could, but she couldn't keep the tension out of her voice.

'What for?'

'You know why.'

He unhooked his percom from his belt and punched out the nine digits as though he was stabbing an insect in his palm. He got the unobtainable signal, so he tried again, slower this time. The same tone. 'Something's wrong with the line.'

He dialled the operator, the same rapid-fire stabbing of the buttons. As he waited for the line to be checked, Julia watched his jaw muscle twitch. Sooner or later this man was going to explode, she thought.

'Check it again, will you,' he said to the operator. He waited for a few seconds, and then slapped the percom shut. 'Her number has been changed,' he said to Julia.

'That's not possible.'

'I know.'

'Are you sure you got her number right?'

'OB7–834–212,' he said automatically.

'Have you checked it?' His look was dismissive, but she persisted. 'Have you?'

He keyed in his mother's name. He looked blankly at the screen, pressed *clear* and then tried again.

'What's wrong?' she asked.

He was staring at the machine in his hand, a frown on his face. 'Her name has been erased.'

'Are you sure?'

He held it up to show her the blank screen. 'No number, no address.' He tried the number once more, and then clicked it shut. He thrust his hands into his pockets in an attempt to disguise his agitation.

Each was waiting for the other to say something, but Julia's nerve held out longer.

'Something weird is going on,' he finally said.

Was this an act of his, conning her into believing him? She couldn't tell. 'Who would want to erase your mother's data?'

'Who *could*? This cost me nearly a week's wage,' he said, indicating the percom. 'It's a thumb-print security code. It's supposed to be unbreakable.'

'Could you try mailing her?'

'She wouldn't check her terminal even if it was on fire. She's the old-fashioned sort.'

'Write to her. Paper mail.'

He snorted. He had never written a letter in his adult life.

'Where does she live?'

'Seattle, Washington.'

'Why not visit her?' Julia's geography wasn't very good, but she knew Seattle wasn't far by North American standards.

'They're not going to let me have furlough just like that.'

'You could ask.'

He didn't bother to reply.

'You could just leave without telling them,' she offered.

'And never work again? Give me a break.' William's percom buzzed and he unhooked it from his belt and flicked it open in one smooth action. 'Yup.'

Julia could tell it was official by the way he straightened in his chair.

'Yes, sir.'

She watched the man nodding, his personal communicator to his ear. A crescent moon of dried blood had formed along the cuticle of one of his fingernails where he had bitten too close to the quick.

He hung up almost immediately. 'Beecham wants to see me.'

The two men were seated behind William, and though the words were coming out of Beecham's mouth, he knew where they originated from. 'Dr Kinderling is concerned about you.'

'Nothing to worry about, sir.'

The project director splayed his fat fingers on the veneered top of his desk as though measuring the span of his hands. 'Two trips, two aborts?'

'I'm feeling fine, sir.'

'Not tired?'

William tried to look as alert as he could. He noticed his shoes were unshined, and slid them further under his chair. 'I'm in control, sir.'

He saw Beecham's glance flick over his shoulder to the two men. William had only seen them out of the corner of his eye when he had entered Beecham's office, but he noticed they were in dark suits. Head office, he guessed.

'Denver is going to take over.'

It was a statement not to be argued with but William couldn't help himself. 'Goddamit,' he said between his teeth. 'Sir,' he added.

'You've done a good job for us.' Beecham linked his fat fingers together as though in prayer. 'A world immersion record, some useful data. Maybe we'll bring you back on when you've had some rest.' He tapped his thumbnails against his front teeth. 'Kinderling will keep an eye on you.' The tone of Beecham's voice suggested sympathy. The men in the suits were making him uneasy.

William waited for more, but the meeting was over. He was halfway to his feet when he hesitated and sat down again. 'Permission to take furlough, sir.' William knew Beecham hated this sort of formality, but he wasn't going to be caught out by the two spies behind him. Again he saw Beecham's eyes move to the men.

'Sorry, son. We need you here.'

'What would you want to do?' The voice came from behind William. Being addressed gave him permission to acknowledge their presence, so he turned to face the two men. One glance confirmed his suspicion: navy blue suits, cropped hair, polished shoes. Security officers. Either that, or CIA. Anything was possible with this amount of money involved.

'Visit my mother, sir.'

'This is a multi billion dollar project,' the elder said. 'A central part of your function is to test the long-term psychological effects of virtual reality systems. I don't have to remind you that you're not just a jockey.'

He paused and William assumed some kind of assent was being anticipated. For a moment the room slid before his eyes like a system malfunction. 'Yes, sir.' Asshole, he wanted to say.

'The tests that Dr Kinderling will perform on you are just as important as any amount of flight time.'

'I understand, sir.'

'I know you're disappointed to be grounded. And I guess it's only natural you want some R & R off the base –' He was being chummy, inviting William to trust him, but William knew better than to drop his guard.

He didn't know who to answer, and directed his response to the older man. 'I would rather stay on the project, sir.'

'You *are* on the project, Mr Morrison,' he replied. 'And you don't expect us to jeopardise security just so you can have a flesh-to-flesh with your mom, do you?'

'No, sir.'

The man nodded at Beecham, indicating that he had nothing more to say. William turned back. He could see from the director's face that Denver's appointment had only one meaning. Once grounded, forever grounded. In three months' time when this project was wound up William would be pensioned off. If he was lucky he could find a job testing civilian programs, if not, he had seen the statistics: 14% dead within ten years, 32% alcoholic or drug addicted. A pension might be enough to afford a protected environment, but problems could come from inside as well as outside.

William went back to his room, selected a braindrain audiotape and lay down on his relaxation chair. He was too restless to meditate, but he made himself keep his eyes open. The music annoyed him, and after a few minutes he switched it off and removed his goggles. He rubbed his eyes, pressing his fingers hard into his sockets until he saw lights spiralling and flashing.

He thought about his mother. It wasn't possible for somebody to disappear in the way she had. Somebody had hacked into his percom and messed with his records. Not only that, but someone had infiltrated Mountain Bell. Why erase his mother's records? This wasn't a prank. Sabotage on this scale carried a five-year exclusion sentence. Whoever ordered it must have top flight clearance – from one of those assholes in a suit, probably. But why would it be officially sanctioned?

He opened his eyes and looked at the red eye of the video camera. Sometimes he wondered if the whole thing wasn't an invention, anyway. The program, Omnisens, the two men from security. It was easy to imagine reaching a hand out and tearing the scenery from in front of his eyes as if it were a computer simulation.

He smiled wryly at the thought. Classic schizoid symptoms: Kinderling *would* be pleased. Finally some data for him.

But it was true. What did he have to go on? Not the evidence of his senses: this chair, these walls, the muffled sounds of laughter from the corridor were no more real than the jungle of the Kogi. And the project's elaborate set up was no more proof of authenticity than anything else.

But what could he do? He knew too much about the project. Industrial espionage was too big a business for them to let him off the base before the package was up and running. How about telling Beecham the truth? Excuse me sir, somebody has been tampering with my files, and has fabricated a hoax book based on my parents' lives. I'd like an apology, a week's rest in Hawaii, and a promise to stop the dirty tricks. How would *that* look on his datafile? Not just schizoid, but paranoid too.

Why not just leave? Go AWOL? Speak to his mother and find out what's going on. They would probably put his absence down to stress. The world record for deep immersion; this was just the sort of thing they were expecting. They'd try and bring him back – with his inside knowledge about the MAYA project, he was worth millions to the competition, but they'd have to find him first. He'd have to get in touch sooner or later, and then they would probably just retire him with a disability pension, and he'd never work again. He'd never work again anyway – he saw the look in Beecham's eyes.

William swung himself out of the chair. It could be easily done and he had a car. If Julia could be persuaded to drive he could hide in the trunk until they were off the base. Drive for a few miles and then he could dump the woman and continue alone. He could be in Seattle in two days. If Julia didn't report him they wouldn't miss him for a couple of hours, and that would be enough time to lose them. He put on a pair of sunglasses and checked his wallet and percom. He considered his reflection in the mirror. Leaving now would just confirm their suspicion that he was cracking up. They were probably right.

13

Julia travelled light. It took her five minutes to stuff all her things into a single suitcase. She checked her watch and then glanced round the empty room. It occurred to her to make her bed, but she dismissed the thought. She wasn't at home now, she owed no one anything. There was no reason for her to feel so guilty. She was breaking no contract, causing no disruption to the project by leaving early. Nevertheless, she decided to leave the hand towel still draped over the video camera, and then shut the door as quietly as she could.

According to the floor plan, the carport was somewhere in the basement. She hurried to the elevator, aware of the sound of voices approaching along the corridor. The elevator was on the second floor and she jabbed the button, staring up at the indicator.

Julia had made a show of hesitation when William asked her to drive him off the base, but the truth was she had found it difficult to hide her delight. From Seattle to Canada was a short hop. She didn't know how much trouble William would get into for this – presumably it was an offence for a bonded pilot to leave without permission – but she didn't care. She had to find out more about the book, and she needed William's help.

The voices were coming closer and Julia pushed her suitcase against the wall, trying to make it as inconspicuous as she could. She closed her eyes to calm herself, willing the elevator to come.

A ping! indicated its arrival and she nipped inside. As she waited for the doors to close a couple of technicians walked past, chatting. They nodded at her as the doors slid shut.

William's car was charging, its doors open, but nobody was in sight. She put the suitcase under the back seat and climbed into the cockpit, moving the seat to fit her. Now what?

As she adjusted the rear-view mirror a movement caught her eye and she turned round. William was hurrying towards the car, a kitbag over one shoulder. He slung it in the back without a word and then opened the trunk. Julia got out to join him. He was wearing a white tee shirt and baggy pants.

The trunk looked too small for a grown man to fit in, and Julia told him so, but he just gave her a blanket and climbed in. He lay down on his side, his knees tucked up to his chest. 'Cover me with the blanket.'

Her hands were trembling as she pulled it over him. 'You'll suffocate.'

'Are you going to help me or not?'

She tucked the blanket round him. It wouldn't fool anybody who opened the trunk.

'Now slam and lock it.'

She gently clicked it shut and climbed back into the cockpit.

She had never driven such a powerful car, and when she started the engine it leapt forward with a jerk. She grimaced, thinking of William in the trunk. She took it easy up the ramp and into the dazzling light of the compound.

At the perimeter gate a guard flagged her to stop. She put the window down and forced herself to smile at him.

'Card please.'

She handed her card through the window, her heart hammering. The guard ran the card through the scanner and then glanced at the license plate of the car. 'This car is not registered in your name.'

'No, it's William Morrison's.' She realised she was biting her lower lip. She licked her lips and increased her smile. 'He said I could take it for a drive.'

'If you would wait a minute please, Dr O'Brien.'

She stared straight ahead while the guard checked the scanner. She was aware of the heat of the afternoon sun. William must be stifling under his blanket. At any moment she was sure the guard would open her door and ask her to step out.

The guard nodded at the scanner. 'I see you have clearance. I should inform you, as a foreign national, that the United States Highway speed restrictions are as follows —'

Julia was deaf to the words he read from the scanner. William must have given clearance for her to use the car. She could see Beecham walking briskly towards the car.

'Dr O'Brien,' he called, waving a hand as though hailing a cab. 'Wait a minute.'

She tried to put the passenger window down, but couldn't find the button. She activated the traffic monitor and radar sensor before she located the right one. She was so flustered by the time it slid open her words came out in barely more than a whisper. 'Hullo, Dr Beecham.'

'Going for a drive?' He crouched down to speak through the window. Julia heard his knees crack.

She nodded hopefully.

'Have you checked that your phone works? And your road map too?'

She looked round the cockpit as if surprised to find herself there. Lifting the phone from its cradle, she listened for a tone. The guard was watching her through the driver's window and when he saw her hesitation, pointed out the button to switch on the road map.

'Yes, everything works.'

'Fuel?'

'Yes.'

Beecham furrowed his brows. 'Would you like some company?'

Her mouth was open to decline when she suddenly realised he was flirting with her. Her smile was genuine for the first time. 'Thank you, but I'd like to be on my own.'

He seemed relieved to hear it, and patted the sill in a friendly fashion. 'Don't go too far. And don't stop for anyone, whatever happens. If you break down, contact the base and stay in the car. If it rains you must keep your windows shut and head straight back, no matter what the air quality monitor says.'

She insisted that she would do so, and then pulled away, smiling at the perimeter guard as she drove through the gates onto the dusty road. She'd made it.

* * *

She stopped a few miles down the road. The metal of the car was almost too hot to touch when she opened the trunk. William kicked off the blanket and swung his legs out. His hair was plastered to his forehead, and his face was alarmingly red. He stretched, breathing deeply for a minute before he spoke. 'Give me a couple of hours before you return to base so I've got a head start.'

She had expected this. 'I'm not going back. I want to come with you.'

'Don't be crazy! You want to get into trouble?'

'I'm in trouble already.'

'No, you're not. Tell them I sprang a surprise on you if you like.'

'I'm coming with you. You need me.'

'I need you? How?'

'I can be at the base in fifteen minutes. I'm sure security would be interested in what I would tell them.'

'You'd blackmail me?'

She shrugged. 'Even a fast car can't outrun a helicopter. You'd be sitting in the guardroom within the hour.'

He studied her for a moment. 'Get in.'

She climbed in the passenger's side and sat back to let the harness buckle itself. She looked sideways at William, his face impassive as he accelerated down the empty road. He glanced at the clock on the dashboard. Six-sixteen. He tapped in their destination: Seattle, and glanced at the ETA as it flashed up. Four forty-three, a journey of just over twenty-two hours. He looked fresh, but she knew that his energy was erratic. He wouldn't want to drive all night.

'How about making a room reservation for about five hours' time?' he said.

Julia ran her finger along the green line of the route. 'St George is six hours away.'

'Okay.'

She keyed in motel information: two single rooms, mid price range. She read the name as it came up. 'The Excelsior. Four hundred and twenty dollars each. Shall I make a reservation?'

'Go ahead.'

She did so, and then put her window down. She wished it were different: tearing through the desert with a handsome young pilot, on a journey to God knows where, it could have been fun. But William was in a bad mood, and Beecham had spooked her. Was it really so dangerous on these roads?

She leant out of the window, letting the warm air buffet her face and swirl her hair round her head. Dangerous perhaps, but she had never realised the desert could be so beautiful. The parched ground stretched in all directions, umber to ochre to silver-white against the horizon, the serious black strip of road slashing through the middle of it. A long way from England. The window twitched below her, and she sat back as it wound up. She looked at William in surprise.

'Put the air on,' he said, directing a vent towards her.

There was little traffic on the road, but he kept his speed down to 65. Highway patrols were getting sterner and sterner and, for the past three years, confiscation of vehicles for speeding had become statutory, even for first offences. William was proud of his car, proud of the fact that he could afford to drive, and he wasn't about to give it all away.

She switched the radio on and listened to a country and western station. There was something funny about the songs; not just the quaint nostalgia, it was the naked emotion that amused her. She turned up the volume so she could catch all the lyrics.

They made desultory conversation for a while, and then fell silent. The drone of the engine and gentle rocking of the suspension lulled Julia into a half sleep, and she snuggled into the pneumatic cushioning of her seat and let William concentrate on the road.

She woke when it was twilight, aware that she had been dribbling onto her front. She sat up and wiped her mouth on her sleeve. 'Where are we?'

William tapped the route display to indicate a name, but her vision was too blurred to be able to read it.

'I slept,' she said unnecessarily.

William said nothing, his body quivering minutely as the seat massager worked its way up and down his back. She dragged herself out of sleep, yawning and trying to stretch within the confines of the cockpit. 'Have you got anything to drink?'

He leant forward to open the glove compartment. The light pencil that came on shone green in the accentuated dusk of the car. She twisted it so she could see into the bowels of the shelf: a can of Coke, a bag of sweets and a revolver. She took the drink and sat back. A few of her friends back home had pistols, but they were fashion accessories rather than anything else. William's revolver looked heavy and serious. It frightened her. She wanted to ask why he carried one – autotheft was a thing of the past, and he would never stop anywhere except in a secure area – but he was still in a bad mood.

She took a swig of warm Coke and offered the can to William, but he shook his head. His eyes were fixed on the road ahead, the dying sunlight glinting off the silver rim of his shades. Such unflinching concentration probably made him a good test pilot, she thought, burping quietly to herself. But wasn't he ever off duty? She drank as much of the Coke as she could, and then not knowing what to do with the can, wedged it between her knees and watched the tangerine sun as it slipped under the edge of the horizon, draining the landscape of its colour. The silhouette of a cluster of half-built cement houses slid by, the sun flashing through their empty windows. She twisted in her seat to see them.

'Do people live here?' she asked. A gang of construction workers paused to watch the car pass, hands shading their eyes against the sunset.

'Earners,' he said brusquely.

They were building a settlement in the middle of nowhere. Tracks branched off the highway, heavy trucks laden with building blocks raising flurries of cement dust. One or two houses had lights in their windows, but the majority were in early stages of construction. They were nearly all the same: cuboid white blocks, flat roofs. Julia was reminded of Greece, Spain perhaps.

'Where do they get their water?' she asked.

'Deep wells.'

'And it's safe to drink?'

'Yeah, and expensive.'

Past the settlement, and the road was deserted again, its old-fashioned asphalt surface taking on a sheen as the sun glanced off it. It could be a river, Julia thought. The Amazon. She suddenly had an urge to get out, to stop for a moment. 'It's so beautiful. Can we stop?'

'Do you have to?'

'Isn't it safe?'

'Look – if you come along for the ride, you've got to travel how I say so.'

'I need the toilet,' she said flatly.

He sighed irritably and pulled off the road, sand crunching under the tyres. He switched off the engine, cutting the dashboard lights. The sudden stillness seemed to darken the panorama as though a blue-grey veil had been lowered onto it. They sat in silence, listening to the ticking of the engine as it cooled. It was like being on the moon, Julia thought. So still, so empty. William's eyes were on the monitor, waiting for a stable reading.

'Can I get out?'

'Go ahead.'

'I mean, is it safe?'

'It's safe.'

She opened her door and climbed out.

The air was warm, and she tilted her head to breathe in the dusk. The sky above her remained pellucid as a bowl of sky blue ink, shading gently darker to a three-quarters moon at the zenith. Not a cloud in the sky, not a mark to be seen. She looked for the evening star, but could only see the distant glint of a jet liner. It was so quiet.

A line of wind turbines stood about a kilometre from the road, their white arms unmoving. There was nothing to hide behind, so Julia checked William was facing the other way before squatting in the sand to pee, her eyes on the turbines.

As she was tucking her shirt back into her trousers she heard the car door slam. She walked towards William, smiling at him, welcoming him to the view. He had taken his shades off and was standing with his hands in his pockets like a man in a railroad waiting room, patient and disengaged.

'Did they really farm this land?' she asked. Beautiful, it may be, but it was a desolate beauty.

William kicked at the packed surface of the ground. 'See this white stuff?'

She noticed that the ground had a white crystalline crust. 'Sand?'

'Phosphate fertiliser.'

She walked away from him but he followed her. 'Why did you come with me?' he called. 'What's in it for you?'

'I don't know,' she lied. She slid one foot over the surface of the ground, breaking its sparkling skin. 'You looked as though you could use some company,' she said reluctantly. She wanted to make this moment of quietness last. Out here, away from the base, away from the rest of her life, she could forget the tangle she was in.

He had his back to the west, his face in shadow, and she couldn't see his expression. 'What makes you think I want your company?'

They heard the sound of a distant car, and both turned to watch the twinkle of headlight slowly grow until it passed them in a flurry of dust and noise. Julia didn't notice the gun held loosely in William's hand.

She waited until it was silent again before she spoke. 'Don't make an enemy out of me, William. We're in this together.'

He snorted derisively. 'You haven't just blown your career prospects like I have. You've got some earner husband back in England to look after you. I'm ruined now – you know that?'

'I know how scared you must be.'

'*Scared?*' He turned on his heel and strode back to the car. He was about to get in when he changed his mind and walked back. When he spoke, his voice shook with suppressed anger. 'You don't know what you're talking about, woman. Those sonsofbitches have been playing games with me. And I guess you're just one more part of the game. Scared? I'm mad as hell.'

'I'm not part of the set up. I'm as confused as you are.' She spoke softly as though she was calming a fractious horse. 'Honestly.'

He stared at her for a moment and then turned back to the car. 'Let's get going.'

They drove in silence for a couple of minutes. She could sense he still didn't trust her, but could think of nothing that would reassure him. 'Did you tell them about the book?' she asked at last.

'No. Did you?' There was a snide tone in his voice, so she left the question unanswered.

'Jarnier,' William said abruptly. 'You seem to know the guy pretty well.'

Julia said nothing.

'He told me the point of the MAYA project was a quest for information. You're the Kogi expert – you might as well tell me what it was now I'm off the team.'

'I don't know what you mean.'

'It's something to do with the map stone, I figure.'

'I still don't understand.'

He sighed heavily. 'They don't have reality holidays in England?'

She mouthed some words, but nothing came out. She hated his attitude, hated the way she let him bully her. Of course they had reality holidays at home, though the closest Julia had ever been to one was a brief immersion in an AV virtual mall. She hadn't enjoyed it: all the food looked plastic and she couldn't tell how fresh the vegetables were. Her kids teased her about it, just as she suspected William would if she told him.

'There's always a point to a plastic playscape,' William explained in heavily patronising tones. 'People get bored with holidays after a while. They like a challenge, a quest of some sort. The MAYA project was a quest for information.' He glanced sideways at her. 'So you might as well tell me what it was.'

Julia's instinct was never again to speak about the Kogi to William. She could not forgive him for his crass attitude towards them. These had been special people; she wasn't about to allow their graves to be trampled by this man. She regretted giving Jarnier so much information about them, even though it was data the Kogi had chosen to give the world. They had shared their culture in the hope it would save modern society from itself. Nobody had told them about reality holidays.

Julia stared out of the window, turning her face from William. What could she say about the Kogi? Was there any way of bridging the gap between cultures, understanding what they meant? How could she tell this man, this epitome of younger brother, what little she understood without corrupting their message beyond recognition?

'So?' William said. He wasn't going to accept silence as an answer.

She searched the landscape for a clue for something to say. The setting sun cast its glancing rays across the spangled surface of the desert, the sand glittering like gold dust.

And so she told William about the Kogi gold, how they saw it as the blood of the Mother, precious beyond money. The Kogi collected gold as an act of husbandry, she said, fashioned figurines into focal points of power which they called Mothers, a concentration of forces where spirit and matter are one. Every plant, every animal, mountains too, have Mothers, the gold figurine being the resting place of its spiritual aspect. If the gold Mother was nurtured, its physical aspect would be nurtured too. If the Mother was abused, it too would lose its power. The figurines were often interred in pots in burial chambers, safely underground doing their work like nuclear reactors. With the European lust for gold the graves had been an irresistible source of revenue for the *guaqueros*, the tomb robbers. For the Kogi the exhumation of the Mothers meant the forces they represented were dissipated, the energy of plant, animal, mountain sapped. Enough of this and the world sickened. Much more and it would die. There had been talk of the Colombian government returning some of the Museo del Oro's vast collection to the Kogi so they could be restored to the earth, but of course nothing had changed, and it was too late now.

She thought William had stopped listening, but after she was silent for a while he said, 'You sound like you believe it.'

She realised she did. She slid her hand into her jacket and felt for the gold cross around her neck that her father had given her.

When she didn't answer he glanced sideways at her. 'And is this a fulfilment of their prophesy?' He was in a better mood, teasing rather than cynical.

Julia let her gaze glide over the horizon. A streak of cloud lay above the setting sun, its underside reddened like a bad watercolour. 'The only thing holding calamity at bay is the spiritual work of the Mama. The planet can't survive without the stewardship of human consciousness. They believe that when the last Kogi Mama died there would be no Elder Brothers left to look after the heart of the world. And when that happened . . .' Her eyes fell to the green lights of the dashboard as she remembered the words of Mama Valencia. As a student she had memorised the words as though they were a poem.

> *When they kill all the Elder Brothers*
> *then they too will be finished.*
> *We will all be finished.*
> *If that happened and all the Mamas died,*
> *and there was no one doing our work,*
> *the rain wouldn't fall from the sky.*
> *It would get hotter and hotter from the sky,*
> *and the trees wouldn't grow*
> *and the crops wouldn't grow.*

'It will all end,' she said quietly. Too quietly for William to hear.

I glance at the clock on the dash. Something has gone wrong with it: it's flashing 00:03. Probably something to do with the battery, I had trouble getting the engine started just now. I forgot to keep the engine running, like they told me to.

It must be nearly twelve o'clock. I'm reluctant to get out of the cab, but knowing Carla, she'll be dead on time with her phone call. I lug the ten-gallon gasoline container out of the back and sit on it just out of view of the shop. After a couple of minutes, I can hear the phone start to ring. I go over and crouch by the shop door, watching Harry through the window. He is in no hurry to answer the phone, pausing to hitch his trousers up and tuck his shirt tails in.

She keeps him talking. In fact Harry settles down on his chair with the phone wedged between his shoulder and his chin, and rolls a cigarette. I haven't seen anyone smoke a cigarette for years. He has his back to me, but I can see him nod his head in agreement with something.

The flickering TV screen is on a level with my eye and I can't help glancing at it. A semicircle of five men and women are sitting in armchairs in what looks like an empty swimming pool. Judging from their earnest expressions they are debating something of great import. It's an arts program, I guess. My gaze flicks back to Harry, but after a moment I find my attention returning to the screen. There's something familiar about it. Perhaps it's a repeat of something I've already seen. And then I recognise one of the participants. It's me.

I lean forward to see better, my knuckles in the snow. It's a younger me – fifteen years ago at least. My hair is fashionably long, and I am dressed in a green suit which I still have. I don't seem to be saying much. When the camera pans onto me, it shows a neutral look I know only too well. The discussion must be on something about which I know nothing. I remember now: it was a review program of the contemporary arts scene. And it *was* filmed in a disused swimming pool. I only appeared once, though the series ran for months. They never asked me back.

What's going on? Am I being beamed a personalised service? Snippets of my past, selected for my delectation? Again I get that feeling of being watched.

I try and stand up, but I'm stuck in a crouch. Forcing my knees straight, I lean so far forward my head bangs on the window. I look at Harry but he hasn't heard me, and continues talking on the phone. What have they got to say to each other that's taking so long? Hardly two words he says to me, and suddenly he's deep in conversation with my wife. I jiggle my legs to keep warm, resisting the temptation to look at the television.

Tacked on the wall to the side of the window display is a travel poster I haven't noticed before. A mystery how it came to be here. It's a SwissAir advert, a ponytailed Heidi smiling into the camera, in the background cows with bells round their necks, in the distance the white-capped Alps. The poster must be thirty years old, but though it's curling at the edges and bleached by the sun, I suddenly want it. The sky is clear blue, the grass green, hopelessly idyllic. I lose myself in the picture, and for a moment I can almost taste the milk, still warm from the cow, smell the brown bread, feel the warmth of the sun on my face.

I wait a minute after Harry puts the phone down, then I put on my mask and go in. The air is so warm I can feel my body sigh with relief. I dump the gas drum by the counter and go to the kerosine heater to warm my hands. Harry is quietly finishing his cigarette, paying no attention to me. I can't bear the waiting any longer.

'Did my wife ring?'

'Yup.'

'What did she say?'

'She wants you to telephone back.'

I eye the phone. An old cardboard sign is on the wall above it:

shrink the world, call a friend. What if you didn't want the world shrunk? 'Is that all? Anything else?'

'She's going to write to you ComSat.'

'I don't have a receiver.'

'She'll send it here.' He raises one eyebrow to indicate the National Mail sign above the counter.

Shall I phone her or not? It would be so easy – so *humane*. But I have rights, too. The right to be left alone, for one. I hesitate, my hand on the phone.

'You're not married are you, Harry?'

'Nope.'

'What shall I do?'

He gives no indication of having heard me. 'What you doing all the way up here, anyway?' he says.

I withdraw my hand. 'I'm just taking a holiday.'

His face breaks into a smile and then it disappears as quickly as it came. It's so unexpected I look at him closely for the first time. The skin on his face is like crumpled tissue paper, criss-crossed with lines. It reminds me of something, but I can't put my finger on it. 'Your missus said you was a bit of a weasel.'

I'm caught by surprise and don't know what to say.

'She said you're a writer.'

'She's wrong.'

'What you writing?'

I don't answer, so he repeats the question, sitting opposite me, arms folded on the counter, waiting. He has all day; he's not going to give up on me.

'I'm not writing anything.' I realise I'm being unnecessarily surly, but I let it stand.

'So, why buy a typewriter and paper?'

'Why all the questions?'

No response from Harry. His face is blank. I feel foolish and unnerved by him; there's a subtext going on here, an undercurrent of conversation that I'm not part of. 'I've got nothing to say,' I reply at last.

His head nods gently back and forward. It's impossible to tell what he's thinking. He points at the plastic drum. 'What's that?'

'You sell gasoline?'

He shakes his head. 'I got none to spare.'

'I need some for my generator.'

He shrugs.

'I've just put in ten gallons. How long will that last?'

'Depends on what you got running.'

'A heater. Some lights.'

'Week or two.'

'A week or two? What am I going to do when it runs out?'

He doesn't propose an answer.

'When's the next delivery?'

'Should be summer. But . . .' The smile again, on and off just as quick, '. . . you come at a bad time. Just you and me left in Tulkina – no gas company is going to send a barge up for two.'

I suddenly realise that I've left no gasoline for my return trip. I've got a 160-mile journey, and a nearly empty fuel tank. Unless I siphon some of it back out of the generator, my two-week ration is more like four days. That is, if I don't want to be stranded here.

'Are you sure you can't let me have any?'

'This ain't California, fella. You turn up here, you gotta come prepared.'

I suddenly feel too weak to stand up. Harry notices and points to a packing case I can sit on. I dab the sweat off my forehead. 'Where has everyone gone?'

'Needles Crossing – the gold mine.'

I remember passing it on my way to Tulkina, the slice cut out of the hillside, the giant yellow mechanical diggers.

'Everyone?'

'There ain't no game here. No caribou, no seals.' His eyes are black, and I can't help wondering what they've seen over the last sixty years.

'How long you planning on staying?' he asks eventually.

'I don't know.'

'Well, you better get a move on.'

As he says the words, there is a change in my internal pressure as though a door has been opened. The image is fully formed and immediate: the trap door of an airplane has fallen off. I'm fifty thousand feet up, and I have no parachute.

What *am* I doing here? If I have only four days to finish

whatever I came to do, then what? I can't go back. Not now, not ever.

'You going to phone your wife?'

I look at the old plastic phone. 'No.'

'What if she phones again?'

'Tell her to leave me alone.' The words have a metallic ring, which seems to hang in the silence that follows. I realise I still love her. But I don't ever want to see her again. 'Tell her nicely.'

15

They arrived at St George's within fifteen minutes of their projected time. The suburbs of the town looked deserted: a maze of potholed streets and defended buildings, piles of trash on the street corners. William felt in his pocket for the reassuring hardness of the gun. He didn't tell Julia, but these little desert towns were getting a reputation for a peculiar type of violence. Not just the brutal gang warfare of the cities, but pointless, almost existentialist crime. It wasn't worth mugging people any more. Nobody in their right mind carried cash or valuables, and a hot car was more liability than it was worth. But that didn't stop drivers being dragged through the smashed windscreens of their cars and murdered. Back roads would be mined with high explosives. Acid spraying, spiking food with poison, dousing with gasoline – it was the new entertainment.

St George's hadn't been route-mapped and Julia had trouble reading the map. She could sense William's mounting annoyance with her, and just as she was about to concede defeat, they saw the hotel.

The Excelsior was part of a chain, almost identical to the one Julia had stayed in on her first night in the States; even the same air freshener in the lobby, she told him. He sniffed, but he couldn't smell anything. They checked in and had their suitcases taken to their rooms by a young Hispanic porter with a wall eye. When she asked for clean towels for the bathroom, he didn't understand her, and William had to translate into Spanish.

'Hokay,' the young man said, his good eye running up and down Julia's body. 'You give good tip, eh?'

William was hungry, so she joined him in the restaurant and

watched him eat his beanburger while the car was driven to the carport for refuelling. They sat in a window seat, looking out at the empty street. Deserted as usual – even without the pedestrian curfew, not many people would chance walking the streets in the dark. The occasional car glided by, their headlights dazzling William and Julia. A glossy Cadillac cruised past, tinted windows hiding the driver.

'Yakuza,' William said between mouthfuls, pointing to the car with his chin. 'Christ knows why they don't wipe those scum away, and leave the rest of us in peace.'

William knew he would regret bolting his food, but he always ate too fast when he was angry. Beecham's face at their last meeting kept returning to him, apologetic and cowed. The company did it to everybody in the end – cut their balls off and turn them into eunuchs. But they weren't going to do it to him. He didn't know what bothered him most – grounding him after four years of loyal service, or the traps they kept setting for him: the assailant, the book, breaking into his private datafiles. They thought they owned you. Fucking Far Eastern work ethic.

He was in half a mind to do precisely what Omnisens was afraid of: contact the competition and tell them what he knew. The design of the exoskeleton alone was worth a tidy bundle.

A movement caught his eye and he turned to see what it was. A white cat running across the road. It was such a surprising sight he was about to point it out to Julia, but then he saw it was a plastic bag caught by the wind. Six hours driving was playing tricks on his eyes. He was experiencing that strange feeling he always had after extended immersion – tired but keyed up, not sure if he wanted to sleep or stay up all night.

Julia noticed his agitation and asked him what was wrong.

'Nothing,' he said automatically.

'Come on, William.'

'I've just blown a good job and you ask me what's wrong?' His reply had more sting than he intended, but he resisted the impulse to apologise. She waited for him to say more.

'I gave my life to that company. I had everything planned, my whole life. Now look at me – beanburgers in Nowheresville.' He had designed his life at eighteen, mapped it out on his PC, and until a day ago he was on target: graduate from college at twenty-four, good job testing commercial programs, buy shares in the company, invest in company retirement plan, retire from piloting at twenty-eight, go into systems engineering, retire with a comfortable pension at forty-five. His record had been spotless till this morning, and having the MAYA project on his CV would impress any future employer. And now this woman had come crashing into his life with a weird book and started to unravel his life. If it was a test Omnisens had designed for him, they were going to be disappointed with its results, but they were way out of line. He glowered at her, but she was looking at something down the street.

'What's that?' Julia pointed to a gaggle of kids fooling round in an aura of neon light.

William twisted in his seat to look. 'Cyberdrome, probably.' He wiped the ketchup off his plate with the bun and stuffed it in his mouth. His nerves were jangled: he knew he wouldn't be able to sleep. He pushed himself up. 'I think I'll get drunk.'

'Is that the answer?'

It wasn't, but it was something to do. 'I'm going out.'

'Where?'

'The Cyberdrome.'

'Let me come with you,' she said.

'Uh-huh.' He shook his head. 'You're staying here.'

'I'm coming with you.'

She looked determined, and he realised why. 'You think I might dump you here?'

'Yes.'

He was amused at the thought. It had crossed his mind to leave her, but he had ruled it out. It would be heartless to abandon such a sap of a woman, alone and without wheels, but to know she considered him capable of doing so flattered him.

'Come on, William, loosen up. You're not the only one in trouble.'

He refused to return her smile.

'Give me a minute while I phone my family, and then we'll go together. Consider it part of my American education.'

He pointed at a videophone in the corner, annoyed and pleased at the same time. 'Phone them, and let's go out.' He saw her hesitate. 'Come on – live long life.'

She winced at the catchphrase. 'Okay.'

Julia got up and he watched her walk towards the phone. She was an unlikely buddy, but perhaps it wasn't such a bad thing that she had come along. He hated being alone. Any company – even a woman like this – was better than nothing.

Three months he had been on the base without a break. Hard to believe it now. Three months without a drink, without walking the street, without playing cyberball with his mates. It had been a good posting, the best of his life; it was every pilot's dream to fly a system this smart. But one part of him was relieved to have left it behind. There was something about the chipped table top of a real diner, old-fashioned gas-powered cars, strangers. The variety here was genuine, the danger real.

She was back in a moment. 'Out of order,' she said. 'I'll try later.'

Julia wanted to walk, but William ordered a hotel courtesy car to take them the hundred yards to the cyberdrome. 'You can't be too careful,' he said.

The security guard at the cyberdrome was polite enough, but his smile had no more substance than the paper jacket which he wore over his bullet proof body stocking.

'Welcome to the MagiCentre. You are in a security zone 4. May I see your cards, please?'

William gave him both cards, feeling the buzz of adrenalin through his body. He was reminded of being a kid, before cards were widespread, sneaking into arcades to blow his weekly allowance in half an hour. He could feel his impatience mount as the guard checked each holophoto carefully, making Julia stand in the light so he could see her better. Nothing was going to hurry the man. He performed his tasks as slowly and as thoroughly as though he inhabited a planet with heavier gravity. He ran each card through his portable reader, and then William and Julia in turn pressed their thumbs onto the electronic pad to authorise payment. Julia was about to step past the guard, but he barred her way with an arm.

'Wait a minute, Dr O'Brien.' He ran a hand-held scanner over her body, looking for weapons. 'Your purse will have to be checked in at reception. Please keep your card carefully concealed except when making payment. And may I remind you that the ingestion of state controlled drugs is an offence, and that this is an alcohol and smoke free zone.' His smile was as automatic as the words he had just said. 'Enjoy.'

The routine was exactly the same for William. He checked his gun in with an unsmiling young woman, and followed Julia into the air-conditioned hall.

It took a few seconds for his eyes to accustom to the gloom. It was bigger than he expected, the designers capitalising on the cavernous room by decorating it as a fantasy cave with shiny blue walls and grotesque rock outcrops. Fibreglass stalactites hung from the roof, some of them almost reaching head height. It was a surprisingly classy hall for such a dusty little town. Computer generated ambient music masked the whirrings and jolts of the kinetic machines as they threw their operators around.

William counted the machines: about twenty joy rides, and probably the same number of full body suits. He didn't know the time schedule for the MAYA system, but it would be only a matter of months before the exoskeleton went into mass production. He could imagine the queues at the travel agents when it hit the market.

Small groups of people surrounded the screens which had been embedded in the walls. Most of it was combat stuff, but there were one or two abstract dance machines for the fantasy freaks. Some people had come in full fancy dress. He recognised the silver cloaks and painted faces of the Fractal Family. One group was wearing animal masks, barking and yelping at each other; another group of young men dressed in leather kilts and fake animal skins were hollering at the gladiatorial contest being shown on the screens in the corner.

Julia had taken his arm when they had walked in, and the more she saw, the tighter her grip became. He enjoyed protecting her. This was a long way from some English college library, this was the world *he* knew. He guided her between the machines, as proprietorial as if he owned the place, watching her face as much as he watched the rides.

He recognised most of the rides. Three of them were Omnisens products, Powerstalker, Entropy, and Black Hole, all pretty basic compared to the MAYA system. It had been a long time since he had seen graphics as basic as this; even in 3-D some of them would be no more realistic than television. But they worked, with the imagination filling in what the visuals lacked.

Julia paused to watch a young woman, almost completely bald, dancing alone in front of a floor-to-ceiling monitor. *Video drug* it said in bold letters on the top of the screen. Another person, her friend presumably, was in a sort of cradle device wearing a helmet, rocking and moaning to herself. Random geometric shapes flashed onto the screen so rapidly it created a stroboscopic effect, and Julia had to turn away.

'Nirvana junkies,' William said. The waxy skin and falling hair was only the beginning. With repeated use, the psychotropic drug loosened more than follicles. You could see the results sleeping under railway arches in piss-soaked sleeping bags.

'It's awful,' Julia whispered.

Three months away from all this, and William could see her point. It looked like everyone's neurotechnological nightmare. But these were the losers and fuck ups, the addictive-neurotics who in the old days would have used gambling or porno or alcohol in much the same way. They were an embarrassment: this wasn't what virtuality was designed for. It was for architects, and biotechnologists, and chemical engineers. It was for travel and entertainment. It was to set people free.

'There will always be victims of innovation,' he said, repeating the standard line. 'Come on, let's move on.'

They paused beside an operator inside a body suit. He was supported by a simple sling device: no haptic feedback at all, purely AVT stimulus. It was a dance-and-flight program, but from the gyrations and pelvic thrusts it was clear what was going on. The screen above the operator was blank, doubtless sabotaged sometime earlier. William considered bringing a guard over, but he didn't want to embarrass Julia. The management probably knew about it anyway, for nothing sold so well as sex. It made him angry to see another program hijacked by a jerkoff, even angrier that he should be breaking the law.

Five years before, when dildonics got out of hand, the Federal government had tried to legislate parameters into programs, but it had proved impossible. Other than precluding virtual disrobing and the showing of certain body parts, there was no possible control over virtual action. A simpler and more effective ploy was to modify suits and ban private shows. Now the internal world of virtuality had to be open for scrutiny; a simple enough matter to sidestep with a screwdriver and a powerful magnet.

'Do you want a go on any of these?' Julia said, nodding at the man in the body suit. Judging from her face, she had no idea what the man was seeing inside his helmet.

He looked around. A two-man capsule was free, and William pointed to it. It was a favourite of his in his undergraduate days – a high speed space buggy chase through an asteroid belt, old fashioned now, but effective. He helped Julia into the back seat and then slid his card into the payment slot. The machine held the card for a second and then rejected it. He wiped the plastic on his shirt and tried again, but it was regurgitated once more.

'Something's wrong with the machine,' he said. 'Hold on, I'll just be a minute.'

He went to the reception and spoke to the manager, a tubby Oriental in what looked like a silk bathrobe. He took the card from William and examined it suspiciously. 'Perhaps you've run out of credit, sir.' The tone of 'sir' made it sound like an insult.

'I have an A3 job,' William said simply. Or *had*, but this fat Chinaman wasn't to know that. Not only was he registered as having a well-paid job, but he had hardly spent a single credit in the last three months.

The manager ran the card through a reader. 'Maybe you shouldn't spend so much then. Your account has been frozen.'

'What do you mean?'

'You currently have no access to your funds,' he said sarcastically. Any pretence at civility had gone.

'I don't believe you.' William took the reader from the man and stared at the message. *Account frozen. Call OS 3692.* He recognised the code immediately: it was the Institute.

'Standard pilot contract,' he muttered. He felt so stupid. Why hadn't he thought of it? They wouldn't just let him walk off the base; and in effect, he had signed a contract that gave them the right to do just this – to freeze his account. They had a legitimate financial leash around his neck, and when it tugged enough, he would have to contact them.

'That's all, buddy,' the Oriental said. 'Bye, bye.'

'Wait a minute.' He had to think. If his account had been frozen now, they must have just noticed he was missing from the base. A six-hour lead was pretty good, but – he winced as he realised his mistake – if they had access to his finances, they would know from his card receipt that he had eaten and bought fuel at the Excelsior. They knew where he was.

William glanced at the manager, but he was met with an insolent stare. He could see two guards approaching across the floor, and he realised he was about to be thrown out. He held his arms up. 'Okay, I'm leaving.' He waved to Julia, who had climbed down from the machine when she had seen the guards walking into reception.

He turned to the manager. 'Let me call for a courtesy car,' he said, but one of the guards was holding his arm. The man was strong, but William twisted out of his grip and pushed him in the chest. 'Back off, fella.'

The guard was taken by surprise, but his partner grabbed William from behind in a bearhug. 'Hey!' He tried to wrestle free and they almost tipped over. The Oriental shot out an arm and held William by the windpipe until the other guard could take William's free arm. He twisted it behind William's back until he yelped.

'Throw this piece of trash out,' the manager snarled. 'Come back when you've got some money.'

'One of your screens is down,' William said, as they bundled him away. 'That's illegal, you know.'

He allowed himself to be escorted to the exit with Julia. The two guards pushed him out into the street and stood in the doorway as if expecting him to charge back in.

Julia tugged him away from them. 'What's happened?'

She couldn't get any sense out of him at first. He wanted to go back in and punch the manager's lights out. 'Goddamn insolence!' He wondered if this was a sign of things to come: no money, no respect.

He explained the situation to Julia. 'I might have gone AWOL, but I'm still an Omnisens employee, and they have the right to freeze my account.'

'What can we do?'

'I've got a fully charged engine, enough for five hundred miles, a bit further if I take it easy.'

'How far is Seattle?'

'Twelve hundred miles. And we can't stay at the motel tonight. They might be on their way already.'

'Okay. But don't worry about money – we'll use my card.'

'Have you given them clearance to your file?'

'Of course not.'

He considered the chance of Omnisens breaking into her file, but thought it unlikely. They were certainly capable of it, but electronic trespass was one thing with a bonded worker like himself, another thing altogether with a foreign national. He realised he had to accept her offer. 'Thanks,' he muttered. He hated being dependent on this woman, but there was no other way. He nodded in the direction of the motel. 'We'd better hurry.'

'Wait a minute.' She went back to the guard at the door. 'Mr Morrison's gun, and my purse please.' She turned back to smile at William. 'Live long life.'

16

They took it in turns to drive through the night. William had
been reluctant to let Julia take the controls, but she'd managed
to convince him she wouldn't crash his precious car, and he
finally fell asleep somewhere past Tonopah.

She was glad to see the dawn. It had been a starry night, quiet
and black and seemingly endless. By five-fifteen, the eastern light
was edging a grey stain into the sky, then it was orange, then
white, until William woke up, snuffling and stiff and blinking.

They stopped outside a rundown diner in the middle of
nowhere. It was a last stop store, which looked like it sold
everything from gasoline to chocolate bars and toilet paper.
It was the only building for miles, surreal in its isolation, and
they stared through the dusty windscreen almost waiting for it
to shimmer and disappear like a mirage.

'Do you want something to eat?' she asked.

William looked at it doubtfully. 'Is it still open?'

It was a mess: a twelve-foot tower of plastic crates looked on
the point of collapsing into the road. Its painted sign was so
bleached by the sun it was illegible. Behind the diner they could
see the carcass of a burnt out Chevy, stuffed to the sunroof with
tumbleweed, as though it were the nest of a monster bird. And
next to it, a sun-bleached trailer with pink nylon curtains, and
no sign of life.

The sun was still slanting long shadows across the parched
earth, so Julia didn't bother with her UV glasses and sun hat
before she got out of the car. William went behind the water
tank to piss while Julia did some stretching exercises, touching
her toes and breathing deeply. She looked at the inverted image

of the diner between her legs. The remnants of pink gloss paint were blistering off its wooden shutters. A solar panel formed a square of light on the roof, next to a patch of corrugated aluminium sheeting which would be as hot as a frying pan in an hour or so. It looked as though it had been abandoned some time ago, and even then hadn't been much of a place.

She stood up straight as a dog started baying from somewhere behind the diner. William came running out, zipping his fly, and looking for a stone to throw. He ran to the car, and she joined him, infected with his fear. The howling mounted as though the animal were in pain, and then an albino bloodhound came into view, lolloping clumsily through the obstacle course of the yard. It stopped about twenty-five feet away from them and paused to sniff the air. The dog lowered its muzzle to the ground, the folds of its face collapsing over its eyes, and then with enormous concentration followed the invisible trail of scent towards the car.

William reached under the dashboard and brought out his revolver. Rabies was bad news in this part of the state.

'Now, you put that gun away, mister.'

The voice was pure hillbilly. It took Julia a moment to locate its source. An old man, a beard halfway down his bare chest, was standing in the doorway of the trailer, a shotgun levelled at William.

'You call your dog off, then,' William shouted back.

The man gave a single whistle, and the dog turned, sniffing the air, its head casting side to side like a radar.

'He don't mean no harm,' the old man said, stepping out of the trailer. He lowered the shotgun, but kept it in the crook of his arm. 'And anyhow, he's as blind as a—' He mumbled something to himself, unsure how to finish the sentence. The dog found its way to the trailer and sat facing the approximate direction of the old man.

William pocketed the gun and shut the car door. 'Are you open?' he called. 'We want some breakfast.'

The old man came out into the open. His hair was as long and as greasy as his grey beard. He wore old-fashioned denim jeans, and was barefoot. Julia could see tattoos snaking up both arms, but from this distance she couldn't make out what they depicted.

'Coffee and toasties.' The way he said it sounded definitive – take it or leave it.

William hesitated.

'Fine,' Julia said. She had no idea what toasties were, but coffee sounded good.

They waited in the porch of the cafe while the old man got dressed. It was seven o'clock, and already getting too hot to stand out in the sun. The occasional car zipped past, but none stopped.

He was wearing shades and a faded Grateful Dead T-shirt when he opened the door. He mumbled something to them, but Julia didn't catch it.

It was dim and cool inside; wooden floorboards, a long dusty bar like the old grocery stores Julia had seen in Ireland. Against one wall were half empty shelves with packets of out-of-date food, cans whose contents were daily simmered when the sun was at its peak. Beams of sunlight shone through the gaps in the shutters, cutting through the air like laser spotlights. A chrome antique jukebox stood by the door.

They sat at the bar and Julia watched the old man as he clattered cups and plates onto the counter. She wondered how he made a living. Even if someone stopped, it seemed unlikely he had anything to sell.

William seemed fazed by his surroundings, and just sat quietly, watching. A copy of an old paperback novel was by his elbow. He stared at it suspiciously and then moved his arm away.

'You folks got cash?' the old man asked, his back to them. His hair was tied in a ponytail.

'We've got cards,' Julia said.

He turned round, his arms folded across his chest. This close, she could read one of the tattoos across his biceps: *Sioux City chapter*, and above it, blurred with age, a winged skull.

'I don't take card money.'

'Of course you do,' William said.

The man looked at William, his eyes hidden behind his shades. 'There ain't no of course about it, mister.'

'But —'

Julia laid her hand on William's arm to shut him up. She knew what he was going to say: *but it's illegal, black market, tax free*. William shrugged, and then got up from his stool and wandered to the door. Julia dumped her shoulder bag onto the counter. 'I've got some ecus. Is that okay?'

'I don't want no foreign money. Dollars is all.'

'Trade you something?' she said.

He hesitated. 'What you got?'

She looked back at William for help, but he didn't notice. 'What do you want?'

The old man sucked some air between his teeth. She could see he was enjoying this. 'Tobacco?'

She shook her head.

'Shotgun cartridges? Whisky? Cheese?'

'I've got a wristwatch.'

'That ain't no good to me.'

William called over from the corner. 'How does this work?' He was leaning over the jukebox.

'It's busted.'

'What's wrong with it?'

'I don't know.'

Julia swivelled her stool round to watch him. 'Could you fix it, William?'

'Maybe. It's probably simple enough.'

'Swap you for breakfast?' she asked the old man.

He grunted a half laugh and turned back to make the coffee.

Toasties turned out to be the trade name of a sort of stale bread pillow filled with fake chocolate paste. She tried one of them, and then let William finish the plateful. The paste stuck to the top of her mouth, and she could feel her teeth smeared with the stuff. But the coffee was real; that would have to do. She had to lose weight anyway.

When William finished his breakfast he went back to tinkering with the jukebox. Seeing Julia alone at the bar, the old man came over. He asked where they had come from, where they were going. She told him.

'Long way.'

She nodded.

'What wheels have you got?'

'The car? I don't know.' She could see its bonnet through the half open door. 'It's silver,' she added lamely.

His eyes narrowed. 'You spend half a day in a machine and you don't even know what it is? Woman, where's your head? It's a Sun Independent.' He called out to William. 'What's the model number of your wheels, man?'

'464,' William called back without looking up.

'Names are important,' the man said to Julia. 'With a name you know where you are.'

There was a heavy silence. 'Is this your name?' she said at last, indicating one of the tattoos on his biceps which said *Jake*. He looked at the name, twisting the skin so he could read it better. 'I guess so.' He watched her as she sipped her coffee. 'So, what you doing with a jerk-off like him?'

'He's a friend.'

'He ain't no friend,' he said flatly. Julia didn't contradict him.

'How much trouble you in?' he asked.

'Why do you think we're in trouble?'

'Tell me you're not, then.'

She was uncomfortable under such scrutiny, and looked away. A car sped past on the highway, a spray of pebbles rattling against the side of the shack.

'Let me show you something,' he said.

'What?'

'Something you ain't never seen.'

She glanced over at William, but he was busy with the jukebox. 'I don't know,' she said.

'I'm giving you a gift, and you don't fucking want it?' The threat in his voice was unmistakable, but it would have been more dangerous to refuse him, so she stood up.

'I'm sorry.' She followed him through the back door to the yard. The dog was lying in the shade, its nose in the dust. Its ears pricked up as they passed but the old man clucked at it, and it lay down again.

He led Julia to a chest-high mound in the middle of a green tarpaulin, weighed down at the edges with rocks. 'That fella,' he said jerking his head in the direction of the diner. 'Is he military?'

'Why do you say that?'

'I can smell the system on him.' He kicked the rocks away from the tarp, and then carefully rolled it back, revealing a gleaming motorbike. 'My baby. Harley D. Electra Glide I customised back in 1980.' He ran his hand over the fuel tank, painted red flames licking along its length. The old man pulled a spotted handkerchief from his back pocket and wiped the high handlebars, blowing invisible dust off the chrome. 'Ain't she beautiful.'

It was a statement that she had to agree with. The leather of the seat had cracked, and the tyres were hardly new, but every part of it that could shine, did so.

He gazed lovingly at it. 'I always keep her tuned and ready.'

'Ready for what?'

'The end of the world.'

A gust of wind span some dust upwards, and she shut her eyes. She couldn't believe she was standing in the desert with a sixty-year-old Hell's Angel having this discussion. She could feel the sun on her neck and imagined cancer cells multiplying by the second.

'You read the *Book of Revelations*?' he asked.

She knew what was coming. The armageddonists had greeted the plague with delight.

'And the third angel sounded,' the old man began, 'and there fell a great star from heaven, burning as it were a lamp, and it fell upon the third part of the rivers, and upon the fountains of waters. And the name of the star is called Wormwood, and the third part of the waters became wormwood; and many men died of the waters, because they were made bitter.' He pointed into the sky. 'That's where the virus came from – outer space.'

She followed the direction of his pointing finger as though she might see the comet itself.

'It's coming, you know,' he said. 'The end of the world.'

For a crazy moment, she thought he might know something, and she searched his face for the answer.

'I don't know when exactly,' he said, guessing her question. 'But when it does, I'm going to ride out in style.'

She smiled at the thought. 'One of the horsemen of the apocalypse?'

'You got it,' he said, pleased she understood.

'And which one are you?'

'War,' he said simply. He surveyed the mound of the motor-bike. 'You think I'm crazy? Too much acid?'

'I don't know.'

'This used to be farmland,' he said nodding at the unending panorama of scrub. 'I used to do good business here from the combine harvesters and the truckers—' He jerked his head to finish his sentence. 'Now it's just settlers and bandits. The last real rainfall we had was six years ago. Now it costs you more to buy drinking water than fucking gasoline. *That's* crazy.'

Julia heard a noise behind her and turned to see William.

'You okay?' he called.

'Yes, thanks,' she said.

He nodded and went back inside. Jake wiggled his eyebrows suggestively. 'You two an item, then?'

'We're just fr—' She hesitated. 'Colleagues.'

He scratched his beard, his expression one of disbelief. 'Give me a hand, here,' he said, unrolling the tarpaulin back over the machine. 'She don't like too much sun.'

Julia helped him, and together they kicked the rocks back in place. It was getting too bright to stay out in the sun, and they went back into the diner. A boy of about ten was squatting on the floor next to William amongst the pieces of the dismantled jukebox. His hair was bleached and dusty, the skin on his nose peeling pink. He looked up at Julia and the old man, and then returned his attention to what William was doing.

The boy reminded Julia of Francis, her eldest son. They were the same age, with the same half-child, half-teenager look to them, growing three inches every year. She felt guilty about not having phoned her family sooner. She'd been away a week, and hadn't called them yet. 'I have to make a phone call,' she said to the man.

Jake pointed to an old-fashioned audiophone on the wall. He saw the doubtful look on her face. 'It'll take your card.'

She dialled her England number.

'Yes?' a man's voice said.

'Peter?'

'Who do you want?'

'Peter O'Brien.'

'Nobody here called that.'

'Sorry, I must have got the wrong—' she began to say, but the man hung up.

She dialled again.

'Yes?' The same man's voice.

'I'm sorry, I think we've been misconnected. I want 762 7422.'

'That's me.'

She didn't know what to say, her mouth opening and closing stupidly. She could hear the man waiting on the end of the line. 'But that's my husband's number,' she blurted.

'01BC 762 7422?' he said, giving the gender and geographic prefix.

'That's right.'

'Don't tell my wife – she'd be jealous.' He waited a couple of seconds, and when she didn't reply, he hung up again.

She looked at the receiver as though it were at fault, and then put it back in its cradle. Surely she hadn't got the number wrong? She fished her diary out of her bag and checked her husband's number. 01BC 762 7422. She'd been married for eleven years, she knew the number as well as her own.

'Oh my God,' she whispered. William wasn't the only one who was losing his family. It was happening to her. Someone was changing their families' numbers.

She took a few deep breaths to compose herself. She didn't want them to see her confusion.

'How you doing, boy?'

She turned to face the room. William was still on the floor, oblivious to the old man.

'I said, how are you doing?'

William glanced at the old man. 'Don't call me "boy".' He nodded for the child to switch on the machine. The lights came on, and the boy clapped.

'You ain't gone and fixed it?' the old man said.

'Let's see.' William pressed a button on the console and waited. Nothing happened.

'You need money for it, mister,' the boy said.

Julia watched the old man take a handful of coins from a drawer and go to the jukebox. She decided that if the machine worked, she would keep the telephone call a secret. If not, she'd tell William here and now.

'Here.' The old man slotted a quarter into the machine, and then ran his finger down the display, choosing what he wanted to hear. He punched two buttons and the machine whirred.

'Goddam, it's working!'

A record slapped into place, and the arm of the record player moved across. A jarring chord of electric guitar burst from the speaker.

The old man thrust his hands into his back pockets and beamed at William. 'Goddam, you're a genius!'

William ignored the comment and screwed the back onto the machine. Julia went over to them, feigning interest in the jukebox. She hadn't seen one of these machines since she was a teenager. All four of them crowded round it, watching the spinning black disc in the middle. Record B16 was playing, and she looked through the list to see its title. The print was now so faint that it was barely legible, but the lyrics of the song were clear enough.

'Wild Thing?'

'You bet. The Troggs, 1966,' the old man said. He nodded at the record, mouthing the words to the song.

William glanced at his watch and then at Julia. 'Let's get moving.'

She got her bag and was about to join him at the door when Jake stopped her. 'What *are* you doing with a cuboid like that?' he said, indicating William.

'He's not military,' she said, knowing she wasn't answering the question. 'He works for Omnisens. He's a systems pilot.'

'A cuboid is a cuboid.'

The boy was outside, tussling with the dog, trying to wrench a bleached ox bone from its jaws. The dog's eyes were white with cataracts: ultraviolet poisoning.

'Thanks for breakfast,' she called back to the old man.

The song was coming to an end, and he raised his hand to wave, his eyes not leaving the jukebox.

She got into the car and looked back at the diner. She didn't know what to think any more. She could feel the limits of her comprehension straining to make sense of this.

The boy had succeeded in wrestling the bone from the dog, and was teasing the animal with it. Its jaws were snapping aimlessly at empty air, spittle flying as it jerked its head about.

William started the car, drowning out the sound of rock and roll. The last thing Julia saw before they pulled away was the boy throwing the bone for the dog to chase. It span in an arc, crossing in front of the sun, dazzling her vision so she had to shut her eyes.

It was less than five minutes later that a maroon two-seater pulled up at the diner and two men got out. It had been fifty years since Jake had trusted a man in a suit, and he wasn't about to begin now. When the elder of the two men asked if a man and a woman had recently been through, Jake answered in Spanish. By the time a tortuous translation had taken place he had decided they were either police or industrial security. He told them, in Spanish, that he had seen nobody all day. He insisted on making coffee for them – no charge. Anything to give the woman and the cuboid with the screwdriver a bit of a head start.

17

Paper and pencil are no less magical than an electronic pad. A long time since I've seen it, but now I look, there seems a startling ingenuity in the way that graphite leaves a visible trail on a two-dimensional surface. Is it the pencil giving, or the paper taking? I bring the paper as close to my eye as I can, tilting the pad at a right angle to my vision, but the mystery remains. Even the faintest of touches leaves a thread of spider's web, but take the tip off the paper and the line disappears. Nothing less than magical, the synchronicity of the line appearing in exact accordance with the touching of paper and graphite. Like falling from a building and discovering that one's descent ends at the precise moment that the ground comes up to meet one.

Now I'm here, alone in my Arctic icebox, I wonder why it has taken me so long to arrive. One part of me has been hungering for this isolation for years. Admittedly, the larger part, the sensible part, tried to smother the urge with protestations of obligation and comfort and sanity, but it only took courage, and less than one might have thought, to leave it all behind. Kicking over the smouldering remains wasn't even one of the difficult decisions of my life. In a few years' time there would have been nothing more to do except collect pension cheques, feed the body, watch television.

No doubt my disappearance will have caused a flutter of consternation in our cosy circle, and I suppose when they find out I'm infected they'll think this is the reason for my desertion. And I suppose at first that *was* my motivation. But now I couldn't care less. So a few years are cut off my life? So I have to live in a bubble? So I sneeze and puke and break out in hives? I'm leaving civilisation behind because I'm disgusted with it.

They might even think my act is one of heroism – an Eskimo sacrifice, wandering off to die in the snow. If only they knew my true reason, I'd be branded something far worse than contaminated. They'd hang a plaque around my neck, parade me round the campus: *subversive*. Not so much leaving a home and a wife behind, but disengaging from the monstrous machine itself – unthinkable. Of course, if I were a Hindu, people would call me a *vanaprasthi* and donate money for my upkeep. But this is the New World, folks.

I go to the window and look out. The suddenness of such unrelenting nothingness is almost intoxicating; that view can swallow you up, trample you into madness. If I spent all day looking out, all I would see is the slowly circling shadow of the factory. I have seen no sign of life through these windows: no people, no animals, not even any birds. Life at its simplest.

I always thought snow was white, but no. It's blue in the morning, white at midday, ochre in the afternoon. At two in the morning when the sun finally gives into the spin of the planet, it's the colour of mercury. It's a blank piece of paper outside my window, just waiting for the sky to scribble on it.

We deserve the plague, every viral cell of it. Not some post-AIDS moral bullshit about divine retribution, but the even-handed comeback of nature. Civilisation is finally dying, killing itself off with an excess of cleverness. And I am at the front of the queue. Good riddance.

For the first time in years I have the privacy to do exactly as I want. No more stepping round obstacles; now I can disengage from the world, go insane if I choose. I don't have to make an effort. I don't have to save the world. There's no one here to care, and that suits me fine. I will go out, not with a bang but a whimper.

A sheen of ice has formed on the inside of each pane, daily growing thicker, distorting the view a little more each time I look out. I have scratched my initials in the ice as though I were a schoolboy.

My window gazing has recently turned into a meditation and a balm for my frown lines. I regulate my breathing, let the tension go from my shoulders, slipping the burden off for a moment. As a child I used to pore over a musty Victorian *Pilgrim's Progress*. The copperplate engravings both frightened and compelled me: this was a world I knew well, a pantomime world where every character was trapped in the role of archetype. And resist it though he may, the reader too, was an archetype – a sinner or saint. I never read the story, still don't know it; my sole interest was in the pictures. Of these, the one to which I returned again and again was that of Christian Pilgrim at the beginning of his journey, up to his knees in the Slough of Despond, bowed under the weight of his knapsack. Even as a child, I understood how heavily consciousness could weigh.

I locate a brown smudge in the middle distance and level my gaze at it. The skill of zazen, like writing a book, can never be completely forgotten. I allow my eyes to unfocus, letting my attention fall into the smudge in the snow. Sleeping but staying awake, waiting for an ultimate disconnectedness, a maniacal unreasonableness: it is these moments out of time that have saved me. *Sunyata*, the void, the Buddhists call it. The pisspot of God. Thanks be.

Last night I dreamt of my school chums. Mike and Jonnie, just as I'd seen them last, age eighteen. It has been years since I've thought of them in my waking life, but there they were, as real and as vivid as if I was still at school. We were driving somewhere in a car, me in the back seat, leaning forward to speak to them. It was night, we were going to pick up some girls, Sarah and – I've lost the other name now. There was a bottle of wine, a joint being smoked. If I shut my eyes now, I can still see the profile of Mike, his wiry hair and glasses, smell the damp car and tobacco smoke. Jonnie is laughing.

I can't believe how real it was. I haven't seen them for forty-five years, but there they were, as complete as they ever were. Not approximations, fuzzed round the edges by the years; no, this was Mike and Jonnie in the flesh.

I can feel the weight of the past pressing against the door of my memory. It's all there, every moment preserved in high resolution, omnisensory Technicolor. But this wasn't like watching a home movie, it was being there. I was eighteen again, and I'd forever be eighteen, driving out to pick up girls with my chums – a trip we probably never took, but no less real for that.

Recently I've been thinking a lot about my school days. Not the really early stuff, but from age twelve onwards. Crewkerne Grammar School, founded 1499, perched like Dracula's castle on top of a hill. The first day, Morning Assembly with masters in their black robes, hymn books with blue plastic covers, fear. The memory is all so wretchedly complete. The roll call at prep – I wonder if I could remember it now? I take my notebook and start typing as the names comes to me. I grope at first, but when I find my rhythm, the names come like the lyrics to a song: Baty, Boyer, Buckton, Busek, Coombes, Cranton, Critchley, Eve, Fell, Gardener, Gibson, Gready, Haig, Harris, Hosken, Hulse, James, Jelley, Jenkins, Mitchell, Perrett, Ward – they are all there. I stare at the list of names on the screen, astonished. I could spend half an hour talking about each one of them, people I have given no thought to for nearly half a century.

Am I the same person as I was then? Is there an unbroken thread that connects me to that brown-haired boy that once answered to my name? There was no break in my past, but in retrospect I was a different person at twelve, at twenty, at thirty-five, at fifty. Am I new born every moment, a different person every day? At times I can believe it, when the past flakes away and it's just me and my nakedness. But then I dream of Jonnie and Mike, and the past is in the present, and there has only been one 'me'. Which am I – particle or wave? Or both?

Sometimes I feel incredibly old; not worn out, but witness to an uncountable number of events. I have lived more than one lifetime in my sixty-three years. There was the young boy, the schoolboy, the student, the young author, the cranky father and disillusioned teacher. If I were to write it as autobiography it would run to a million volumes.

Only one million? I recently estimated the number of times my heart has beaten. The answer? At eighty contractions a minute for sixty-three years, the sum total is two and a half billion, or so. Extraordinary to think that a piece of equipment could perform so consistently well, and without apparent wear. But I suppose the body, like the self, is under constant construction, new cells replacing old. Heraclitus said the physical body is like a river: it may look the same from moment to moment, but its configuration is forever changing. We never see the same river twice.

The physical continuum of the body is an illusion. Ninety-eight per cent of the atoms that make up the aching structure of my body, if I am to believe the physicists, were not here a year ago. With every intake of breath I inhale 1000000000000000 atoms that have been present in the body of every human being who has ever lived. Take your pick: Genghis Khan, Tutankhamun, Julius Caesar, Marilyn Monroe, Gautama the Buddha, the first cave man. And I wanted to be alone!

So, whose heart is it that is beating? Mine or one quadrillionth of everyone who has ever lived? And where did they get *their* atoms? From the star dust of the big bang. Twenty billion years ago. No wonder I feel so old.

Two and a half billion heartbeats, one for every eight years of the universe. Coming up with that figure got me wondering: perhaps we all have a roughly equal number of heartbeats per lifetime. Perhaps the horse, the fish, the stick insect (whatever its equivalent to a heartbeat may be) all have their two and a half billions worth of longevity. If that is so, then perhaps the biological clock, rather than the horological clock, determines their experience. Perhaps no absolute clock exists for them. Perhaps the giant tortoise with its sluggish metabolism is aware of living no longer than the mayfly for whom every second is a week.

And how about Toto? Does its heart beat *allegro*, time inching past its hooked nose, one hour to my fifteen minutes? I must seem like a bradycardiac giant from its perspective of the light fitting.

I think about Harry Homme. His fist-sized heart is beating too. At this very moment, it is contracting and relaxing, squeezing its requisite number of pints of blood into the aorta, keeping the machine going.

I suppose the Eskimos, like the Kogi, would say that trees and mountains and oceans are as alive as anything that walks and flies. If that is so, then what kind of metabolism do they have? If high tide and low tide are the systole and diastole of an ocean, an equivalent heartbeat of twice a day, how old would an ocean be at sixty-three? It takes some time to work it out, but eventually the number glows on the screen in front of me: 2,721,600 years. Is that the lifetime of an ocean?

I've taken to braiding string. I've knotted three lengths of twine to the window and I am slowly working my way across the room. It'll take me for ever to reach the end, but the repetitiveness is therapeutic. I remember now that I used to plait string as a child; all the pleasure of knitting with none of the complication.

Whether it's the illness or lack of food, or the twenty-hour daylight, I don't know, but I've been feeling increasingly light headed. Perhaps it's just the letting go. Of what? Time.

If I can keep the body from demanding too much attention I can escape from past and future. Standing at this table, cutting bread for toast, slow sawing motions, my whole body, the whole room directing its force along the plane of the knife, I can hear the footfall between each moment. Tricky to achieve, maddening to sustain, living in the present is like balancing a pole on the end of your nose, forever on the edge of crisis: unknown, unknowing, unidentified, longitude and latitude collapsed into a single point. And like the pole balancing trick, too sudden a movement will bring the thing crashing to the ground. Thus, these thoughts, and I'm on the passenger train of fantasy, destination nowhere. A light touch is required. To find yourself, lose yourself. To be sane, go crazy.

Carla would hate me for this. Time is the wool of our lives, start tugging and the whole fabric unravels until we're standing naked in the face of the void.

The smoke alarm starts howling, and I realise I've burnt the bread again. The sound is stunningly loud. It feels as though it's inside me, subcutaneous electrodes screaming up and down my meridians. I cover my ears and wait for it to finish. I eye the sprinkler above my head. At least it's a dry attack.

The noise has set Toto squawking.

'Fuck the bastards!' I imagine it crying. 'Fuck the bastards!'

I stand on a chair and try to smash the smoke alarm with a broom handle, but it's screwed to the ceiling and is apparently indestructible.

I decide to go out and leave it to howl to itself.

18

They stopped at a motel at midday. William was prepared to drive on, but Julia insisted they have a break. She was right. They had driven nearly a thousand miles in eighteen hours; there was no point in exhausting themselves. Seattle wasn't going to go away, and if she used her card, the base shouldn't be able to trace them.

The only room they could find was a twin on the ground floor with a faulty light switch in the bathroom. The receptionist assumed they were there for sex, and told them they could push the beds together if they wanted. They booked the room for the afternoon and Julia paid for it.

William automatically switched on the TV and then lay on his bed fully clothed while she took a shower. He flicked through the channels with the remote and then turned the sound down and stared at the ceiling. If they slept a couple of hours and left straight away, they would be in Seattle by nightfall. And then hopefully, this whole crazy episode would end. The paperback was still in his pocket, and he ran its pages between his fingers. He wanted to phone his mother again, get it over with, but he resisted the temptation to try. Her number didn't exist, he reminded himself. Something had happened to wipe out all trace of her.

Julia came out of the bathroom in a loose cotton tunic, a towel wrapped round her head. She was sexy in a matronly sort of way, he decided. A bit on the fat side, but she had good skin, nice hair. She sat on the bed and bent down to dry her calves, her necklace falling out of the neck of her dress, swinging with the movement of her arms.

He had been avoiding the question ever since they'd left, but in the stillness of the room it clamoured for his attention. He watched her as she towelled her hair dry. Why had she insisted on coming? It was he who had gambled his future work prospects, but this escapade would hardly look good on her datafile.

'Why don't you have a shower?' she said without looking at him. 'It'll make you feel better.'

He said nothing while she brushed her hair out. She had the same colour hair as his mother. He glanced at the TV screen: a public service announcement about property protection. 'Why have you come along with me?' he asked at last.

She faltered for a moment in her brushing.

'Has Beecham set you up for this?' he said.

She tied her damp hair back with a scarf and turned to face him. She held his gaze for a moment to let him know she was telling the truth. 'No.'

'Then what the hell are you doing here?'

She went to her suitcase and slid her hands into the middle of her clothes. She brought out a book, dog-eared and yellow, its cover stuck on with tape. He took it and stared at the cover. The same author. He looked at her for an explanation.

'I found a copy of this four years ago in a junk shop in London. I don't know why I bought it, but—' She stopped and shrugged.

'But?'

'It's the story of an English woman called Kate who meets an old Irish man, Michael O'Brien. They spend a year together, she gets pregnant, he dies, end of story.'

'And?' Some part of him knew what was coming next.

'My father was Irish and died before I was born. My mother was forty years younger than him, called Kate. His name? Michael O'Brien.'

He didn't want to hear this, but he had to know more. He indicated for her to continue.

'Your parents are not the only ones who have been written about,' she said. 'All the detail in the book exactly fits the lives of my mother and father: the same location, the same dates – everything.'

'Are you sure?' His throat was constricted, and his words sounded choked.

'I haven't checked with Kate, but it's just as she told me.'

He looked at the publication date. 'When were you born?'

'In 1989. The same year the book was published.'

Why didn't you tell me this before?'

'I didn't know if I could trust you,' she said simply.

She sat on the edge of her bed and stared at her bare feet. He noticed she was wearing a ring on her little toe. 'I checked out other books by this author. I'd heard of the one you read but I couldn't find a copy. And then it turns up on my bedside table the first night at the base.'

William studied her face. It must be a set up. It all dovetailed too neatly.

'I stayed awake all night reading it,' she continued. 'And when I met you the next day, I realised we were in the same situation. Both of our parents' lives have been turned into novels by the same author.'

William scanned through the author biography on the inside cover. Not much to go on. A couple of previous books, date of birth: 1957. He made a quick calculation; he would be sixty-three now. 'Who is this guy?' he asked, indicating the cover. 'Did you check him out?'

'There wasn't much to discover. He hasn't published anything for years. The last anyone heard of him, he was living in West Canada.'

William opened the book at random and read a couple of paragraphs. The book smelt of pepper. 'You've been carrying this around with you for four years?'

'I hoped I might be able to find him.'

'So *that*'s why you've come with me. You want me to drive you to Seattle. Just a few hours from there to BC.' He didn't like the idea of being used, but at least he had an explanation. 'If it's so important to get to Canada, why didn't you try before?'

'Until a couple of days ago I thought it still could be a coincidence.'

He tossed the book into the suitcase. 'Where is your mom?'

'In England.'

'What does she say about this?'

'We don't talk any more. I guess she doesn't know about the book. She never mentioned it.'

William closed his eyes to concentrate. This was like one of those brain teasers, easy to solve as long as you kept your thoughts focused. 'She must have met the author and told him about meeting your father.'

'And he writes it as a novel and publishes it in the same year?' The tone of her voice was clear: impossible, it said.

'What other explanation is there?'

'I don't know. But think about it – how is it you can't get in touch with your mother?'

'Some technical screw up, probably.'

Her blank look suggested she knew something she wasn't telling him.

'What is it?' he asked.

'And when I phoned my husband,' she said carefully. 'Why wasn't he there?'

'He was out?'

'The number I dialled was somebody else's.'

'I don't understand.'

'Somebody else has got my husband's number.'

'That's not possible.'

She didn't bother to answer. It was possible, because it had happened. He got up and walked to the TV. He stared at the screen for a moment, and then switched it off with the toe of his shoe. He could feel her watching him, waiting for his next response. 'There's a rational explanation to this,' was all he could think of saying.

He paused in front of the mirror and glanced at his face . . . he looked worried. 'It has to be a set up by Omnisens.'

'They plant a book in a bookshop four years ago, and I just happen to come across it?' She shook her head. 'Are they really that clever?'

'Then it must be you.'

'Oh come on, William.' She sounded as though she was scolding as child.

'No – listen. You get some hack to write a book copied from my life, make it look thirty years old. Then do the same with yourself. It's easy enough.'

'Why would anyone want to do that?'

'It's all about mind games. Just seeing how much I can take.' His certainty made him vindictive, and for a moment he considered how he could best hurt this woman. He wanted to smash up the room, destroy something.

'This isn't part of the project,' she insisted. 'Or if it is, nobody has told me about it.'

'I don't believe you.' He crouched by her case and ran his fingers along its rim. 'So, where's the microphone?' He tossed her clothes onto the floor piece by piece, shaking the folds out of her shirts, looking in shoes. He rattled her holoplayer. 'In here?'

Julia was saying nothing, her arms crossed over her chest. He reached for her, but she stepped back. 'Or are you wearing it?'

'Piss off!'

He lunged for her and caught her wrist. She twisted out of his grip. 'Keep your hands off me.' She went to the door and stood with her back to it, one hand on the door knob.

William knew he had gone too far, and apologised. He looked at the mess on the floor and started to pile it back into the suitcase.

'Leave it,' she said.

He hesitated and then got to his feet. He couldn't meet her eyes. 'I'm going back to the Institute. I've had enough.'

'They won't be able to answer your questions.'

He shrugged. He'd made up his mind.

'I've been looking for an answer for four years. Don't put yourself through that. If there is an answer, it's in West Canada.'

'I'm going back. If you want to come with me, I'm leaving at six.'

The maroon two-seater slid along the highway as smoothly and as silently as a drop of oil down a blackboard. A perpetual sunburst from its rear windscreen was visible as a glint across the valley floor. The Harley Davidson which followed it hung well back, matching their speed exactly.

William was too agitated to sleep for the rest of the afternoon. He left Julia in the room, and wandered round the motel complex under the speculative gaze of the security cameras. There was no other rational explanation: it had to be her behind this book thing. He was being tested, and he'd fallen right into their trap, believing everything they'd put in his path. And now he had allowed himself to be persuaded to leave the base.

William went to the games room and watched some kids playing a sensex game. He sat in a corner cubicle, staring dully at the flashing sign on the screen: *insert your card*. He considered going up to the room to wake her, tell her they were leaving now. It was probably too late to retrieve his place on the project, but if he turned back straight away, he might still have a job.

It was the only rational explanation, but still he had difficulty believing in her duplicity. She was playing her part too well; she looked as confused as he felt. He lifted the head set off its cradle and examined it. Cheap LCD screens, one of the speakers cracked. But looks can deceive, he muttered, replacing the head set. She had put up a fight when he said they'd be going back, but that was only to be expected.

He went to the bar and ordered a whiskey. It was only when the bartender placed it in front of him that he remembered he couldn't pay for it.

'Charge it to Room 121,' he said, showing the man the room key.

As William watched the bartender key in the price on his console, he felt a sudden urge to get drunk. 'And one for yourself,' he added.

'Thank you, sir.'

By six o'clock William was so drunk that when the bartender refused to serve him any more he accepted it without complaint. He felt better now that he'd made up his mind. As the bartender helped him up the stairs he explained his resolve. 'That's what I'm going to do. Go back to the base, turn myself in, blame that woman. They'll buy that won't they?'

The barman had no idea what he was talking about, but he knew drunks well enough to agree with him.

''Cos it's all a set up, isn't it?'

'One more step and we're there.'

'You too, probably. You with the Institute?'

The man rapped on the door and Julia opened it.

'We're going back,' William announced. 'And you can get fucked.'

His legs were sagging now, and Julia had to take his other arm. They led him to the bed and let him drop onto it.

* * *

The maroon two-seater swung into the long driveway of the motel and parked by the steps which led up to the entrance. Two men in dark blue suits got out and stretched, surveying the front of the building. It was mock Victorian, built at the turn of the century, but already mouldering under the onslaught of acid rain. Its stone cladding had come away in places, a drainpipe swaying in the wind. Broad steps led up to a pair of ostentatious doors at its entrance. The younger of the two took the steps two at a time and had to wait at the top for his colleague to join him. He pushed open the front door, stepping to one side for the older man to pass.

Jake waited until they were out of sight and then drove his bike to the side of the motel. He parked in the shade of a yew tree and was about to link a heavy chain round its back wheel when he changed his mind. There was nobody about, just the sound of a baseball game on the radio through one of the open windows.

He knew the maroon car would have sophisticated alarms, so he was careful not to touch it. He considered it for a moment and then looked underneath before returning to his bike. Taking off his leather jacket and then his T-shirt, he winced at what he was about to do. He took a last look at his T-shirt and then unscrewed the cap of the gas tank and stuffed the shirt into the tank, leaving a piece showing. While the gasoline soaked into it he put his jacket back on. He pulled the shirt out of the tank, careful not to drip the gasoline and took it over to the maroon car. He didn't bother to check if anyone was watching, but lay on the ground and wrapped the wet shirt round one side of the back axle, squeezing the material so that the tyre stood in a puddle of gasoline. He took a box of matches from his hip pocket and broke three match heads off, forcing them into the tread of the tyre.

He knew he didn't have much time. The motel had four floors. If the woman and the kid with the crew cut weren't on the ground floor, they were fucked. He hurried to the end of the building, treading flowers in the beds under the windows. The first two windows he looked through showed empty rooms. The curtains of the third were drawn and he knocked on the pane until someone pulled them to one side. The man looked sleepy, angry at being woken. Jake ignored his complaints and tried the next window.

When Julia pulled the curtains aside she was so surprised to see Jake she laughed. He could see the cuboid was asleep on the bed. He gestured impatiently for her to open the window.

'What are you doing here?'

He pointed past her to the door. 'Whoever's on your tail, they are just about to come visiting.'

She looked at the door and then back at Jake.

'Believe me, babe. I followed them here. I don't know what shit you're in, but whatever it is, it's just about to hit the fan.'

'He's drunk. Help me get him up.'

Jake wasn't as young as he used to be, and it took him several goes to climb through the window. While Jake pulled William to his feet, Julia tried to stuff their belongings into their bags. 'Forget that!' he snapped. 'Give me a hand here.'

He was holding William in a bear hug, bracing himself against the deadweight. William was barely conscious, mumbling into Jake's neck.

'How did they know I was here?' she asked.

'You use your card?'

'Yes.'

'There's your answer.'

They managed to get William halfway to the window when there was a knock on the door. They froze.

William was coming to, blinking and smacking his lips exaggeratedly. He realised he was being held up by two people and swayed away from them to see better. The three of them staggered for a moment. There was another knock on the door.

'Hold on a minute,' Julia called. She nodded at the window. It was no easier now that William was coming awake. They had to chivvy him towards the window, hissing into his ear to be quiet. Julia climbed through the window first and then Jake tipped William out. He fell onto his side into the flowerbed. The knocking at the door had become insistent.

'Get the car,' Jake growled. 'They're going to bust this door down soon.'

Julia ran to their car and reversed through the low hedge right up to the window. Jake helped William to his feet and steered him into the passenger seat. He was just about to slam the door when there was a shout from the window.

'Hey!'

Jake ran back to his bike and she slammed the car into first and pulled away, the passenger door flapping open. They bumped over the hedge, narrowly missing the maroon two-seater. She took the curve of the drive too fast and mounted the curb, bumping back onto the road after ten yards.

The two security men were slower. The elder of the two must have had leg trouble because he had to be helped through the window. By the time they had started the car, both Jake and Julia had reached the main road.

Jake reached over and slammed the passenger door shut.

'I thought you were saving her for the end of the world,' Julia shouted, nodding at the bike.

'This *is* the end of the world!' he called, roaring away up the hill. Julia followed him, doubling back past the motel. Out of the corner of her eye Julia saw the maroon car reverse, and then the rear burst into flames. Jake had seen it too, and circled his arm in the air in a victory salute.

19

Travelling faster than any bird, you glide above the tree tops, banking your wings like a jet pilot. Mist hangs in patches above the forest, ionised air so sharp you have trouble breathing it in. The white limbs of a dead tree reach from the sea of leaves like the arms of a drowning man, but you zip past them, flashing above the foliage.

From here no wildlife is visible, just the waves of tree tops, a million shades of green in the dawn light. Only condors would dare fly above the protection of the forest canopy, but the sky is empty. You can see the curve of the horizon, the orange morning sky above the mist. You bank and roll, spinning the horizon like a wheel.

And then you're in the forest, slipping through boughs heavy with fruit and monkeys. Lianas, bright red fruit, huge yellow mushrooms, leaf mould a million years thick; you can smell it from here.

A leaf, so green and perfect you almost want to cry out, its veins, tiny translucent stripes. Closer, you can see the yellow speckle of pores, sucking in the dappled sunlight. Your gaze travels along its stem, to twig, to branch, to limb, and you see for the first time, a plant as a creature, as alive as a cat or a dog. You study the bark of the tree; it has a presence, not a character, something grander than that. A spirit.

The roots of the tree are like flying buttresses, rising three feet out of the ground to anchor the skyscraping tree top. You're standing between them, sheltered in their embrace. The exposed wood of the roots is old, the bark like an old man's skin, and you run your hand along its surface. The wood is as hard as stone. You want to embrace the trunk.

And then the map stone is in front of you. Grey and weathered and crossed with Kogi cicatrices. You run your fingers along the etched lines, the stone spongy beneath your touch. You allow your fingers to trace a shape, a trail of green paint left on its surface. You don't know what you're writing, but it's a word. It's the answer to an enigma . . . You'll have to stand back to read it, but your finger hasn't finished. You press harder, hurrying to complete the pattern, and then you realise it isn't stone at all. It's animal tissue. Cod roe, white and fleshy. Your hand recoils and you step back. It's a human brain, capillaries lacing its surface. The carved lines are the rucks and folds of its surface. The lines are moving. It's alive.

You're facing Mama Francisco. He is standing in front of you, looking directly into your eyes. You can't tell the meaning of the expression of his face: it could be amusement, it could be melancholy. He chews a wad of coca slowly and then dips his stick into his mouth before slotting it into his *poporo*.

We are the elders.
We are elders of all,
with greater knowledge, spiritual and material.
Serankua tells us
that he created us
that he created the earth
that he made the sky.
He is called Serankua.
He made us to care for the creatures, flowers, nature.

Thus it was.
The Elder Brother was there to protect the earth,
because the earth,
it is our Mother, earth.
Without earth we cannot live.

You're in the desert, flying above sand dunes, the sun hot above you. You follow the course of an escarpment, and then bank away, wingtips nearly touching the ground. You twist, once, twice, the sun circling in your visor. You straighten out, still travelling at high speed, and you realise you are above an ice flow. The landscape is flat and featureless, the snow blue-grey. A speck in the distance catches your eye and you turn towards it. It grows steadily until you realise you are approaching a settlement of some sort. A cluster of single storey houses, formed in a cross. You dip your wings as you flash above them, and then continue out over the frozen sea.

He woke with a start, light flashing over his face. 'What is it?'

'Checkpoint,' Julia said, winding down his window.

It took a second before his hangover hit him, and then he wanted to be sick. He gritted his teeth, holding the nausea down.

The state line. He squinted against the bright light of the clearing shed. He was aware of a guard approaching his window so he clicked open his security pouch and handed his card to her. It was like a filling station with its floodlit concrete and queuing cars. The shed was warm, a smell of hot rubber in the air. He wondered whether he was going to be sick or not.

'You okay?' Julia asked.

He grunted. The dream was so vivid he could still feel the tilt of the aircraft. It was like coming out of deep immersion, a transferral so rapid that his senses took a few seconds to catch up with each other. He closed his eyes, but the blackness swayed and he opened them again.

Julia was fiddling under the dash for the catch to open the trunk. He leant across her to do it, unaware that his arm brushed against her breast. There was an acid taste in his mouth, and he needed to wash.

Normally he would have supervised the inspection of the trunk, but he didn't know if he could get out of his seat, so he adjusted the rear-view mirror to watch.

'What is your destination, please?' Only the lower half of the guard's body was visible through Julia's window.

'Seattle,' she said.

'Purpose of journey?'

'Recreational.'

It took a second to sink in. 'What!' William twisted in his

seat to look at her. The sudden movement made him wince. 'Seattle?'

The guard's head came into view as she bent to look at him. 'Is there a problem, sir?'

The mask which covered the lower half of her face gave her the look of a lizard and for a second William thought he was hallucinating. 'No problem.' He turned to Julia. 'I told you we were going back to the Institute!'

Julia smiled up at the guard. 'Excuse us for a minute, please?' She tried to put the window up, but the woman's hand rested on it. 'Don't make a fuss!' she hissed at William. 'Let's just get through the border, then we can talk about this.'

The guard hunkered down and was looking suspiciously at William. 'A firearm has been registered on your datafile. Do you have it with you, sir?'

William hesitated and then gave the woman the gun. He stared ahead at a floodlit signpost as the guard checked it. *Welcome to the State of Washington*. It should have read California. Julia had tricked him. There was a puckered hole of a shotgun blast through the 'o' of *Welcome*.

William's gun was returned, and the barrier lifted. They drove in silence until they were out of the border compound.

'Okay. Stop the car.'

She pulled over and switched the engine off.

'So, what is this? Kidnap?'

Julia tried to get out of the car, but she caught the loop of her belt on the harness and for a moment she struggled before unhooking herself. She swore under her breath and got out of the car.

William turned to watch her as she opened the trunk and took out her case. Cars zipped past, swirling her hair in their wake. He got out with difficulty and rested his arms on the roof. He realised he was still drunk. 'What are you doing?'

She hefted her case onto the off-side of the car, ignoring the traffic that sped past. 'I'm going to Canada!' she shouted above the noise. Even in the reflected light of headlights he could see the anger in her eyes.

'How?'

'I'll hitch hike.'

'Don't be a dirk! You want to get murdered?'

She ignored him and stalked away from the car, her case banging against her legs. She gestured at a passing car, and it sounded its horn, a doppler whine as it disappeared into the dark.

William knew better than to wrestle the case from her, but he stood in her way. He had to steady himself against the crash barrier.

'Look,' she shouted. 'For four years I've been haunted by this book. If you don't come with me, I'll go on my own.'

'Get in the car. Please.' His legs were beginning to buckle.

'Bugger off.' She started down the road, but changed her mind and turned back to him. 'Why have you got to be so controlled all the time? You're not the only one who's scared and confused!'

He tried to placate her. 'Don't give me a hard time.' As he said the words, images started filtering through his hangover: being bundled into the car, a chase. He sensed they were in more trouble than he realised. 'What happened back at the motel?

'You don't remember?'

'Don't play games – just tell me.'

'Jake – remember him? He set fire to the security officers' car.'

'What security officers?'

'The ones who have been chasing us for two days.'

'Shit! An old guy with a limp and someone about my age?'

She nodded.

'Put your case back and get in.' He saw her hesitate. 'We're going to Seattle.' If the Institute was on his tail, that could only mean one thing: big trouble. He walked back to the car like an invalid, not bothering to see if she was following him.

William let her drive, the darkness flooding into his body, slowly easing away the toxins that had lodged in the space behind his eyes. A local jazz station was playing Miles Davis. He was about to switch it off but he changed his mind. He could sense Julia listening to it. Cat's eyes flicked past, green-red, green-red; the headlights of approaching traffic like aircraft coming down to land.

The images of the dream were still fresh in his mind: the jungle, the map stone, flying over the desert, the Arctic wasteland. The dream had been as vivid as being hooked up to the machine. More than a dream, it was real. He could still feel the granular surface of the map stone, the flashing landscape as he flew above it. There had been a question, standing in front of the map stone. But what?

He scraped the fuzz off his tongue with his teeth. He wanted to be back in cyberspace. He wanted to escape from all this, go back into the limitless expanse of the parallel world.

Reality-casualty, he mouthed at the rain-splashed windscreen. Classic first symptoms of cybermania: preferring the virtual to the actual. He stubbed the thought out as though it were a cigarette.

When they reached Seattle city limits the car was waved through the checkpoint, their registration automatically noted and filed. The suburbs stretched for miles: football parks, shopping malls, house after identical house, as though a giant and unimaginative child had made a sandcastle town. The city had been road mapped so Julia was able to follow instructions for the city centre, the synthesised voice purring directions in her ear like a solicitous friend.

Fifteen minutes into the city limits and they were buzzed over the car speaker by a citizen's patrol car. William scanned his rear-view mirror for the car. It was always difficult to spot these civilian security men. He guessed it was a beaten up Ford two cars behind him. William brought the mike down to face level and gave him his card number. There was a moment's pause.

'What are you doing in town?' the voice crackled over the speaker.

'We're visiting family.'

'Name and number of passenger.'

They were unable to verify Julia's credentials; their hackers not up to breaking an international security code. There was silence while they digested the information. William wondered if they would be hassled, but the voice on the speaker sounded respectful. 'Do you know your way, sir?'

'Yes, thanks.' William's security status had clearly impressed them.

'Have a nice stay.'

They were overtaken by the Ford. The printout on the back window flashed 'KEEP SEATTLE CLEAN'.

It had been raining, and the sidewalks were dark and deserted. William checked the air monitor. A red light flashed: contaminated air. Without Julia seeing he took the revolver out of the glove compartment and slipped it into his jacket pocket. People were desperate in areas like this, so many of them on their way out, so much rage, that anything could happen. It was no use relying on the police for protection. They had withdrawn to the city centres, their zone of authority contracting as the disease expanded.

A raised barrier across a side street pointed skywards, a couple of red lights still blinking on and off, a deserted guard post on either side. Julia asked him what it was, and he told her: an old-fashioned plague area. When the virus had first struck, people thought they could confine it by confining its victims, but air was breathed by everyone, and no wooden barrier would prevent that. When secluded areas had been introduced there had been riots, poisoning of city reservoirs, spiking of soft drinks. Now the disease was too widespread for people to try to control it. This city, like all big cities, was contaminated, the only safe zones were in buildings, and even some of those wouldn't have air-con, just primitive dry air ducts, a stack of tinder waiting for a match to be thrown. In the poor districts there was nothing to prevent its spread; most of the houses were undefended, and short of working and sleeping in a mask, contagion was inevitable. He had heard rumours that giant lime pits had been dug outside D.C. and New York to deal with the mounting number of plague deaths.

Now they were closer to the centre, a few people were visible on the streets, hooded and masked, presumably licensed night workers. It was raining hard, the sidewalks spattered with a firework display of reflected light. It was a long time since William had been in a city; he'd forgotten how bad it had got.

The car purred to a halt at some lights and he watched a man hurrying to cross in front of them, his face sinister under his one-piece rainhat. The lights changed and, as Julia accelerated away, the tyres caught a puddle and sprayed the man. He skipped clear of the car, gesturing angrily at them.

William still hadn't told her, but he couldn't remember where his mother lived. He had the idea it was somewhere near the university, but when he groped for the address he found nothing. It wasn't just the hangover, it was as though his memory, like his diary, had been erased. He should know Seattle well. He had studied at the University of Washington, lived in the city for four years. So, why didn't he recognise any of this? Why was it as though he was travelling into someone else's life? A wave of nausea swept over him as though he had tumbled too many times in the exoskeleton.

They came out at Elliot Bay, the left side of the road as black as the sky, the pinpricks of ferry lights blinking like stars. He wanted to put his window down and breathe the salty air to clear his head, but the air hazard light was still on. It was safe in the old days – he remembered that much. Breathing down lungfuls of Pacific Ocean air, running barefoot along the beach. But had that really happened? Or was it just an image from a movie? He admitted the feeling to himself for the first time: he was scared.

'Let's stay the night here,' he said, indicating a high rise parking lot by the waterfront.

'What for?'

'We can't check into a hotel. They're tracking your card as well as mine.'

'Why can't we go to your mother's?'

'That's the first place they'll look.'

'We'll have to go there some time. Why not now?'

'Just do what I say,' he snapped.

Julia pulled up at the side of the road and looked at him. 'What's the problem?'

He knew he would have to tell her. The tic in his eye started up again, and he held his fingers against the twitching muscle to still it. 'I can't remember her address,' he muttered.

He could see her formulating and then abandoning questions. 'Do you recognise any of this?' she said at last, indicating the street, the waterfront.

William looked around. It could be anywhere. 'When we get to Sector 1 I'll know where we are.' It didn't sound convincing, but it was all he could think of saying.

She checked her mirror and then pulled into the cavernous

mouth of the parking lot. The inside was lit only by small roof bulbs, and the beam of the car cut through the gloom like a searchlight passing over piles of trash. It was only when one of them moved that she realised there were human forms amongst the cardboard boxes and rags. On the second level a group of people stood around a campfire, the smoke hanging in layers like a heavy fog. Julia drove past them without looking, and up to Level 3. William told her to park in the corner, facing outwards. As she switched the engine off, her arm caught the car horn, making her jump.

'Are you sure we'll be safe here?'

'We'll be okay.' He reached for the headlights and turned them off. No point in advertising their presence. 'We can take it in turns to stay awake.' He took the gun from the glove compartment and put it on the dashboard. 'You know how to use this?'

'No.'

He showed her how to take off the safety catch. 'Squeeze the trigger, don't pull it.' He saw the look on her face. 'Just look like you mean business – you don't have to fire it.' He checked the doors and windows were locked, glad of the bulletproof glass that protected them. 'Now, you get some sleep. I'll wake you up in four hours. Tomorrow when it's light, we'll have a look around and I'll get my bearings.'

He could see she was scared, and he took her hand, squeezing it clumsily. 'We're nearly there,' he lied.

He left it half an hour, and then when he thought she was asleep, he turned on the route planner. He brought up the street plan for Seattle and studied it, looking for something to trigger his memory. Some of the street names seemed familiar, but he couldn't be sure. Streets called Jefferson, Union, Pine – what cities *didn't* have those? He could be looking at any city in any state.

He ran through his options: his mother wasn't listed in the directory, banking and medical files were off limits. The only legitimate way he could access data was through his own personal files, and those had been wiped. There was only one option left untried – family friends. He could contact them. They were still on his file, and they were bound to know where she was living. But how could he explain that he didn't know his mother's address?

He scrolled through his diary, looking at the names. Who were all these people? Jackie and Fell Burlance? Had he ever heard of them? The Freeflight Foundation, Manray Scott, Pat Andersson? Name after name he measured against his memory, and none of them fitted. This was somebody else's datafile. He realised his hands were clammy, and wiped them on his trousers. Somebody had substituted a bogus program; somebody was still working on him, adding pressure until he cracked. Sonsofbitches.

He switched his diary off and closed his eyes. He was stiff with sitting in the same position, his kidneys hurting. For a moment he thought of giving in, dialling the Institute and telling them where he was. He glanced at Julia, her breath coming gently. But he wasn't alone: she seemed to be in the same position, no less confused than him. As he watched her, he felt his resolve strengthen. Only when she gave in would he admit defeat. He wouldn't allow them to break him this easily.

They could tamper with his datafile, but his memory was his. He tried to picture his mother, bring forward anything from his past, but all he had was fragments. The detail was there, he could feel it, but when he tried to pin anything down, his attention dissolved. Stress, he concluded, was playing tricks with his memory.

He checked the air monitor and then got out of the car and stretched. He was hungry and thirsty, still ragged with a hangover. The sound of laughter echoed from upstairs, and it seemed to him it was mocking.

He suddenly realised how he could find his mother's address. Access public files; nobody could tamper with those.

He slipped back in the car and switched on the on-board computer. Hands trembling with excitement he slid his card through the reader and keyed in: *University of Washington*.

The menu came up immediately:

Administration

Admission

Degrees awarded

Library

Personnel

Research Facilities
Subject

He tapped *Subject*. The screen changed, white letters against a blue background. He only needed to read the start of the list to find what he wanted:

Architecture
Art
Biology
Computing

Computing brought up the screen:

Degrees awarded
Staff
Student list
Supporting Research Institutions

Now would be the test of his security status. He hit the wrong entry and had to cancel the screen. He tried again. *Student List*. The screen changed. He'd got in.

Please key in Year of entry and Name

William typed in 2012 W. Morrison. The machine seemed to hesitate, and then:

Morrison, William
Degree: MA
Subject: computer simulation
Year of entry 2012
Year of graduation 2016
Grade: pass
Address: Newton Hall, University of Washington

He swore. Only his term time address had been entered. He half-heartedly tried *More*, but the screen twitched and remained unchanged.

He cancelled the information. He'd lived near the university. He *had* lived with his mother, he could remember that. He screwed his eyes shut, trying to snatch details from the flashes of light he saw. It was a big house, wasn't it? Single storey, no, a large apartment near the bay. An orange-tiled roof. Palm trees.

'Palm trees?' he said aloud. In Seattle? Almost as though someone had taken his head and turned it, he found his eyes drawn to the glove compartment. He reached forward and took out the courtesy card the motel bartender had given him. Turning it over he saw a photograph on the back of an orange-tiled hotel block, palm trees framing its view of the sea. The legend under the picture read: *Hotel Miranda, Hawaii. Part of the Valdar chain of five star hotels.*

'Shit!' he said.

This was the longest Julia had ever been away from her kids. Frances, Catya, Jed and Patric, she repeated their names, trying to bring a glimpse of their faces to mind. She wished she had brought some photos of them, but she'd assumed she would see them on the videophone. She longed to talk to them, but after her experience at Jake's, she wasn't going to try again. For as long as she could put her inability to contact her family down to a technical error she could retain the foundations of her identity. If her children were just a memory, what would happen to her? She wouldn't think about it.

She looked at the man beside her. With his face in repose he looked younger, the parking lot's night lights erasing the frown lines from his forehead. The green lights of the dash picked out the fake pearl buttons on his shirt, twinkling with the rise and fall of his breath. She suddenly realised he was awake. His eyes had opened and he was watching her.

'Are you awake too?' she asked.

'Yes.' There was a whirring noise as William's seat rose to a sitting position.

'Can we talk?'

'Go ahead.'

She brought her seat up beside his. She was glad he was awake. She hated this concrete lot. It was like being interred. They gazed into the gloom in front of them. 'Do you have a girlfriend?'

'Nothing serious.'

'Will you get married?'

'I was planning to marry at thirty. I guess that's unlikely now.'

'Why?'

'Who's going to employ me after this? And what girl will go for a non-earner?'

'You'd be surprised.'

'Is that a compliment?'

She laughed quietly. 'Are you scared?' she said after a moment.

He inhaled deeply before he answered. 'Confused. You?'

'I'm terrified.' Saying the word brought home how true it was. Suddenly a wall of her life had fallen away, gusts of agoraphobia plucking at her clothes. She had always wanted to be free, but not like this.

William patted her hand and she instinctively moved to take his, but he had withdrawn it as quickly as he had offered it. 'This map stone of Jarnier's,' he said. 'Did he invent it?'

'No,' she said, surprised. 'It's real enough.'

'What's the deal with it?'

She took a towelette from her bag and tore open the plastic seal, the smell of eau de cologne flooding the car. She wiped her face with it and then held the cool cloth over her eyes for a moment, gathering her strength. 'It's not a map as we understand it. It doesn't show any physical terrain.'

He took the towelette she offered and rubbed his own face, then rolled his head until his neck cracked. 'Go on.'

'It's thought to be a repository of stories, a sort of ideogram, I think. The Kogi had no written language, remember.'

'So, what is it – hieroglyphics?'

'Not really. They've been spoken of as "thought lines" – representations of ideas that can be deciphered in any number of ways.' Julia knew they had no way of understanding this, but she was happy to take her mind off herself for a moment. 'The map stone is a story book which is different for everyone who reads it.'

'That doesn't make sense.'

'It did to them. The Kogi didn't see the world in set terms. The phenomenal world wasn't the real thing for them – it was just a trace of reality.' She sensed that William, too, realised they were on the edge of something, that somehow this related to the whole puzzle of the books.

'What was real to them?' he said.

'The thing that underlies the phenomenon – the noumenon. They called it *aluna*. Mama Francisco mentioned it when you went inside last time.'

'He said *aluna* was the Mother. But you said the Mother was these little gold things.'

'Their language is impossible to translate. Their nouns are so—'

she groped for the word, staring into the darkness, '—vague, the best translation is only approximate. It's as though they are speaking in metaphors, where everything can mean everything else.'

'Softies.' He glanced at her, but she was looking out of the window. 'So, why call it a map?'

She didn't tell him she had seen his anxious study of the street plan. 'A map is something to help you find your way.' She laughed gently in spite of herself. 'As I think we're beginning to realise.'

20

The fuel gauge on the generator indicates it is three-quarters full: about twelve gallons, I estimate. The halftrack can probably do twenty miles to the gallon, and there must be a gallon or so already in its tank. That means if I keep eight gallons back for the journey to Inuvik, I'll still have enough gas to keep the generator going for a week.

I tried Harry again, offering to pay him double for some gasoline, but he denied he had any to spare. A lie, of course – the fifty-gallon drum out the back sounded pretty full. I ended up shouting at him and stomping out of the store. He's playing some sort of game with me: nobody is *that* obtuse and stubborn.

The wind has picked up again today. He said summer was on its way, but other than the lengthening days there is no sign of a thaw. I hurry into the shelter of the factory and take the elevator to the second floor. I'm feeling ill and miserable, a piercing headache from the cold.

Carla has written to me, a flimsy sheet of ComSat paper I immediately folded and put in my back pocket. It arrived two days ago, an hour or so after she phoned. I assumed Harry had read it, and asked him what it said, but he told me he couldn't read. Another lie, I suspect. Nobody can run a store and not read. I was going to throw it away, but I couldn't bring myself to. Though I don't want to read it, I do want to know what is happening with Carla. I should have quizzed Harry with a bit more assiduity.

At the store this morning I felt my eyes being drawn to the travel poster in the window, and after some vacillation asked Harry if I could have it. I've brought it back with me, but now I'm in two minds whether to pin it up or not. I unroll it and

I'm in two minds whether to pin it up or not. I unroll it and hold it experimentally against the wall. One picture won't hurt – I don't have to look at it. I tack it to the wall, and spend a few minutes studying it. If that was a door, would I walk through it? The sunshine, the scented air, the happy girl with her ponytail – it looks too good to be true. But if it *was* true? It looks like Eden. I take Carla's letter out of my back pocket and, without unfolding it, tack it beside the poster. I'll answer that question later.

I've developed my thermopane construction a bit further. The plastic sheets were helping to keep the frost out, but as I move around so little, I decided to reduce my living space, so I've hung a sort of tent from the ceiling. The table is too big to fit inside it, but I have room for the mattress and the electric heater and a few bits and pieces.

I'm getting thinner and weaker with every day that passes, even light exercise wipes me out now. I've stopped taking the capsules: rumours of them being expensive placebos seem accurate.

It doesn't take me long to discover a drawback of living and writing under plastic: beads of condensation form on the inside of the tent, but they seem to run harmlessly downwards, absorbed by the floor boards. One major advantage is that I can function free of my mask. I can also avoid being bombed by bird shit.

The ice on the inside of the windows is half an inch thick now, bulging in the middle as though a jellyfish has been stuck on every pane. The effect is to diffuse the light with a blueish tint, strangely restful. Not being able to see out is a minor nuisance but I have made an eyehole through the ice by heating a silver dollar coin and pressing it to the pane, something I remember from Hans Christian Andersen. I gaze through it at intervals throughout the day like a submarine captain checking his course. Sometimes I feel as though I have been frozen inside a glacier.

The daylight is now almost perpetual. I can't tell whether it's morning or evening, not that it makes any difference – there is still no wildlife outside, nothing to distinguish midnight from midday, and Harry seems to be open all hours. My clocks have all gone wrong. The cold, I presume. I guess Harry's are no different.

Julia and William, my newest progeny, are keeping me at it. I run my fingers over the pile of paper on the table: ten, fifteen-hour days at the typewriter, my fingers burning with chilblains, I don't know how the story will end, but I imagine there will be enough forward momentum to complete it. I won't finish it before the gasoline runs out, but I'm writing as fast as I can.

Moving characters round an imaginary world is simple enough; it's the ideas with which I'm struggling. Why call it a map? William asks. I don't know. What is a map? A representation of reality, I suppose. Its purpose being to negotiate from confusion – being lost – to knowledge, arriving. A useful definition, because the more I think of it, the more inclusive it seems. Art and cartography; myth and religion; scientific theory and numbers; language and philosophy. All tools to negotiate our way through the maze. All maps.

What is the map stone, though? It really *does* exist – standing at the entrance to *La Ciudad Perdida*, the lost city. I've seen photographs of it: there it stands like a mossy dolmen, those infuriating scratches cut into its surface. Is its function to represent reality, to somehow decipher the chaos of the cosmos into something a mind can grasp? A story.

I can feel my own bubbling up of recognition. Perhaps this is what I'm trying to say, that the first function of story telling is to make the incomprehensible comprehensible. To give some shape to formlessness. And so William and Julia, my ink and paper puppets, ten microns thick, are made to dance on my behalf.

All maps are symbols – they represent reality. As far as I understand the Kogi, every thing – not just language, not just thought – is a symbol. Sensory input included. What we perceive is not the real thing, but the shadow of the thing, just as a word is a shadow of an object. Our sense data, like our language and thought, is a map of reality: it tries to show what is 'out there'. And the map is not the thing. Younger brother has created a philosophy based on an illusion: that we can believe the evidence of our senses, that the visible thing is the thing itself. I suppose we have Empedocles to thank for that. William accuses the Kogi of being mystics (or, at least he would have if I'd remembered to include it), but the opposite is the case. The transmitted through the exchange of sodium and potassium ions in our visual cortex. Neither do we hear things, smell things, taste things. Even touch is an illusion: not the thing itself, but the trace. Virtual reality, the blind eye and echoing ear of Parmenides.

A tiny white feather floats past my face, caught in a beam of sunlight. It lands on the blank sheet of paper in front of me, casting a perfect, elongated shadow. The feather, no longer than my fingernail, is almost invisible on the paper, but its shadow is distinct, each barb detailed against the white background. The shadow is more real than the substance. I study it for a minute and then blow it away.

The question William was reaching for is very simply this: who am I?

What can I, his author, say in response? You are a creation of mine, I could say imperiously. I am your lord and master.

But that's missing the point. William is asking questions on my behalf. Who am *I*? Me. The author.

Sometimes when I look inside myself, I see nobody there. I am an automaton, a wind-up toy. I keep realising I've just done something – eaten a can of spaghetti for instance – and have no memory of it. Even with the taste of tomato sauce still on my tongue the meal is less of a recollection than a conclusion. Sometimes I catch myself in the middle of an action – brushing my teeth, shaving my eyebrows, shovelling snow into a bucket – and force myself to concentrate. This is a lifetime I'm shovelling away. And do I care? Sometimes yes, sometimes no.

I don't really know what's coming next with William and Julia. I have enough bits of plot to take me forward, but I feel like I'm laying railway tracks ten feet ahead of the steam engine, too busy keeping the machine on the rails to see where we're going. I've a feeling we're heading for quicksand.

When I've had enough of writing, I return to my braid. The rope is coming along. I'm on the second phase now: braiding the braids. It's producing a cord the width of my little finger. Still not strong enough to hold any weight, but it's getting there.

21

He didn't have anything to go on. The more he tried to examine the fragments of a life in Seattle, the more they evaporated like the wisps of a dream. At first he thought he recognised the town in the daylight, but then he wasn't sure. Things had changed. A new road system had been built, a shopping complex too. They could be in any of a hundred North American towns. William recognised the Needle, but it was such a well-known sight, he would have seen it in photographs.

Walking the streets wasn't helping; the more he saw, the more confused he became. He said nothing to Julia, turning decisively at street corners as though he knew where he was going, but he was walking further into a maze.

He found himself scanning the people they passed, looking for a familiar face. He *had* lived here – the university records proved it. So, why didn't he recognise it? Why was it like walking through a plastic playscape?

The more they walked, the more he realised he was lost. He grasped for logical hand-holds that could pull him out of his confusion, but he was numb, incapable of thinking properly. He was aware of the back of his shirt sticking to his skin with sweat.

As he turned at an intersection, squinting against the dazzle of reflected light from a wall of windows, William realised that for the first time the intrigue existed solely behind his eyes. Even if Julia and the book were a set up, that didn't explain being lost in a city he knew well. It was *his* memory that was failing; even Omnisens couldn't change an entire cityscape.

He couldn't walk and think at the same time so he paused,

pretending to look in a shop window. He considered the logical options. They could have given him some kind of psychotropic drug which was affecting his memory. He thought back to breakfast: coffee and a doughnut. It could have been spiked with something. But this amnesia had started earlier – yesterday, and anyway, how could they so selectively wipe his memory? Everything else was there, just the memory of Seattle and his mother was gone. He didn't feel drugged either.

He wondered if he was in some kind of hypnotic trance. Easy to do. And you could be as selective in your brainwashing as you liked. Dr Kinderling could be behind this, tinkering in his smarmy mid-Atlantic way. But surely he would know, have some sense of a veil being drawn over his eyes?

There was one last option: that Seattle, Julia, this body he saw now was all part of a virtuality program.

He could see his reflection in the window, Julia standing next to him. It didn't feel like virtuality. The detail was too good; it was too untidy. He raised his hands to his head. No tell-tale feel of a helmet.

'What are you doing?' she asked.

He ignored her. If this was a playscape, she'd just be one of Jarnier's puppets. He studied his hands, rubbing the skin to feel for a glove. If this was a program they had made a significant breakthrough – somehow they had compensated for CR encroaching on the experience. If he was wearing a glove, it was undetectable.

He stooped to study the sidewalk. A piece of grit, a tiny styrofoam ball, dust. He saw a woodlouse in the gutter and picked it up between finger and thumb. It rolled itself like a miniature armadillo, and William flicked it around his palm. The detail was perfect. He rested his thumb on the insect and pressed hard. He felt the crack as the louse was squashed and then studied the juicy smear in his palm. This was not cyberspace; no system would have covered such an eventuality.

'What's wrong?' she asked.

'I don't know.'

'What do you mean?'

'I don't recognise anything.' William turned and walked blindly away. He was aware of the tall buildings leaning over him; straight lines as sharp as a knife, the wedge of sky like a blue painted ceiling. He was on the edge of solid ground, and it was running out. The further he walked towards the horizon of the future, the softer the ground was becoming. If he progressed any further it would be quicksand.

He was aware he was walking too fast for Julia, but he didn't slow his pace. She had taken his hand, and had to skip to keep up with him. He could sense her anxiety like a pulse of electricity up his arms.

Though the air monitors on the poles were silent, there were few people on the streets, and most of those were wearing masks. Three months out of circulation and William noticed the difference. Had things really gotten so bad? Necessity was apparently becoming a virtue, face masks becoming increasingly fashionable: animal shapes, fluorescent patterns, tiny gold and black face pads. Some people wore full helmets, antennae rising from their ears like comic book Martians.

William shook his hand free of Julia's. He could feel her anxiety infecting him. He had to stop and think. How many people were in the city? Half a million? What chance of finding someone who knew his mother? He made quick calculations: average number of friends and acquaintances, say, two hundred. The chances of finding someone who knew her, one in five thousand. Stop five people a minute, a thousand minutes. Sixteen and a bit hours. A couple of days' work.

He caught the arm of a passing woman. She was wearing an old-fashioned pollution mask and a pair of dark glasses, just the end of her nose and cheekbones visible. Judging by her clothes she would be a teenager.

'Excuse me,' he said. 'Can I . . . ?'

Her hesitation was momentary and then the young woman twisted her arm out of his and hurried off. He watched her striding away, glancing over her shoulder when she'd put a safe distance between them. William tried someone else, an old man with broken teeth and stubble on his chin.

'I'm looking for Connie Morrison,' William said.

The old man shook his head. The question hadn't registered. William cast around the sidewalk and then approached a young family: father, mother and two kids, each with matching helmets.

'I'm looking for Connie Morrison.'

The man's voice came from the speaker in his mouthpiece. 'We're just visiting. Ask a police officer.' The man gathered his children to him like a protective duck and they waddled after him, away from the madman with the woman plucking his sleeve.

He turned angrily on Julia. 'What is it?'

'What are you doing?'

He looked at Julia. It was a sunny day, and her UV glasses cast a yellow stripe across her eyes. He suddenly realised how exhausted he was.

'What's happening to you, William?'

He met her eyes for a moment and then turned away to stop another passerby. Julia grabbed his arm and forced him to face her. Even through his mania he could see he was frightening her.

'We're lost, aren't we?'

It was all collapsing onto him: the buildings, the fake blue sky, the faces behind their masks, this woman in front of him.

He glanced at his wrist watch. They'd been walking over an hour, and he hadn't seen anything he knew for sure.

'Let's go to the university,' she said. 'At least we know where it is.'

When he didn't protest she took his hand as though he was a child and led him to a bus stop. They rode the bus to the university, sitting side by side in silence, William staring out of the window. He searched the street signs and shop fronts for something he recognised, but it all looked like a dream. The buildings and cars were pixels, infinitesimal pinpoints of light; the super processor of his brain gluing them together to give the illusion of solidity.

When the bus stopped by the main gates of the campus and he failed to recognise it, he could feel the heat flooding up the back of his neck making his scalp prickle. Public records said he had attended this campus for four years, but he had never seen it before.

This site was a security zone 5, and the armed guards on the gate were taking no chances. Everyone must be cleared and accounted for. As an alumnus, William was confident they would let him onto the campus, but he wasn't sure if Julia would be admitted. His card was passed through the reader without any problem, and he was let through, but Julia was asked for the purpose of her visit. When she hesitated the guard presented her with a multiple choice selection, one of which was as a guest of an associate member. Citizen William Morrison apparently still had enough security clout to be trusted not to smuggle in subversives. The metal doors swung open and Julia stepped through.

Once they were on the campus, they didn't know what to do. They bought a cup of coffee in the canteen and sat under an awning outside. The tables were covered with paper tablecloths, red and white checks that made William's vision dance. He sprinkled brown sugar over the top of his cappuccino, and then stirred the foam under.

'If those goons are still on our tail,' he said, 'it's only a matter of time before they turn up here. They'll guess I was heading for Seattle, and they knew I studied here.' He tried to disguise the tremor in his hands as he lifted his cup to his mouth. For the first time in his life, he realised he was losing control. Even the Institute training program, the extended immersions hadn't disoriented him in this way. Something was happening that he didn't understand. And he was afraid. He wanted it to end. He wanted Julia to smile suddenly and explain it was all a test, that this was Michigan or Denver, that he had passed with flying colours.

She must have sensed his disquiet, because she squeezed his hand across the table. He felt her wedding band against his knuckle, and he was glad of its reassuring solidity. He searched her face, looking for something but not knowing what.

'Why don't I recognise anything?'

'I don't know, William.'

'How can you can forget where you lived for half your life?' He was sinking; he could feel it. He took an old-fashioned ink pen from his pocket and began sketching on the tablecloth. There must be a logical explanation for this. 'What are the options? One: this is a conspiracy. Two: this is cyberspace. Three: I have amnesia.' He stopped to think, pen poised and then crossed through the first two sentences.

'Four options,' Julia said. 'None of this is real.'

He tapped the pen against the second sentence. 'It can't

be cyberspace. No system would have this degree of resolution.'

'That's not what I mean. What if living in Seattle was a kind of dream?'

'Oh brilliant!' he said sarcastically. 'That solves everything. And my mother? Your family? They're a kind of dream too?' He was suddenly angry at her. 'Is this your answer?'

'Not a dream exactly.' She cast about for the right word. 'Maybe they really *do* exist, but only —'

'But only in the pages of a novel?'

'I don't know.'

'So, they are all fictional characters? Or are you just a figment of my imagination too?'

She didn't answer.

'How can we be the children of imaginary parents? Has that little impossibility crossed your mind?' He could feel his body taut and constrained, his fingers gripping his coffee cup too tightly.

'Okay, okay.' She held her hands up, suddenly defensive.

They finished their coffee in silence, watching the criss-crossing of students across the quadrangle of concrete. Even as William said it, he realised it *was* possible, at least theoretically. Chop matter down to its smallest constituents, the particle physicists argue, and it becomes virtual, popping in and out of existence, obeying no knowable law of time and space. All this, they would say – the table, the coffee cups, the leafy profile of a tree against the blue sky – they are all real, but their subatomic worlds exist somewhere between reality and unreality. Every molecule of Julia's face is a galaxy of spinning particles, none of which could be exactly defined. According to dear old Heisenberg you can measure position or momentum, but not simultaneously. Move towards the definition of one and the other recedes.

He could remember his college quantum theory well enough. Phenomena manifest according to the collapse of the wave function of possibilities. Light exists in mutually exclusive forms, particle or wave, depending on the experiment. Reality is not a thing but a process, a perpetual construct that exists only in relation to an observer. The universe is chaos until perceived.

He ran his pen nib along the tablecloth with such force that the paper tore. 'I have a joke,' he said grimly. Julia turned away so he rattled the table until she looked at him. 'Aren't you going to ask me what it is?'

'Go on.'

'When is a table not a table?'

She made no answer.

'When it's an envelope. Or should I say when it's a table tennis ball. Or when it's a goldfish.' He looked at the ruined nib of his pen and threw it away from him so hard that ink shot out of the end, spraying an arc of blue specks across the paving slabs.

'What are you talking about, William?'

'I'm just welcoming you to the Kogi world of incommensurable nouns. Where everything can mean everything else.'

His body felt as hard and as artificial as a suit of armour, caffeine dissolving the kinaesthetic glue that held William in place inside himself. He was nothing more than an ephemera, a mayfly batting its wings against a steel cage. He forced himself to think. All this talk was nothing more than *theory*. The world is the world is the world. Subatomic particles may pop in and out of existence like the lights of fireflies, but they are as real as is necessary. The laundry truck by the entrance gate which was backing into a loading bay was a product of the process of observation, existing only because its wave function had been collapsed by his observation, but if he stepped in front of it, he'd still be killed.

William suddenly had an impulse to be in the company of Mama Francisco, back in the dusty compound of the Kogi village. *He* would be able to supply an answer. Those watery, distant eyes knew things beyond the grasp of logic. William battled to dispel the image of the old Kogi Mama from his mind. This was crazy – he knew the man was just a creation of Jarnier's, part of the problem, not the solution, but he seemed so *real*. In his job, William had encountered dozens of computer generated characters, but none of them had approached the apparent authenticity of Mama Francisco.

He bit his lip until it hurt, using the virtuality pilot's 'ejector seat', as they called it. Nothing like pain to bring you to your senses, remind you of what's real.

'What are you thinking about?' Julia asked.

'The Kogi.'

'Me, too. Listen – have you heard about *seivake*?' Julia asked.

He made no sign of having heard her, but she continued anyway. 'The Kogi believe the purpose of life is spiritual evolution, that when we die we must have achieved three things in our lifetime.' She counted them on her fingers. 'We must become like a child, they say. Whole, complete. Secondly, we must renounce everything we know, forget everything we have experienced. And third, we must become 'cold' to our emotions.'

William struck his spoon against the rim of his cup, making an unexpectedly pure ring. 'And this is an advanced society? At least we've beaten senility in ours.'

'Don't be stupid. They're not senile.'

He raised an eyebrow at her rebuke. 'And when we get these things?'

'Then our soul can achieve its highest goal – returning to the great Mother.'

'Why are you telling me this?' He placed his feet squarely on the ground as if he could anchor himself that way.

'Becoming like a child, forgetting our past—' She hesitated, but then decided to push ahead. '—isn't that what's beginning to happen to us?'

He studied her eyes. She was serious. 'You're enjoying this, aren't you?'

'I think we should try to find the author.'

'Return to the great Mother, is that it? You're cracked.'

'What else can we do?'

'Find the author, is that it? Pin this bastard down and beat the truth out of him?' His vehemence shocked even William. He paused. It wasn't such a bad idea. 'Do you know where he lives?'

'I couldn't find his address. I tried everything.'

'His publishers?'

'He hasn't written anything for years. All they know is that he emigrated to West Canada.'

'What about directories, societies, that kind of thing?'

'I spent months searching.' She shook her head. 'No luck. It's as though he's disappeared.'

'So you don't even know if he's alive?'

'He's alive.'

'How do you know?'

'I just do.'

Sometimes he wanted to shake some sense into this woman. 'What are you suggesting we do? Just turn up and ask around? West Canada is a big place.'

'We can find him.'

'How can we find him in a whole country, if I can't even find my mother in a city the size of Seattle?'

'Trust.'

'Trust? Trust what?'

It was her turn to get angry. 'If I could weigh it and measure it and give it a number, I would,' she snapped. 'But I can't.' She lifted her glasses for a moment to look him in the eyes. 'Things have a habit of falling into place.' He wasn't convinced. 'Don't worry.'

'I'm not worried, I'm being rational.' He looked away from Julia, towards a group of students in the distance. Either this woman was a total flake or she was coming apart at the seams.

The light was more like a spring day than summer: bright and sharp as a razor. The students were fifty metres away, but he could see every detail of them. He watched them approach, studying them as if trying to understand something about them.

William realised his eyes were on one of the group. Older than the rest, a man of about his age, a mature student probably. As the group approached, the man waved.

'Bill!'

William was too surprised to say anything.

'It's me – Mersey. The gate told me you were here.' He walked up to their table and held his hand out for William to shake. He automatically took it. 'I wasn't expecting you this early.' The group had carried on, but the girl had stayed beside the man and was looking at William speculatively. 'This is Alix.'

William looked up at the girl and shook her hand. The sun was behind her and he couldn't see her features.

'Bill's come to look over the work we're doing. We did the same degree together,' the man explained to her. 'And then he went off and sold his soul to Omnisens.'

William forced himself to smile vaguely. He had no idea who the man was.

'And you must be Dr O'Brien,' Mersey said, holding out his hand. 'Are you a flier as well?'

She shook his hand. 'Just William here.'

'Four years as a flier and not locked up in the rubber room yet?'

William looked at him blankly.

'Joke, William,' Julia said. There was a pause as they waited for William to say something.

'Are you still studying here?' he ventured.

'I'm teaching. My first year.' He turned to Alix. 'I'll catch up with you.'

William watched the girl hurrying after her friends. He guessed she was one of his students. Mersey pulled up a chair and sat down.

'Do you work in computer simulation?' she asked.

Mersey was confused for a moment, and his eyes flicked from Julia to William. 'I'm sorry, I thought you were part of the team.'

'I'm the project anthropologist.' She paused. 'For the MAYA project.' Another pause. 'I came along for the ride.'

Mersey nodded, a smile returning to his face. 'Welcome to the University of Washington.' He turned to William. 'Would you like to see the lab now? I have a free afternoon.'

William didn't react, but Julia suddenly got to her feet. 'We'd love to.'

William looked up at Julia, startled. She caught his eye and glanced meaningfully towards the gate. At first he didn't understand, then he turned round to look behind him. A maroon two-seater had parked beside the entrance gate and two men in dark blue suits were speaking with the security guard. He could see the guard shaking his head and shrugging. He got to his feet.

They followed Mersey as he strode towards the science block. It meant walking closer to the gate, and while William pretended to shield his eyes from the sun, Julia walked behind him, obscured from sight. As they passed through the glass doors of the science block, he turned and glanced back at the gate. It looked as though an argument was taking place between the security guard and the older of the two men. There was a shout and the younger man pointed directly at them. William hurried inside the building, glad of the automatic lock which clicked shut behind them.

22

The lab was a mess: metal benches piled with equipment, cables across the floor. At one end, mechanical engineers were working on a pressurised body stocking. Mersey paused in front of them and explained the system. William had heard of the idea; it used hydraulics rather than the cumbersome exoskeleton that he was used to. Weightlessness would be achieved by immersing the flier in a liquid medium, air fed through the helmet.

The computing was impressive. Judging by the new equipment, the system would have been augmented within the last four years. Still nothing to match the Omnisens capacity, but in relay it would do a pretty good job.

'How's the MAYA project going?' Mersey asked. 'Or aren't you allowed to talk about it?'

'You'll hear about it in time.'

'I'm told Jarnier's being a bit of a pain in the ass.'

'You know him?' Julia was surprised to hear a familiar name.

'Everyone in IP knows him,' Mersey said using the old-fashioned Japanese term: Intimate Presence. 'He came to visit a couple of weeks ago.' He laughed. 'Nobody told me about the hair.'

William nodded vaguely. What was Jarnier doing here?

'He was so interested in the work we're doing on brain maps,' Mersey explained to Julia, 'he sent his ace pilot along. I'm honoured.' There was an edge of sarcasm in his voice.

'Brain maps?' said Julia. 'What's that?'

'The UN Circuitry Database is located here,' William said, safe in the knowledge that he was right. 'The world's most sophisticated atlas of the brain.' He wandered to the window and looked out. The maroon car had gone.

'You're designing a brain?' she asked Mersey.

'Mapping it. The brain is the most complex structure in the universe, impossible to replicate.'

A poster of a Buddhist mandala was taped to the wall, and Julia paused to look at it.

'We've been researching the impact of religious art on brain waves.'

William could see why Mersey was treating him as a colleague rather than a friend. Any university computing faculty was divided into two sects – hard and soft – and this campus was probably no exception. Mersey was clearly one of the softies; religious art was just up their alley.

William ran his hand along the moulded plastic of the terminal's casing. 'Everything has a number.' He could hear the petulance in his tone.

Mersey chose not to hear him.

'What did Jarnier want?' Julia asked.

'I'm surprised you haven't been informed.' He paused, a worried look on his face. 'This isn't classified, is it?'

William shook his head. It probably was.

'He's exploring the creation of a virtual 4-coordinate paradigm of metaconsciousness.'

She squinted as she translated it. 'A brain?' she said.

'Not exactly. He called it a "map stone".' He looked from William to Julia, registering the surprise on their faces. 'Didn't he tell you all this?'

It hit William with a physical force, the question that had hovered on the edge of his mind since this whole thing had begun. He couldn't believe it of himself, but there it was, the words he had been writing in his dream: who am I? If he wanted the answer to that question, he would have to find the author. And if he wanted to know where the author lived, the answer would somehow be in the map stone. It had been staring him in the face all along. Jarnier has set this whole thing up. Why call it a map? Because it showed him the way.

'Is it possible for me to use the mainframe?' William asked. 'I need to get into the system.'

Mersey was so surprised by the request he could only look blankly at William. 'Do you have access?' he said after a moment.

'You can lend me your ID.'

Mersey's eyes automatically flicked towards the technicians. 'Are you crazy?'

William didn't know what to say.

'What are you up to, Bill?'

Julia was shocked to see how tense William had suddenly become. A tic had started in his left eye and he was plucking at his lower lip with his teeth. 'I just need to get back inside,' he said. 'Don't ask me why.'

'But you don't have access.'

'I can get in. Just let me past the rack and I can do the rest.'

'I'm not going to lose my job for you, Bill.' He shook his head. 'Sorry.'

Julia could see the chance slipping away from them. She smiled at Mersey. 'You don't have to know about it. You can just bend the rules a bit.' She didn't know what she was talking about, but she trusted William. They had to get in.

'You're going to have to leave.' Mersey's tone had become chilly. He held his hands out to usher them out.

He stopped, and was staring at William. Julia turned to see what was happening.

William's gun was held out of sight from the mechanics, pointing from his hip straight at Mersey. For a moment Julia thought he was going to fire. Mersey looked from one to the other. 'What's going on?'

'I've got to get into the system.'

'William?' Julia hissed. 'What are you doing?'

Mersey looked more surprised than afraid. 'Are you going to shoot me?'

William's face was white. Though his jaw was set, his eyes betrayed his vacillation. The gun wavered, but at this range he couldn't miss.

Julia realised he was about to change his mind. She held her hand out. 'Give me the gun.'

William didn't take his eyes off Mersey. She stepped into his line of vision and held her hand out for the gun. He gave her it as though he was a child.

Julia turned to face Mersey and the man's face dropped. It was her turn to point the gun at him.

'If you don't do what he says, I'll shoot you myself,' Julia said. She was so nervous she was holding her breath. For a moment the three people stood facing each other like actors who had forgotten their lines. Julia could hear the murmur of conversation from the technicians at the end of the lab. They hadn't realised what was happening. 'What do we need to do, William?'

'Give me security clearance to use the mainframe,' he said after a moment.

She could see he wasn't thinking clearly. 'How do we do that?'

He seemed to snap to. 'Where's your office?' he asked Mersey. 'Room 201.' He pointed.

'Let's go.' Julia jerked the muzzle of the gun to one side. She followed Mersey out of the lab, the gun pressed in his back, so close behind him their legs clashed.

His office was small and untidy; papers and bits of hardware strewn across the desk. Julia indicated for him to sit in the chair, and William locked the door behind them. She gave him the gun which he pocketed almost sheepishly.

Julia felt hopelessly amateur, dizzy with fear. She couldn't believe she had pulled a gun on another human being, been prepared to shoot him if he didn't obey her. Things like that didn't happen to people like her. She was Dr O'Brien, PhD, an English anthropologist and mother; but for a moment she had been so afraid of things going wrong that she could have killed another human being. She was cold and sweaty now, still feeling the unpleasantly heavy piece of tempered steel in her hand. The gun had turned her into someone else, someone she didn't recognise. She was shocked at how easy it would have been to pull the trigger. The cartoon man in front of her would have fallen down, cartoon blood spilling out at eighteen frames a second. Rewind it, and he'd have leapt to his feet, walking backwards through the lab out into the quad.

If only. Julia looked at William, wishing she could rewind it back a week. She could have ignored the book on the bedside table, had nothing to do with William. She could have declined the offer of work from Omnisens. She could have not gone into that book shop four years ago on the Charing Cross Road and bought the story of her mother and father. But she had, and now she was locked in a stuffy room, expecting two security men to kick in the door at any moment.

William indicated the glowing monitor in the wall. 'Give me clearance to use the mainframe.'

Mersey hesitated, and then tapped a couple of digits on the keyboard. 'Card, please.' He held his hand out without looking at William. He slid the card through the reader and gave it back to William. 'What time do you want access?'

It would be safest later in the day, when the lab was empty, but they couldn't wait that long: The security officers might be back at any moment with gate clearance. He would have to go for it now, and hope the machine wasn't being used. It was highly likely that they had cancelled his key, in which case he would have to do some snooping until he found an open window, if one existed. It could take hours, and then there was no guarantee he'd get in. Even if he could hack into the system, it would only be minutes before he was discovered. 'Straight away,' he said eventually.

Mersey leant forward to the microphone. 'Mersey Kritsinger. Department of Computer Simulation.'

The monitor blinked its acknowledgment. *Good morning, Mr Kritsinger.*

Mersey ignored the obsequious voice. He pushed his chair back from the desk and indicated the keyboard to William. 'You're past the rack. The rest is up to you.'

'This may take some time,' William said to Julia. 'We'd better tie him up.'

Julia picked out a length of electrical wire from the jumble of equipment on the desk.

'Don't touch that, please. I've been working on that for a week. Use some tape.' Mersey opened the desk drawer and gave her a roll of black masking tape.

Julia wanted to apologise as she taped Mersey's arms and legs to the chair, but she restrained herself. Now was not the time to lose her nerve. She couldn't bring herself to gag him. He was compliant enough, bemused rather than intimidated by the situation. She felt gullible and weak, accepting his promise not to call for help, but there was too little resolve left in her to insist. This wasn't how it was supposed to be. According to holo-film philosophy, she should have blown him away by now, or at least have stuffed a pair of socks into his mouth to stop him calling out.

William had moved his chair to the desk and was working, his head bowed towards the keyboard.

'I'll need a datasuit,' he said without looking round. 'Is there one in the lab?'

'Yes.'

'We'll need two,' Julia added.

'You'd better stay on the outside.'

'Why?'

William didn't answer, all his attention on the lines of numbers on the screen.

'Why?' she repeated.

'Someone has to keep an eye on Mersey,' he said at last.

'He's tied up.'

'Anyway,' he said, 'it's not possible for two people to go in together. Damn!' The screen cleared. *Access denied.*

'Yes, it is,' Mersey said quietly.

'It is what?' he said irritably.

'Possible for two people to go in together. Ten people can go in.'

'But the program's mono,' William said.

'So what? She'll just have a basic body picture, but there's still full somatosensation.'

William was reluctant to approve. 'She's never flown virtually before. The last thing I need is someone freaking out.' He turned to her. 'It might involve complicated procedures. You wouldn't know what to do.'

'How complicated can it be?' Mersey said, teasing. 'What do you have? Twenty verbal commands?'

'I'm coming in with you,' she said.

William bent over the keyboard and went back to work. 'Okay.'

'Are you going to tell me what you two are up to?' Mersey said. He looked at William but he was engrossed in his task. He tried Julia. 'Well?'

'We'll tell you when we know.' She admired this man's cool. He was sitting comfortably in his chair as though nothing was out of the ordinary.

'What's so important about the map stone?' he persisted.

She shook her head. '*You* tell us.'

He thought about it for a moment. 'It's neither a map nor a stone. It's a metaprogramming technique using bio-feedback, translating brain signals into responses. Simple idea, brilliant technology.'

'A machine that talks to itself?'

'No,' William said without taking his eyes off the screen. 'It's you talking to yourself.'

Good evening, William.

She spun round. She saw William's face first, blank with surprise. Then the face on the screen. She knew who it was without being told. Jarnier.

Well? Aren't you going to ask me how I am?

William found his voice. 'How did you know I was going to —'

Jarnier supplied the word William was reluctant to use. *Hack in? I guessed that a bright boy like you would eventually get round to it.*

Julia moved behind William to look over his shoulder.

Is that you, Julia?

The mini camera above the monitor panned to look at her.

The face on the screen was as she'd imagined. A child prodigy grown up: cheerful, a hint of mania in the glittering eyes. A halo of orange hair filled the top half of the screen. Julia forced herself to smile. 'Pleased to meet you.'

I'm sorry it had to be like this.

'Does Omnisens know you're talking to me?' William said.

The figure on the screen shook his head. *It's our little secret. Is Mersey there, by the way?*

'Yes.'

The camera scanned the room. *Where is he?*

Julia realised she was blocking its view of Mersey. She turned quickly, keeping her body between the camera and Mersey. She pulled his chair closer to the monitor and then stood aside.

What's going on?

'I'm being held hostage.'

Jarnier laughed. *I want you to link them up with the two helmets we worked on.*

'I can't. I'm taped to the chair. Bill pulled a gun on me.'

William! Where's the art of persuasion? Is that all they taught you at the Institute? His head nodded for a moment while he paused to think. *If William frees you, will you play along? No alarm bells?*

'Am I going to get into trouble for this?'

Sweetheart, you'll get a Nobel prize. He paused to watch Mersey's reaction. *This engagement will be untraceable.* He leaned towards the camera. *I won't tell if you won't.*

'But how can I link both of them?'

That's where your Nobel prize comes in.

Jarnier tugged his collar into view and they saw he was in his bath robe. *Give me five minutes, William, and I'll meet you inside.* The image of Jarnier loomed larger until just an eye filled the screen. *Trust me.* The eye winked.

'You want us inside the MAYA programme?' William said.

You've got clearance. You, too Julia. Oh, the password you were looking for was 'scumbag.'

The screen went blank. The three people looked at each other. 'Let's go for it,' Julia said.

William and Julia held a muttered conference about Mersey. Trusting him was a chance they would have to take. William suggested taping his mouth until they were safely in the lab, but Julia pointed out that while they were inside he would have every chance of alerting security. And they could hardly wheel him around the corridor with tape over his mouth. They would have to trust him.

Mersey's wrists were exceptionally hairy, and Julia tried to ease the tape off without hurting him too much. William reluctantly pulled the gun from his pocket. 'We're in enough shit already,' he said to Mersey. 'Don't give us any trouble.'

William opened the door, looking left and right. He beckoned for Mersey to lead the way, and they followed him out. The corridor was empty and they reached the lab without being seen. Julia was aware of the video cameras hanging from the ceiling following their progress, but the gun was out of sight and Mersey was giving no indication that anything was out of the ordinary.

The technicians had gone, the room silent except for the high-pitched buzz of three monitors which lit the lab with a theatrical green glow. William closed the blinds and switched the main lights on.

'Where are the suits?' William asked.

Mersey took two datasuits out of a metal cabinet, checked their sizes, and gave Julia the smaller one. 'Suit up.'

Julia changed into her flight suit behind their backs while William studied the helmets. 'What is this – Brain Pong?' he said, indicating the attachment to the side of each helmet. Every undergraduate had played the game at some time. Tricky stuff, it required focusing your thoughts in a way most people were unaccustomed to. After a while you got the hang of it, and the game lost its appeal. Clever, but hardly breakthrough material.

'It's got a bit more class than that.' Mersey smiled. 'As the man said, this is where the Nobel prize comes in.' He helped Julia on with her helmet. 'Don't worry, it's very simple,' he said when he saw her face. 'It converts your brain waves into an electronic pulse which will be visible on screen as a green spot. You'll understand it when you see it.'

William saw from the screen that a second input was available. The first was marked *Morrison W.*, the second, *O'Brien J.* Tiny lifelike representations of them stood side by side like dolls waiting for their strings to be pulled.

'You've been body mapped,' he said, surprised. 'When did they lasergraph you?'

'When I first got to the base.'

'Why didn't you tell me?'

She shrugged. It had never occurred to her that it might be of any significance. It had only taken a minute, and she had forgotten about it. But now she realised she had been written into the program. When she entered the virtual world, she wouldn't just have a standard body picture, but a tailor made facsimile. She had been expected, and somebody had put a lot of work into her welcome.

They decided to use the recliners. They wouldn't have full

haptic feedback, but it was simple and quick. They clicked their helmets into position and lay back. William had left one of his datagloves off so he could unhook them if necessary. He gave the thumbs up for Mersey to activate the system.

23

You find yourself in the *nuhue*.
You're pleased to be back,
something inside you relaxing
in the smoky gloom of the
ceremonial hut. Sitting on the
bench to your right is Julia.
The body image lacks some detail,
but she's recognisable.
Are you okay?

You notice there is no voice
print out on the screen.
Mersey must have switched it
off. It's hard to tell from
Julia's face what she's feeling,
and as she doesn't answer, you
ask again.
Are you okay?

Yes, she says.
You are tapped on the shoulder
and you turn to see Mama
Francisco behind you.
Francisco.
Jarnier, actually.
The old man looks around at
the hut and smiles. Jarnier?
What the hell is going on?

I did a good job, didn't I?

You find yourself in the *nuhue*.
The surprise is so shocking that
you shut your eyes for a moment.
When you look around it's like a
dream. It's just as
you had imagined: the woven palm
walls, the floor of packed earth.
You look at your body. The detail
is good, but the quality is
alien. You flex your fingers and
watch your body image do
likewise. William's here,
sitting next to you. He looks
odd, like a waxwork dummy.

Are you okay? he says.
You realise he's talking to you.
Yes.
You jump. A Kogi Mama is behind
you. His eyes are glittering.

Francisco, William says.
Jarnier, actually.
It's the Mama you studied at the
base, your favourite. He
looks so real. Now he's saying
he's Jarnier?
I did a good job, didn't I?

He holds his hand out for
Julia to take.

Welcome to cyberspace.
Julia is having trouble
coordinating her movements.
She stands up, but the hut is
too low and her head
disappears. Jarnier chuckles
quietly.
Sit down.
You take her hand and guide her
until she is sitting beside you
in the bench. You speak.

*Before, was that you? Or
was Mama Francisco an
anthropoid?*
*No, I've just borrowed him for
a moment. I thought it would
be more fun than a simple body
form.*

He must have had trouble
covering his tracks. This
is a complex procedure, hard
to see how he could keep it a
secret.
Question time, I suspect.
He smiles at you then Julia.

You're being very quiet, Julia.
There is a long pause, while
her mouth works. She looks
more attractive inside than
out, the flaws ironed out. Her
skin is flat and smooth, android
looking.
Who are you? she says.
*Straight to the heart of the
matter. Good. I haven't been*

He's holding his hand out to
you. Suddenly you're unsure how
to move.
Welcome to cyberspace.
You can feel the straps of the
recliner pinching you. You want
to get to your feet. You push
out and your perspective changes.
You can see the sky.

Sit down, William says.
Somebody grabs your hand and
pulls you down. You're sitting
on the bench again. William is
speaking.
*Before, was that you? Or
was Mama Francisco an
anthropoid?* he says.
*No. I've just borrowed him for
a moment. I thought it would
be more fun than a simple body
form.*

He rattles the stick in the
poporo. You can't believe it.
This is just like being there.

Question time, I suspect.
He looks so kind. It's hard to
believe he doesn't actually
exist.
You're being very quiet, Julia.
You don't know what to say. Or
even if any words will come out
if you try and speak. William's
not being much help, just gawping
at you.

Who are you?
*Straight to the heart of the
matter. Good. I haven't been*

completely honest with you,
or with the Institute, come
to that.

You are aware of the metal
support of the recliner
digging into your back, and
you change your position.
What is Jarnier up to?

You see, I am Omnisens. Or,
majority shareholder, at least.

He pauses to look at you,
waiting for your reply.
You're too stunned to say
anything.
I made my first million at
fourteen, my first billion
by the age of twenty-one.
Unfair, I know, but – there's
gold in them thar hills.
He taps his forehead.
This system is my baby.

You've been running the
project?

You can't believe it.

The MAYA project was my
choice, the map stone my
design.

This isn't a reality
holiday, is it?

No. It's a training tool.

With what purpose?

Julia has explained about
seivake?

What the hell is he talking
about?

completely honest with you,
or with the Institute, come
to that.

This is astonishing. That such an
alternative universe should
exist, with such complete
believability. The man really
does look real.

You see. I am Omnisens. Or
majority shareholder, at least.

Omnisens? A Kogi Mama is telling
you that he's a multi-billion
dollar company?

I made my first million at
fourteen, my first billion
by the age of twenty-one.
Unfair, I know, but – there's
gold in them thar hills.
He taps his forehead.
This system is my baby.

You've been running the
project? William says.

This explains a lot.

The MAYA project was my
choice, the map stone my
design.

This isn't a reality
holiday, is it? he asks.

No. It's a training tool.

With what purpose? He sounds
angry.

Julia has explained about
seivake?

Yes, she says.

*So, the point is we can return
to the great Mother?*

If this was for real you'd
take a swing at the bastard.
He's been playing with you.

Otherwise known as the author.

Your hand is on your helmet,
ready to rip it off.

Wait a moment, Jarnier says.
Julia has some questions.

Do you know about the books?
she says.

Yes.

Is this part of the . . . ? she
says.

Yes.

So, what's happening?

*For that, you will need to
take a step further.*

Into the map stone? she asks.

She's ahead of you, William.

Jarnier stands up and turns
round. You follow him out
of the hut. You're pissed
at this man, but glad to be back
here amid the dust and the
livestock. You ignore the people
staring at you. Julia is hurrying
to catch up with him. You're not
close enough to hear her
question, but Jarnier's answer
is clear.

Yes.

*So, the point is we can return
to the great Mother?* he says.

Otherwise known as the author.

Francisco laughs. He sounds like
a teenager.

Wait a moment, Francisco says.
Julia has some questions.

Do you know about the books?

Yes.

Is this part of the . . . ? You don't
know what to call it. Project?
Program? Game?

Yes.

So, what's happening? he asks.

*For that, you will need to
take a step further.*

Into the map stone?

She's ahead of you, William.

The old man gets to his feet and
indicates for you to follow. The
light outside the hut is bright.
He is walking quickly and you try
to catch up with him. You are
walking like an automaton.

Where is the author?

He exists in an infinite
number of locations.

How can we find him? she asks.

All the answers are in there—

He is pointing to something.

He exists in an infinite
number of locations.

How can we find him?

All the answers are in there —

The map stone. You catch your
breath. You never expected it to
be so beautiful. Its surface
seems to fizz and shimmer, but
when you look closely you can see
the cicatrices are moving. The
lines are not just on the
surface, but penetrate into the
depth of the stone. They are
like the criss-crossings of a
complex 3-D wiring system.

He turns to wait for you
to catch up.

It's hard to think of this old
man as the face you saw on the
screen. He seems so wise.

You're at the map stone.
You're reminded of your dream,
how the stone turned to flesh,
like a giant maggot. Its
surface convulses, and you're
suddenly scared. You want to
get out of here. The stone is
taller than you remember, as
broad as your arm's span. The
lines etched in its surface
are dissolving into fragments.
Slowly at first, then faster,
the fragments shift and
circulate, like smoke particles
in a chamber.

The stone has the texture of
sandstone. You can feel heat
radiating from its surface. The
lines have broken into dots which
dance before your eyes. At first
it seems random then you realise
they are forming back into lines.
It seems you can hold them in
place by concentrating.

Jarnier's voice seems to come
from everywhere.

What's happening? Any shape
forming yet?

What's happening? Any shape
forming yet?

No.	*No,* he says.
Can't you see the lines? she says.	*Can't you see the lines?*
For a moment you see them, but then you lose your focus and the movement of fragments becomes chaotic again.	Yes, there they are.
Look, she says.	*Look.*
She traces a line across the surface of the stone, and suddenly you see what she means. There is a complicated network of lines covering the whole stone.	The stone seems to buzz under the touch of your finger like fizzy sherbet.
I've got it.	*I've got it,* he says.
There is something familiar about the interconnections, a shape you recognise.	
Is it a word? she says.	*Is it a word?*
You suddenly realise what it is.	
It's a highway system. Look— You trace the long line on the right side. *You can see the outline of the coast. This must be route 101. I guess this is SF, here LA.*	*It's a highway system. Look —* *You can see the outline of the coast. This must be route 101. I guess this is SF, here LA,* he says.
You trace your northward journey from the base to Seattle. *We're here.*	*We're here,* he says. There is a network of roads above where he is indicating. *This must be Canada.*
This must be Canada, she says.	
You tap the stone on the nexus of three roads. *And this is Vancouver.*	*And this is Vancouver,* he says.

It's as though you have pressed a button on a TV. The lines change, snapping into a different grid.

Is this Vancouver, do you think? she says.

Yes, look – here's the Bay. And this must be Victoria Island.

This is where the author is living, she says.

You scan the map, looking for clues. There are no names to the streets, no areas marked. You point to a peninsula on the west.
What about here?

Why do you say that? she says.

I don't know. Do you know what it is?

I think it's the university, she says.

Congratulations! It looks like you've found him.

It's Jarnier. The map disappears and you're face to face with the form of the Kogi Mama.

The author lives in the university? she says.

If you say so.

What the hell does that mean?

I can't explain. You can only understand the answer if you

The lines disappear, a fresh pattern in their place. This is more ordered, more geometric. A street plan.

Is this Vancouver, do you think?

Yes, look – here's the Bay. And this must be Victoria Island, he says.

This is where the author is living.

Your eyes are drawn to an area on the western tip of the city.

What about here? he says.

Why do you say that?

I don't know. Do you know what it is? he says.

I think it's the university.

Congratulations! It looks like you've found him.

You're facing Mama Francisco. You raise your hands to shield your eyes but the gloves clash against your helmet.

The author lives in the university?

If you say so.

What the hell does that mean? William says. He looks peeved.

I can't explain. You can only understand the answer if you

can understand the question. And if you can understand the question, there is no need to ask it.	can understand the question. And if you can understand the question, there is no need to ask it.
	You catch hold of his arm and he smiles enquiringly at your hand. You let go. Who is this you're talking to: Jarnier or a Kogi Mama?
Some yes/no answers, she says. *Please,* she adds.	*Some yes/no answers.* *Please.*
Go ahead, but make it quick. We don't have much time.	*Go ahead, but make it quick. We don't have much time.*
Is the author real? she says.	*Is the author real?*
Yes.	*Yes.*
Are we creations of his?	*Are we creations of his?*
Yes.	*Yes.*
Can we exist without him?	*Can we exist without him?*
No.	*No.*
Can he exist without us?	*Can he exist without us?*
Good question. No.	*Good question. No.*
Is he God?	*Is he God?*
Define your terms.	*Define your terms.*
You are mesmerised by this conversation, unable to take in what he is saying.	He holds his hand up to stop you. You can see he is laughing at you.
No, don't bother. I'm out of my depth here. You'd better ask him yourself.	*No, don't bother. I'm out of my depth here. You'd better ask him yourself.*
This is bullshit. We're going to get arrested as soon as we step off campus,	*This is bullshit,* he says. *We're going to get arrested as soon as we step off campus,*
Oh, your two pursuers. Nothing	*Oh, your two pursuers. Nothing*

*to do with me. You can thank
Beecham for that.*

Can't you do something?

*I'll fix the databank so they
think you're somewhere else.
You'll need clearance to get
into Canada.*

And my banking account?

*I'll unfreeze it. Now get the
hell out of the system before
somebody finds you.*

*to do with me. You can thank
Beecham for that.*

Can't you do something? he says.

*I'll fix the databank so they
think you're somewhere else.
You'll need clearance to get
into Canada.*

And my banking account? he asks.

*I'll unfreeze it. Now get the
hell out of the system before
somebody finds you.*

24

I wake up to find something heavy lying across my face. I grab it and hold it away from my face so I can focus on the object. It's somebody's arm. I shriek and throw it away from me as hard as I can.

I sit up and look to see where it has landed. It's lying on the bed beside my body, waxy palm upright. I recognise the hand. It is mine. I think.

I run my free hand up the arm to my shoulder. It hasn't been severed. I squeeze the arm, but there is no sensation. I can only assume it has been numbed through lack of blood.

I try moving the fingers but they are paralysed. The arm is not just numb – it's not mine. Though I can see it is attached to my body, I have a moment's panic when I realise I will have to carry a stranger's arm around with me for the rest of my life. Although one part of me recognises it, another part cannot believe it has any connection with myself. I start massaging it with my other hand, but it's like a dead man's arm. The thing is inert.

Gradually at first, and then in a torrent, blood flows back into it, pins and needles coursing down my arm, magically returning it to the rest of my body. It's painful now, but at least it's mine.

To take my mind off the pain I study the beads of condensation which have formed on the inside of my tent. I reach out and flick the surface with a free finger, starting a race between two drops of water. One of them stalls, so I flick again and it jiggles sideways, merging with its opponent and sliding at double speed out of my field of vision. The pain in my arm is almost unbearable, and I cradle it to my chest, waiting for the buzzing to subside.

Lying on the mattress with the typewriter on my knees has

made it easy to drift in and out of sleep. I don't know how much I've been sleeping. My clocks have all gone wrong, and the daylight is almost twenty-four hours now, but I guess I'm just cat-napping, seemingly every hour or two. Dreaming, too. Nothing of great import, mostly fragments and irrelevances. A lot about the book, sometimes difficult to disentangle from what's real. One dream I'd like interpreted however: riding a white horse, bareback, along a series of corridors, leaping ridiculously small obstacles. And I, the rider, am crying, almost in agony, 'Yes, yes!', water pouring from my throat like a drowned man.

Enough. I kick the flap open and shimmy off the end of the mattress. My arm is heavy and still buzzing, and I let it hang from the shoulder like a leg of mutton. I scoop some snow from the bucket into the kettle and warm my good hand on it as it boils.

Sleeping and writing, I have reduced my life further. Even my occasional excursions have come to a stop. The weather seems to be getting worse. Summer is apparently a time for snowstorms and mist, sometimes for what seems like days at a time. I don't want to waste gasoline driving the halftrack, so I stay in the warm, heating dollar coins to keep my eyehole in the window free.

But when the sun shines I can see more and more islands of black in the white sea. The thaw is on its way. Soon the road will be open and Tulkina will have its three month acquaintance with the rest of the world renewed.

I haven't seen Harry Homme for a while, and neither have I seen much of Toto. I thought it might have gone, but on my rare trips out of the tent I see that the white slugs of shit are still mounting. As are the letters from Carla. When the first one arrived I wrestled for a couple of days as to whether to unpin it from the wall or not. In the end I decided against it, but just as I couldn't bring myself to read it, neither could I bring myself to destroy it. Two more have since arrived. Harry Homme has taken to delivering the letters, sending them up in the elevator so I can collect them with barely any effort. He also brings bits and pieces of food – strips of some kind of dried meat and salted fish. At least, I assume they are food; they look no more edible than archaeological finds.

Sometimes I wonder what is in the letters. The first probably pleads for me to come home, the second I guess gives me the benefit of the doubt about the arrival of the first, the third comments on my ignoring the second. I estimate that one more will arrive and then she'll give up. Carla may be devoted, but she's no fool. I don't know what I'm afraid of finding in them – open wounds, muscle cramps, migraines. Pain, certainly. I have no photograph of Carla, and I am unable to bring her picture to mind. I could describe her, but she has gone, fled from my memory. Does this mean I don't love her? Does this mean I don't know who she is? I *don't* know who she is. For twenty-five years another man has lived my life for me, fathering two boys, building my home. He has sent me reports, and I am authoritative about the domestic details, but I have yet to meet any of these characters. I'm talking about my family as though I've invented them, God forgive me.

Apart from Harry's contribution, food has almost run out, but I'm eating almost nothing, and my stores will last a few days more. Stopping the capsules has, as I expected, made no difference. The worsening of symptoms is no swifter than before. I have no energy, but I guess that's because I have no appetite. A nuisance that I seem to be allergic to bread now. At least, the last time I ate some, I threw up. I'm still in nothing more than discomfort. I feel strange rather than ill. It's the cold which is bothering me. Even with the electric heater inside my tent, the air is never more than tepid. Outside the tent, there is a permanent frost. My tinned food is crunchy with ice, the slush in my water cistern still frozen. This is officially summer, I'm told. We must be somewhere in May. How did people ever survive an Arctic winter? Perhaps they hibernated. Not a bad idea: sleep until the world has burnt itself out, be reawakened when it's all over.

Regret, I suppose, is the larger part of my feelings now. I have made a mess of things, a cell of a body who has likewise made a mess. It could all have been so beautiful, but we blew it. Damn.

I wash my hands of you all. I will die here with my travel poster and my peephole through the window. Damn.

And meanwhile the book looms throughout my waking time, William and Julia emerging from the page like grotesque mud skippers from primordial slime. Not fair. Sorry, folks.

I don't know what I'm doing, still don't know where I'm going. All this epistemological wandering – does it make any sense?

Either technologically or philosophically? Probably not – even the Pacific rim whizz kids haven't got a computer capable of a sensible conversation. Something like the map stone would take a central nervous system jack to run the thing, and I can't imagine anyone volunteering to have a DIN plug inserted under their occiput. I *can*, but I don't want to.

That's irrelevant, anyway. Do the ideas make any sense, *that's* the point. The questions, I can ask on three fingers. One: do I, like a hyperallergic Schrödinger's cat, exist in an infinite number of worlds, my location dependent on the observation of William and Julia? If they perceive me to be in Vancouver, does that mean in some parallel universe another me is in Des Moines, Iowa?

Which reminds me of the Zen parable of the kitten. Two monks arguing over ownership of a kitten, the abbot cuts it in half, gives a piece to each monk with the question: where is the kitten now? Is there an answer to that? I don't know. Did the kitten cease to exist? If so, where did the kittenness of the kitten go? Into *aluna*?

The second finger: can I, their author, exist without Julia and William? Jarnier seemed to think not. Does that mean that I and my creatures are literally – every pun intended – co-dependent? Without the world (and William and Julia are an integral and unsubtractable part of the world) I cannot exist, because self can only exist in relation to other.

The third finger: am I, however you are pleased to define the term, *God*? Not just in the world of make believe, but really, in some true sense?

A fourth question, dammit: is there a difference between the world of make believe and the real thing?

One more, I realise. The pinkie: does it make sense to ask these questions at all?

Questions, questions, questions. Let's get on with the story.

And anyway, who the hell is Jarnier? And why does he seem to know more than me?

They left the university at three o'clock. It was a cloudless day, scented with fresh mown grass etc. There was a scraped clean look to the sky, just a single trail of vapour from a high flying jet. There had been a lull in activity at the campus, the bright sunlight keeping people indoors, and it seemed unnaturally quiet. William paused at the doorway before he stepped out; there was no sign of the security men. Jarnier must be as clever as they said if he could break into the central Databank and fix information.

They had been inside for nearly five hours. Mersey had begun to tape the transaction but the screen had gone blank as soon as they had entered. Mersey had been worried for their safety, but Jarnier had reassured him over the videophone: this was to be expected, he'd said. Trust me. Mersey had checked their biofunctions at twenty-minute intervals and spent the rest of the time staring at the screen. He had decided, whether Jarnier agreed or not, to unhook them after two hours, and then three, and then four. If Jarnier *didn't* know what was happening, he would have two psychotic casualties on his hands and a lot of explaining to do.

And then without warning, the screen had flickered into life – a snowstorm of static and white noise – and Jarnier was telling him to unhook them. William and Julia were disorientated at first, nothing unusual after such an extended immersion, but he checked their reflexes nevertheless. After a few minutes it was clear they had suffered no ill effects. Whatever they had gone through hadn't done them any harm.

He had gone to the vending machine in the corridor to buy

some glucose drinks, and when he came back to the lab they had been plugged into a private videoline, presumably talking to Jarnier. He had sipped the sweet juice and watched their faces under the masks. Was there some kind of conspiracy of silence? Wasn't anybody going to tell him what was going on?

They had detached their videophones at the same time and closed the line down.

'Well?' he had asked. He hadn't been about to report them, but they owed him *something*. He had put his career on the line by being party to an unauthorised interface with a private computer system. Now Jarnier was refusing to answer any questions, and William and Julia either didn't know what had happened to them, or they were playing it so close to their chests, they might as well be deaf and dumb.

Mersey drove them back to the parking lot. His car was an old diesel model, an impressive luxury considering the road tax he would have paid, but William paid it no attention. He sat in the back, biting his fingernails while Julia pretended to find interest in the passing scenery.

They said nothing to each other until they were safely locked in William's car.

'I don't know whether to find this funny, or freaky,' William said. 'God is a sixty-three-year-old novelist?'

'Is that what Jarnier meant?'

'The author is supposed to be creating us. I'd say that's pretty divine.'

They stared ahead at the cement blocks of the opposite wall. There were too many questions to know where to begin.

'Our parents' lives,' William began slowly, 'were they documented, or created by this guy?' If they took their time, he thought, they might get the right questions, if not the right answers.

'If they are fictional, that would explain why we can't contact your mother – or any of my family.'

'And we're not real, either?'

'We *are* real, but . . .' She tried to suppress a smile.

'But we are being controlled by a higher being somewhere in Vancouver?' William was buzzing. He should have been tired –

five hours in the machine, no sleep for twenty-four – but he was twitchy with adrenalin. He knew she was trying hard not to laugh.

'You never thought you were in charge of your life, did you? *I* never did.' She sounded drunk. 'But Jarnier also said the author doesn't exist without us.'

'So?'

'Doesn't that make *us* equally divine?'

'Not if he's the one in charge.'

'Maybe he's not.' she said. 'It was us who located the author in Vancouver, remember.'

He shook his head. 'I don't buy that self-metaprogramming stuff. No matter what they say, the world doesn't behave like subatomic particles. If the author is in Vancouver, we didn't put him there.'

'My brain is going to explode,' she groaned, holding her head in her hands, laughing.

'Mine has already.'

Julia wanted to hug him. His very first joke. 'Do you think Jarnier knew where the author was all along?'

'He must have – it's his program.' William brought up the city plan of Vancouver on the road map. Sure enough, the university was on the western peninsula of the city, just as they had inferred from the map stone.

'If the author *is* there,' she said, 'how did we manage to pick the right spot? It was us, remember, who made the choice.'

'Subliminal suggestion? They can get pretty clever.' He looked sideways at her. 'I realise, by the way, what the quest in the MAYA program was for – it was *knowledge*.'

Julia didn't understand what he meant.

'I thought it was *data* they were looking for. Facts, information.' He hadn't made the distinction until now. He couldn't believe how dumb he had been. 'Jarnier's right – it *is* a training tool. This is the whole point of the program – to reach some kind of understanding about all this.'

He was suddenly buoyant, almost happy. He started the engine, letting it idle for a moment. He was about to pull away when he turned to Julia. 'You don't really believe this writer is creating us?'

'What other explanation is there?'

The car was thoroughly searched at the West Canada border. Normally Julia would have been intimidated by the uniformed officials, but even when she had to empty the contents of her pouch onto the Customs desk, she didn't lose the liquid feeling inside her. She had been harbouring the warmth in her belly for the entire journey, not wanting to disturb it by sudden movement or conversation. She wanted to keep it for ever, and she smiled at the Customs officer's officious manner.

The only thing she could liken virtuality to was a fainting fit. She had been prone to fainting as a teenager, and though she hated it, the moment before blackness struck her on the head she had often experienced a split second orgasmic convulsion, a red tide of heat that ripped through her.

Face to face with the map stone was similar, but there was another side to it. As she waited for her visa clearance, she tried to pin it down. Unlike the throbbing headache and eviscerated feeling after a faint, she was left with this heat in her belly and the sense of being poised on the edge of something. She felt as though, with the slightest nudge, she would fall forward into space. Something had opened up for her.

It was a belief of Julia's, buried so deep that she was mostly unaware of it, that the final evolution of the human being was not ectomorphic super-brained sainthood, but *flight*. Not mechanical air travel either, not a laboured flapping of wings, but gliding and swooping. Deep immersion had confirmed it for her. With her street clothes and her sagging breasts she was just a clay figure, but hooked up to the machine, she felt something so alien to her waking life it almost couldn't be named. Freedom. This was what she was looking for – to escape the tyranny of gravity. She wanted to fly, she wanted to be free. Free of being responsible for four children, free of worry, free of her body. And one day, her secret fantasy said, we will all be able to fly. Like angels.

William had told her that their financial status would be checked, and that if his credits were still frozen he would be turned back. But after his gun had been impounded and the car vacuumed clean by an Aboriginal Canadian, they were informed they could stay for the maximum thirty-day period. Jarnier must have freed up his banking account as he said he'd do. William was so relieved he insisted on paying Julia's thousand dollar visa fee.

Driving north into the afternoon sun, Julia imagined the road stretching into a network of other roads, a vascular system with vehicles for corpuscles. They could drive for ever, circle the body of the planet in perfect comfort.

The list of faculty members was posted on the wall by the administrative office of the Arts building. Access to the campus had been unchallenged; Jarnier had prepared their path well. Julia ran her finger down the list, but the author wasn't mentioned. William almost seemed pleased, wanting to believe they were on the wrong track, but Julia trawled through the names again until she found a Creative Writing tutor. There was nothing to be lost by asking if anyone knew him. The photograph beside the name showed a youngish woman with blonde hair pulled back into a bun. Professor Lara Lacey, room 641. They took the elevator to the sixth floor and found her room. It was nearly six o'clock, but there was a chance she would still be there.

Professor Lacey was reading something from a sheet of paper, and indicated a chair without looking up. She was obviously expecting someone else. 'Sit down, please. I'll be with you in a minute.'

It was only when she realised that two people were standing in front of her desk, that she looked up. She was older than the photograph implied, the hair brown not blonde. Julia could see she was struggling to adjust her thoughts.

'Professor Lacey?' Julia smiled, giving the other woman no time to question their motives. 'I'm Dr O'Brien, and this is William Morrison of the Institute of Computer Science.' She had decided that the stamp of academia would help pave their path. 'I'm sorry not to have made an appointment, but we've only just arrived in Canada.'

The woman behind the desk was looking puzzled, but not unfriendly. 'How can I help you?'

'May we sit down?'

The professor indicated the chairs as though Julia hadn't seen them. Julia laid two books on the desk in front of the woman and then sat next to William. 'Do you know this author?'

The professor glanced at the books. 'Of course. He worked here until recently.'

Julia didn't know if she was relieved at finding someone who knew him, or disappointed that he had gone. 'He doesn't work here any more?'

'He left a month ago.'

'My colleague and I are very interested in finding him.' She looked at William for agreement, and he smiled hopefully at the woman. Julia had made him shave and change his shirt before getting out of the car. She hoped she didn't look as manic as he did.

Lara Lacey was still trying to grasp who these people were. She straightened the papers in front of her. 'Why do you want to find him?'

William leant forward and Julia caught a whiff of sweat. 'We are preparing a paper on the levels of reality in fiction, and as you know, he did some interesting work in the field.'

They had prepared the excuse beforehand, but now he said the words, it sounded patently like a lie.

'The Institute of Computer Science?' She sounded suspicious.

'University of Southern California.'

The professor turned one of the books over and read the reviews on the back. 'I can't tell you where he is.'

'Did he resign?' Julia asked.

'Not exactly.'

'Fired?'

The woman hesitated, and then decided that she had gone too far. 'I can't give you that information.'

'Why was he fired?'

'He wasn't fired.' She pushed the books across the desk to Julia, inviting her to take them back. Julia ignored them.

'What was it then? Sick leave? Sabbatical? Suspension?'

Julia could see the academic in the professor weighing which response to give. The answer she gave was judicious rather than surly. 'That information is restricted. If you want to know more I suggest you contact his wife.'

'And her name is?'

The professor stood up, signifying the interview was at an end. 'Carla Shoal. You might know her from TV.'

They found her address with no difficulty, and drove to the suburb where she lived. William parked in the driveway and they sat watching the house in silence. A cherry tree had been planted too close to the porch, and the steps up to the veranda were dotted with squashed fruit. Julia checked the air monitor and then wound her window down. It was quiet and windless, as though the neighbourhood was holding its breath.

There was no doorbell, and Julia wondered what to do until William pointed out the old-fashioned door knocker. She knocked twice and stood back.

The woman who opened the door was in her late fifties, a light-skinned South Asian. She smiled questioningly.

'Ms Shoal?' Julia said. 'Is your husband at home?'

Julia liked her immediately. The older woman was the perfect counterpart to the ethnic decor of the house: warm and welcoming and faintly aromatic. Her English accent was a surprise to Julia. They followed her to a room at the back of the house which looked over a small garden. Julia let William do the talking while she looked round the room. It was bare to the point of being spartan. A sofa and an armchair, a woven rug on one wall, a few books on a shelf, a yucca plant in the corner. She noticed some dried rose petals lying in the lap of a white marble Buddha. Julia instinctively knew whose room it was: the author's, *her* author's. She could feel her heart pounding in her chest. At any moment he could walk in.

Julia didn't want to lie to Carla, but when William explained that he was a research student writing a thesis on her husband, she let it pass.

'Are you a student too?' Carla asked her. The tone of the question implied incredulity.

'No.' The word slipped out, and Julia could feel the conversation suspended until she qualified herself. She turned to William. 'I want to tell her the truth.'

And so she did. She kept it as simple as she could, not

mentioning the project, that William didn't recognise a town he should know, that they couldn't contact their families.

Carla was less surprised than Julia had expected. 'So you think my husband has somehow written the story of your parents? Yours too?' she said to William.

'Yes, ma'am.'

The woman accepted it with no comment. Julia noticed that what she thought was a mole on her nose was a diamond nose stud.

'We want to talk to him. Do you know where he is?'

'I'm worried about him,' she said after a moment. 'I haven't seen him for a month.'

'Where is he?' William asked.

'He's gone to a small town in the Northwest Territories.'

'He left his job?'

'He just didn't come home one day.'

'Why?'

Carla hesitated. 'He's infected.'

Julia caught her breath. 'Oh God,' she whispered.

'I'm never going to see him again.' She went to the window to hide her tears. William and Julia stared at her back, not knowing what to say. 'The only thing he cared about was the garden. It's getting a bit out of hand now.'

Julia joined her at the window, standing so close their shoulders touched. A wooden hut was at the end of the garden, saddle backed and raised off the ground like a Japanese tea ceremony house. 'Is that where he worked?' she asked gently.

'Yes. He was planning a novel, the first for years.' She turned from the window, back in control, and sat down. 'He's a bastard.'

Julia glanced at William who was looking though the titles on the bookshelf. Yellowed paperbacks on quantum theory, popular works on AI and computer simulation. Simpleton's science, full of wishful thinking and wild assertions. A well-thumbed paperback about the Kogi caught his eye, but he left it on the shelf. This was getting too weird.

'He was never satisfied,' Carla said. 'He would never just accept things the way they are.' She glanced at William and Julia for confirmation, but they offered nothing. She looked angry now, contemptuous. 'He always said he was alone. Now he's proved it.'

She was determined not to cry, and she cast her eyes around the room, her glance pausing at the Buddha. 'Apparently he borrowed the keys to a friend's place, took a plane and left. He won't answer my letters.'

'You know his address?'

She nodded and then rose abruptly. 'Let me show you his work room.'

They followed her through the sliding doors to the hut at the end of the garden. It was uncarpeted and smelt of pine. Garden tools were stacked against one wall, a writing desk by the window. It was an undefended building, a viral trap whenever it rained. Julia could see William surreptitiously checking his wrist monitor.

'He spent almost all his time in here,' Carla said. A bunch of rotting carnations stood in a glass vase on the table. Julia could smell the brackish water from where she stood. 'I don't know if he got beyond writing notes.' She scuffed her hand against the papers on the desk, accidentally knocking one of the sheets onto the floor.

Julia bent to pick it up. She turned the paper over and scanned the almost illegible handwriting. The words were tiny, obviously written at different times and in a variety of colours: green, blue, red, pencil, green again. They were notes about some kind of fiction, references to a text and books. She read a line to herself. *This is one possible future – don't restrict yourself to what you want, or even what you foresee.* Another line. *A man dreaming he's a butterfly, or a butterfly dreaming he's a man.*

Carla was looking through the window, back at the house. Julia caught William's eye and indicated the sheets on the table. A notebook with a red cover was visible among the jumble, and she slid it out. William stood behind her, reading over her shoulder as she flicked through the pages.

This is his one last book – of course he's reluctant to finish it because that will be the end of his life. Therefore he will try and postpone events.

The daughter? Married with kids. The son? Realisation that his story has been written undermines his grasp of who he is, so he disintegrates, throwing in his job. He tries to rationalise it in any way he can – a conspiracy, he becomes paranoid.

Julia let William take the book off her, and closed her eyes. She could feel his breath on her bare neck. 'Did your husband ever mention us?' she asked.

Carla turned to face them. She had been daydreaming, and she looked vague. 'I'm sorry, I don't remember your names.'

'Julia O'Brien and William Morrison.'

'The daughter of Kate and Michael O'Brien,' she said to Julia. 'The son of James Morrison and Connie.'

'So you know about it?' Julia said.

'I've read the books,' she said simply. 'But I don't think he ever mentioned you.'

'Did he talk about the book he was planning?'

'No. He never spoke about his work.' Julia held Carla's gaze.

'I want to come with you,' Carla said. 'You *are* going to go?'

'Yes.' They turned to look at William. He had taken the notebook to the window and was flicking through it. His hands were shaking so much he tore one of the pages as he turned it over.

'Chapter thirteen,' he read aloud. 'She loves the outdoors, he hates it. She wants the window open/to stop the car – he reluctantly agrees. The skeleton of a wooden farmhouse. "This used to be farmland". Drive through the night. J dozing, waking in the dark. W asks about the map stone – the end of the world.' His voice was taut, strangled. He let the book drop and then rubbed his eyes fiercely. When he lowered his arms, his eyes were red. He looked exhausted. 'There's no denying it now. He's been writing about us. The whole thing has been a fiction – this too.' He span round, checking the corners of the hut. 'What does he use? Hidden cameras? Or does he write about us as it happens?'

He scrabbled through the papers on the desk. 'Perhaps I can find out what happens next.'

Julia stilled his hands, but he pulled away from her.

'I'm finished. You can do what you want.' He was on the edge of tears. 'I've had enough.'

He stumbled out of the shed, knocking a plant-pot off the bench. He slammed the door behind him but it swung open and the two women watched him hurrying away.

'I don't understand,' Carla said.

There was no point even beginning to explain. Julia took Carla's hand. 'I want you to come with us as well,' she said. 'We'll find your husband together.'

They found William in the car. He was crying, his breath coming in pants. Julia called his name, but he didn't hear. His face was white, sweat standing out on his forehead. She peeled his fingers off the steering wheel, damp stripes on the plastic where his fingers had gripped.

'I can't—' he began.

'Don't try and talk,' Julia said.

He allowed the two women to help him out of the car and they led him back to the house. He lay down in a bedroom while Carla drew the curtains and Julia sat on the edge of the bed, watching him. His skin was waxy, his breathing erratic. Tears stood out in the corners of his eyes, two diamonds in the dusk of the room. 'I can't go on,' he said quietly. 'I've had it.' His eyelids closed for a moment, but then sprang open again. 'I should find it funny, I guess. There's no reason not to.' He started crying again, his laugh turning into a sob. Julia laid her hands over his eyes and he let his lids close.

'Your hands are cool,' he said. 'I'm so tired.'

Julia waited until he was asleep, and then joined Carla in the kitchen. The older woman was cooking something in a microwave, watching a pot circling on the turntable. 'I'm worried about him,' she said with her back to Julia.

'He'll be all right.'

'I mean my husband.' She took a sudden inbreath as though she was smelling flowers. 'I want to see him again. Even if he's going to die. Just once more.' The oven pinged and she opened the door and took out a tea pot. When she turned round Julia saw she had been crying. 'We can't leave things the way we have.'

They sat opposite each other at the table, waiting for the tea to brew. 'We can fly north to Inuvik, and then drive to the town,' Carla said. 'Apparently the roads are clear now.'

'Why didn't you try and contact him?'

'I did, but he didn't answer.'

'Couldn't you have gone on your own?'

'The network wouldn't have given me time off.' Carla saw her disapproving look. 'They would have sued me for breach of contract.'

'And now?'

'I don't care about the network.'

They booked two seats on the plane for the next morning. Julia felt guilty at leaving William behind, but he had reached the end of his tether. She wondered if she was doing the right thing – perhaps she could return to her life and forget this ever happened. But did her life still exist? Was this all she had: the kitchen table, the company of another person, the memory of the journey she and William had taken together? What would the Kogi say? Everything exists in *aluna*. Some things manifest, some things do not.

Carla showed Julia to the spare room. The pink bedspread on the bed reminded Julia of her daughter's, and she felt a surge of home sickness. She was missing her kids more than she realised. Please God, she thought. Let me see my kids again. Let them be real.

Dizzy with exhaustion, she just wanted to curl up on the bed and sleep. 'Did your husband tell you the name of the novel he was writing?' she asked Carla before she closed the door on her.

It was a second or two before Carla answered. 'The book? I think he called it *Twenty Twenty*.'

26

If I turn to look at my past, I can only catch glimpses of shapes as they dart into shadows. I know there is something there, but it defies my attention. And strain my eyes though I may, the future is like a snowstorm, mental white out. I am balancing on the tiny point of the present, unsure of myself. But even though I'm running out of ground on which to stand, I find myself not afraid, but more vividly alive.

I feel sorry for Julia. Pulling the rug from under William is performed with a certain satisfaction, and I have no qualms about it. I'm getting my own back, I suppose, on those who have crossed me. But Julia has become a friend, and here I am, refusing her access to the rest of her life. Will she ever see her family again? It's within my power to make this happen; I may have to stretch a credible point or two, but I could work something out. I feel guilt at animating a character only to dash her hopes. What sort of sadist am I?

A clumsy one, I suppose. This story has begun to slip its lead. William and Julia coming across a page of my notes was not expected. Likewise Carla asking to come to Tulkina. I expected her to stay behind. Now I'm going to have to handle three people instead of two (William is going to reappear at the breakfast table and change his mind about going with them. Julia is glad of the company, as is Carla, who secretly finds the young pilot attractive. Dammit – see what I mean? My wife is chasing my own characters.)

I spend my days on the mattress, sleeping and dreaming, writing and thinking, venturing only to the window to monitor the melting ice. The shore line is clearly visible now, each day the pack ice moving closer to the horizon. If I open the window I can hear the cracking and growling as it breaks apart, a giant creature sloughing its skin. The Mother is coming awake.

The weather is mostly misty, but when the sky clears the sunlight is unremitting: no dawn, no dusk, just a slight dipping and rising of the sun. The sun is so low in the sky its beams are levelled directly through the glass, sometimes making the room so bright I have to wear shades. The ice on the window is melting quickly, puddles on the windowsills overflowing onto the floorboards.

I am astonished to see grass showing through the snow under my window, patches of brilliant green in the bright sunlight. Birds have arrived, mostly gulls. I take more pleasure than I can say, watching their circling and diving after fish in the bay.

Now I think of it, I haven't seen Toto for a while. I search for him, but all I can see on the light fittings are cobwebs. I would dismiss the bird as an hallucination were it not for the evidence of the shit it left behind. I never did understand how a green parrot came to feature in my life.

My food is at an end. All I have left is a tin of Yannoh coffee, a few dried apricots and Harry's archaeological find. The rest of the food I can't keep down for more than a few minutes. I could last for a couple of days, but if I don't go to Harry's now, I may never have the energy.

The sun is warm out of the wind and I'm reluctant to take the halftrack, but I don't have the strength to walk. There's no point in saving gas any more; I've long since passed the point of no return. I couldn't even get a quarter way to Inuvik, so I might as well use the halftrack until the tank runs dry. I can't believe Harry won't rescue me if I'm in trouble.

I switch on the engine, but it doesn't even turn over. I don't know what else to do but tap the starter button until something happens, but after a couple of jabs I find I've jammed the plastic cap into the hole. I prise it out with a fingernail, and then catch the back of my head on the rear-view mirror as I sit up, knocking my hat over my eyes.

I do a little dance on the pedals, hopeful that something will happen, but their only response is to squeak. I'm aware of muttering to myself. I can hear the rasp of my bristles against the upturned collar of my coat as I open and shut my mouth.

I'll have to walk. The snow has turned to slush, islands of ice between giant melt water puddles. I don't trust that my boots are waterproof, so I step carefully around the pools, tiptoeing through them when I find myself cornered. If I take it slow I can sort of glide over the ground. If it was windy, I'd be knocked over, but it's so still I can feel myself lifting off the ground like a helium balloon.

By the corner of the factory I catch a whiff of sewage. My honey bags must be defrosting – something Harry had warned me about. I'll have to ask him what to do with them. I don't suppose I can bury them, the ground will still be frozen. As I float past the houses on the main street, I can see the garbage exposed by the melting snow: cardboard boxes, a tractor tyre, rusted gasoline drums, Coke cans. The stuffing from a rotting mattress is being tugged out by a dirty brown gull. Beside most of the houses is a similar pile of bright orange sacks, some of them burst, staining the ice brown. The sun has hatched swarms of mosquitoes which dance over the surface of the pools of water. I can hear a buzzing inside my head. Almost music.

Harry is loading up the back of an old gas-driven pickup with boxes. I stay on the opposite side of the street, keeping away from the smoking exhaust. After a minute he sees me watching, and he waves.

'Anything you find, you can keep.' He jerks his thumb towards the open door of his shop.

I daren't get any closer to the truck. I'm already nauseous from the fumes. 'Can you turn the engine off?' I call to him.

Harry hops over the tailboard and reaches into the cab. The engine coughs and stops. He waves the air ineffectually, trying to disperse the smoke.

'What's happening?' I call.

'I'm moving south.'

I nod, thinking I must have misheard him.

'This town is all yours.'

I slip my mask on, cross the road and follow him into the store. The shelves are empty.

'Another letter from your missus,' he says, handing me a ComSat sheet.

I'm too surprised to do anything other than take it from him and put it in my back pocket. I stand aside to let Harry pass. 'What's happening?' I ask again. There's something I'm not understanding.

'I'm going to live with my son-in-law.'

'What for?'

'This is a shop, not a museum. There ain't no one left to sell to.' He pauses and points vaguely over my shoulder. 'The oil company has killed off the Delta, and it ain't never coming back to life.' He studies me, his face creased into concern. 'You ain't looking too good, fella.'

'Aren't I?' Now he mentions it, I feel like shit.

'You want any of this stuff?' He nods at the miscellaneous packets and cans on the counter.

'I came for some food.'

He puts down the bundle of axe handles he's carrying and lifts a cardboard box off the floor. 'This is all there is.' He gives me the box, but it's too heavy and I nearly drop it.

'Whoa boy!' He takes it from me.

I read the upside down label on the box. A case of creamed rice pudding. 'I'll just take a couple of cans.' I put one in each pocket and lean against the counter.

Harry watches me, but says nothing, then carries on shifting stuff from the shelves. My eyes and nose are watering in the warm.

'You're going to have to clear out,' he says with his back to me. 'This town is dead.' He takes a pot off a shelf and squints at it. 'You want some white paint?'

I do, actually. 'Thanks,' I say, indicating for him to put it on the counter.

'I mean it. When your gasoline runs out, you'll be a goner. There ain't nobody going to come and rescue you.'

The look on my face must be plain.

'You've already run out of gas?' he asks.

'A couple more days, I expect.'

'Pack your bags and come with me.'

I can't think what to say. 'The story's not finished yet,' I offer at last.

'Well, hurry it up. I can stay another day.'

'Thanks, but it's nothing to do with me. It could take weeks – I'm just a spectator.'

'You don't understand, fella. The chances of anyone coming up here, summer or winter, are slimmer than nothing.'

'I'm not ready to go back.'

'What's so important about this book?'

'I don't know.' I do, but I won't tell him. William and Julia, I realise, are my last chance to stay alive the few years my illness will allow. I have given them the unenviable task of trying to convince me it's worth living a second longer than is necessary. The irony of starving to death to find out the answer doesn't escape me. 'I'm trying to work something out,' I say to Harry.

He looks at me doubtfully. 'How long is two cans of rice going to last you, friend? You want to kill yourself in the trying?'

Maybe, I think. I've yet to see.

'Face it. You'll last a couple of weeks, maximum.'

I try to laugh, but it sounds more like a bleat.

'What's so funny?' he says.

'I'm infected.'

'I know that.'

It takes me a couple of seconds to digest this. 'So, how long have I got? Five years if I live in a bubble?'

'What about Carla?'

'I'm not going to live in a bubble. And I'm not going to infect her.'

'That's good of you to make up the woman's mind.'

'What do you mean?'

'You asked her what she wants?'

My head is aching with a sinus headache. I don't need this inquisition. 'Thanks for the paint, Harry,' I say. 'Thanks for everything.' I mean it.

I pick up the can and head out of the store. As I'm leaning into the door to push it open I hear the voice on the TV. A woman's voice, a soap opera by the sound of it. 'Should I stay or should I go?' she is saying.

Amen.

I have to stop and rest five times on the way back to the factory. In the end I dump the can on the sidewalk and sit on it for a breather. The virus is increasing its hold. I'm wearing out.

I stand up and check my reflection in the window of the old school house. I've aged. My cheeks have hollowed, and something seems to have happened to my eyes. *Yin sanpaku*, white slivers of eyeball visible under my iris. Beware, say the Orientals, death is stalking you. Kennedy had eyes like this before he was assassinated.

Am I about to die, is that it? Are my eyes telling me I have already made my choice – to stay with my novel at the cost of my life?

I leave the can of paint on the sidewalk and start towards the hills. I have to negotiate a boggy area at the bottom where the air is thick with swarming insects. Trying to hurry through, I sink up to my shins in freezing water. I'm too tired to scramble out, so I let water flood into my boots. I want to lie down.

I lose one of my boots to the bog, but I'm as cold and as wet as I can get, so I carry on up the hill.

I had no idea it was here, all these seeds waiting for the winter to pass so they could burst into their brief Arctic summer. I recognise saxifrage, and some kind of heather with tiny white bell flowers. A bird is startled by my approach and rises flapping from the ground, heavy and clumsy.

It's a struggle to get there, but I eventually make the top. Tulkina looks like a model village from up here, little cardboard bungalows and the sugar cube factory. And beyond is the sea, a fringe of gravel beach, islands of ice sliding by in the current. I thought if I travelled far enough I would escape the machine, but even this distant outpost has been colonised. Beaufort Bay is poisoned, seals are dying from toxins, trash washes up on every shore in the world. The conquest is complete: younger brother has completed the job.

I find a mossy hollow like the palm of a huge hand, and lie in it out of the wind. The sun has a watery halo, the sky grey-white and cloudless. An arrow of ducks flies slowly out to sea.

I doze in the sun until I hear Harry's pickup starting up. I consider getting to my feet to watch him go, but I'm too tired to get up.

The road out of Tulkina is a thin black strip; the truck is like a toy shining in the sun. It stops at the foot of the hill and Harry gets out and I see him looking around. I suppose he must have seen the path my footprints made up the hill, because he skirts the bog and starts up the hill. His stride is swift and easy.

He says nothing, but squats beside me, watching the view. I am intensely aware of him, the leathery brown skin of his hands, the blue neckerchief, his battered cowboy hat. The heavy folds at the corner of his eyes makes him look more Chinese than Inuit.

'Beautiful,' he says at last.

I look down to the sea, the black waters of the bay. 'Yes.'

'So, you're staying?'

'Yes.'

He notices my wet sock, and kneels down to unroll it from my foot. I watch him, surprised. He unpeels each of the three layers until my foot is exposed. The skin is white, frail looking – the foot of an old man. He squeezes the water out of each sock and lays them on the heather, parallel to each other. Untying his neckerchief, he flaps the folds out of it and then dabs my foot dry, gently drying between the toes. I'm empty inside, a hole in the middle of my chest through which a breeze is blowing. Harry wraps my foot in the neckerchief, tying it at the ankle.

'Thank you,' I whisper.

He waits a moment and then pushes himself to his feet. We shake hands and then I watch his back as he half runs down the hill to the road. He starts the truck and drives away. I can hear the sound of the engine for minutes after it is out of sight. Then there is a lull in the cawing of gulls, and silence.

I could have made a friend out of Harry, but I'm glad he has gone. I want no witnesses. I have the town to myself, possibly the most northern man on the American continent.

Am I alone now, sitting here on this hill? Is there nothing to connect me with Harry, with Carla, with this gull who is riding the thermals above me? Or is Mama Francisco right? Is there really a parallel spirit world in which separation has no meaning?

The Christopher Columbus culture sold us the philosophy of dualism: the phenomenal world is its totality, we were told. Your God is transcendent and heaven is another place. There is no spirit at the heart of matter, no noumenon, no Mother to care for. Just pillaging.

Beneath the touchability of this hill and the sea and Harry Homme and everything lies the dimension of *aluna*, the life force, the Mother, intelligence. The moss is so green, so succulent, I *will* believe it.

Opening the trellis gate to my room, I am overwhelmed with happiness. The room is warm, my things are in place. The air seems to hum with life. The halftrack is empty of gasoline and I'm falling over the edge. If I let go, I might just fly.

27

Julia hated flying. At the airport when she saw the sixteen-seat jet that would take them north to Inuvik, her newfound equanimity, which she had assumed was hers to keep, wavered. When she saw the other passengers waiting to embark, it vanished completely. Twelve expensively dressed Korean game hunters, overexcited and tipsy from the flask that was being passed around, were having porters load and unload leather cases of rifles and fishing poles from the luggage trolleys. Though the air was clear they all wore fancy masks in what she could only guess was the style of theatrical characters. One of the men winked at the women, but Julia pretended not to have seen. She despised their braggadocio and stupid guns. They would have paid tens of thousands of dollar credits for a licence to kill a moose, perhaps a hundred thousand for a bear, and people treated them as though they were movie stars. Reality holidays were supposed to limit the influence of tourists like these, but when money spoke, the world still sat up and listened. What are a few dead moose compared to all that foreign exchange?

They had left William sleeping at Carla's house. Julia had written him a note saying she'd contact him as soon as she had any news. She felt guilty about leaving him like this, but he had reached the limit of his endurance. Julia thought that if it weren't for Carla's company, she too might abandon the search. After all, why should she have to crack this puzzle? She could return to England, consign this episode to the drawer marked 'inexplicable', and get on with her life. She had four children to bring up, a loving husband. At least, she thought she did.

A shout made them look up. William. He was striding across

the departure lounge, his sack over his shoulder, smiling. She found herself on her feet, hugging him. 'I'm so glad you changed your mind.'

She expected Carla to share her delight, but she looked doubtful. 'Are you sure you're up to this?' Carla asked.

He looked alert, better than Julia had seen him look for days. He was wearing a fresh shirt, one of the author's, she guessed.

'I've never felt better.'

'What's happened?' Julia asked. She sat down, still holding his hand.

'I figured that if I didn't try and understand what's going on, this would just be a flight in a plane.' He shrugged. 'I like flying.'

He looked different, his skin glowing as though he had been scrubbed and powdered. *Seivake*, Julia thought. The first step: becoming like a child. He certainly looked younger. She thought of the second step: forgetting everything you know, renouncing all knowledge, including the way things should be. Was this what was happening to him?

When they boarded the plane, Julia was so anxious she couldn't make her fingers work, so William buckled her safety belt for her. When he saw her eyes shut as the engines started, he took her hand and didn't let go until the plane had finished climbing and the pressure of her grip lessened.

It had been an overcast day, low cumulus cloud shrouding the airport, but they had risen through it and into brilliant sunshine. William unbuckled his harness and stretched his legs. Something had happened yesterday: a fuse had blown, one part of his brain ceasing to function. He couldn't believe how relaxed he felt. As long as he didn't attempt to net the butterflies of thought that flitted at the corner of his attention, he felt solid, assured even. He was not going to seek an answer, just follow the path that was laid out before him. He felt as though he had shrugged off a heavy weight and for the first time in his life was walking unencumbered.

William loved riding above the clouds. As a child he had always wanted to reach out and touch them, and he found himself doing it now, brushing the Perspex window with his fingertips. He had always wanted to be a flier. This was his domain – the pale blue horizon, the dazzle of light off a wingtip. They skirted a towering column of woolpack cloud, brilliant white. Its bulbous billows looked substantial, a resting place for angels, but the closer to the cloud they came, the less defined it was, until in the midst of it, what had seemed as tangible as cotton wool was nothing more than formless vapour.

The islands of green visible through breaks in the cloud became more frequent, until the cloud petered out and there was nothing between them and the prairie below. William searched the landscape, but the plane was flying too high to see its shadow. He was aware of Julia craning to see over his shoulder, so he sat back to share the view.

He looked back to check on Carla, but her eyes were closed, apparently asleep.

They passed over what looked like a desert: the wheat fields of British Columbia, the bread basket of the north. William pointed out a coniferous forest. It was as clear cut as a jigsaw piece; from here you couldn't see the impact of acid rain. A lake, as neat as any cartographer's drawing, divided the forest in two. And then they were over the mountains. Shaded on one side by the afternoon sun, capped in white, the range looked like a grey-brown ploughed field with just a dusting of snow. There was no scale to the sight, nothing to which they could relate it. William felt he could bend down and scoop a handful of soil, the 2734 metres high Mt Dubose, according to the holographic indicator on the window, held in the palm of his hand.

His gaze fell to the hands folded in his lap. He looked at the creases across his knuckles and they were the same as the river valleys in the mountain range. He studied his hands, the faint criss-crossing of veins visible below the surface, and for the first time he realised he did not own his body. This body was no more his possession than the view through the window.

He felt his perspective change. It was not a shift in visual orientation; it was something else. Some part of him was watching the world over his shoulder. The jet rose over a thermal and he was aware of his body riding the swell. An orange had bounced off a tray a couple of seats in front of them and was rolling down the aisle. He felt himself reach across Julia and catch it. As he looked at the orange in his hand, something opened inside him.

This orange was charged with a force, the same force that was holding the plane above the ground. The same force that animated his body. He looked at the fruit as though it was a bomb about to explode.

His attention stepped back again until he was outside the jet, aware of it travelling through space, the mountains and plains below the jet, the soil beneath the plains, the rock beneath the soil. He wanted to tell Julia what was happening, but there were no words he could use. He had no locus any more. His body was sitting next to her, but he was not limited to his body. He was everywhere. He was not in the world – the world was in him.

Julia knew something was happening to William. In the bustle at Inuvik airport, he stood like an island of quiet, a smile playing on his lips. He had hardly said a word in the plane, not eaten anything either. She slid her arm through his. 'What is it?' she whispered.

'I can't say.'

Carla was recognised by the young woman porter who took their cases and she was obliged to sign a paper napkin for her. Julia was amused to be in the company of someone so famous, but felt too foolish to ask Carla the reason for her fame.

The cold surprised them as soon as they stepped out of the airport building. They hurried to the parking lot where they collected the all-terrain camper Carla had booked for them. The road map informed them it was two hundred and fifty kilometres to Tulkina. The roads were mostly clear of snow; the most they would meet along the way was axle-deep slush. Looking into William's face Julia realised she would have to drive.

Inuvik was the centre of a hydroponic farming area. They drove past acre after acre of plastic sheeted fields and long, low packing plants. The horizon was low and the pale grey sky hung over them, unmarked by bird or cloud. It was half an hour before they reached countryside.

He tried to tell the two women what he had felt on the plane, but words tripped him up. The further into a sentence he ventured, the further he strayed from what he wanted to say.

Julia listened carefully, her eyes on the road, leaning towards him in her concentration. She knew what he was trying to say. She too had felt it. Once, when walking in a wood, she had unexpectedly witnessed her attention flying away from her like a quiver of arrows all fired at once. Suddenly she was no longer herself; not the thinker, but the thought. That was all there was: thought. She had never told anyone about it, kept it close to her, afraid of desecrating it with explanations, but it had changed her life. For that moment, she had known there was more to her than society allowed, and though the vivid shades of that experience had leached over time, its pigment still coloured her life.

'Can't you see, this is just—' He paused for so long that Julia turned to look at him. 'It doesn't make sense – do you understand?'

She held her hand out to him, palm up, and he took it.

'I'm beginning to.'

Carla had taken over at the wheel, and Julia rested her head against the window, watching the road behind her being pulled out of the wing mirror. She was happy, she realised. Happy and also something else, something she couldn't put her finger on. The road was lined with fir trees and they flicked past the edge of her field of vision. She thought back to her experience in the wood. Were the Kogi right? Was reality something which could only be perceived directly, spoken about metaphorically? Was it only in the gaps between words that true meaning could be found? It didn't make sense, of course, because sense was something alien to the experience. *Maya*: the apportioning, labelling, discriminating intellect, the net thrown over the world. God bless Jarnier and his game playing. The project *was* a training tool, the novels part of it. And it was working, for she and William were both learning something, something beyond words to explain.

Over the last few miles, the road and verge had become powdered with white. At first she thought it was frost, then she realised it was chalk dust. Heavy trucks passed them at intervals, a spume of dust following like a pursuing devil trying to catch up.

When they turned the corner and saw the quarry, she gasped at the contrast.

'Stop, can you?'

It was so white it looked like a glacier. Carla brought the camper to a halt and she opened her window. The quarry dropped away from the road to their left, a man-made valley, half a mile across and stretching out of sight in front of them. It was like something from the moon: a huge white crater with stepped sides, platforms of rock in the distance on which tiny yellow excavators worked like mechanical birds, pecking away at flesh. The gulf from one side to the other was broken by pillars of reddish stone, hundred of feet high, as broad as an office block. A river, unnaturally straight, had been cut though the middle of the valley. She traced it to its source, a two-hundred-foot waterfall dropping so steeply that it was shrouded in a permanent mist.

'What is it?' she asked.

'Gold mine,' William said from the back seat.

The rumble of thunder reached their ears, a puff of smoke in the distance. Julia opened her door and got out. It was cold here, a sharp metallic smell in the air. She walked as close to the edge of the road as she dared and looked down. It was like looking down the side of a mountain, scree gathering around any available shelf.

William and Carla joined her. They both walked past her to the lip of the road.

'Careful,' Julia said automatically.

'Come to the edge,' he said. 'It's beautiful.'

'I'm afraid,' she said.

'Come on.'

'I might fall.'

He beckoned her and she came. Standing between William and Carla, she held onto an arm on either side and leant as far out as she dared. She imagined what would happen if she fell forward. Would hands catch her, the hands of everything around her? She realised what the unfamiliar sensation was that had started at the Customs post. She felt safe.

She breathed the cold air deeply, feeling the burning at the back of her nose. Looking down she saw the upturned roots of a dwarf pine reaching towards her like the arms of a drowning person.

If we plant an orange tree and then pull it up by the roots it will die. Digging out the earth's gold is the same. It could die. Gold has its own thought and it can speak. It is a living thing. They must stop stealing it. If they take all the gold, the world will end. They are cutting off the flesh of the Mother's body.

Julia suddenly realised what she had to do. She undid the top buttons of her jacket and slid her hand under her shirt. Her fingers found the medallion her father had given her, warm between her fingers. She unfastened the hasp and slipped it out of her shirt. William looked enquiringly at the necklace in her hand. It was a Celtic cross. The gold was worn, its surface buffed by a multitude of tiny scratches. It was her most precious possession, the only thing of her father's she had. It had been a gift to him from the Bishop of Galway. Her father, if she could believe the book about him, had never finished his training for the priesthood. Yet he had kept this sign of his faith, worn it every day until his death. Julia closed her hand over it, hiding it in her fist.

'Help me down,' she said, holding her free hand out to William. She stepped over the crash barrier, facing out into the white canyon. It was not too steep to negotiate. She chose her spot and, letting go of William's hand, she half-slid, half-climbed, until she reached it. A boulder jutted from the surface, a huge block of chalk, and around its base the ground was deep with shingle. Ignoring the sharp edges of the stones cutting her fingers, she scraped a bowl into the mound and then placed the cross inside it. The gold was orange in the shadow of the boulder. She took a last look at the cross and then brushed the stones into place and scrambled back to the road.

William and Carla had returned to the camper and Julia paused to look back across the quarry. Suddenly it was as though she was standing on top of the paramo, snow-capped peaks in the distance, silence. As though something had grabbed her ankles, she felt a surge of energy rising from the ground, up through her legs to her groin. She felt rooted to the spot, part of the landscape. Before she knew what was happening, the feeling uncoiled itself into her belly and then up into her chest. For a moment she was frightened at the thought of it reaching her head, but it was too strong to resist. Her body was singing with power. As the rod of energy moved up her neck, she felt the hairs on her nape rise. When it reached the crown of her head she felt a breeze on the back of her neck, her vision click into preternatural clarity. She felt very tall, thinner than she normally was. She scanned the landscape as though someone had taken her head in his hands, and then she saw a flash of light, like the sun on a distant lake.

She knew what it was. It was what the Kogi called *munse*, the dawn light of the great Mother, shining through a crack in the world. The landscape *is* the great Mother, she realised, whether scarred with a Caesarean quarry or immaculate as it was before younger brother. The last Mama had gone, the world was in decline, but though worlds would come and go, the Mother would always be here. The Mother is all that is.

After the road branched, they found themselves alone. An old-fashioned road sign indicated that Tulkina was 133 kilometres away. The on-board computer couldn't give them an ETA and Carla asked William to work it out. She had reduced her speed; the road was neglected here, cracked apart by frost, in some places just loose gravel.

She thought he hadn't heard her, and turned to look at him.

'Midnight,' he said.

She looked at the clock. 9.16.

The road was following a narrow valley, and the sun dropped behind the hills, light flickering through the trees on the horizon. They would be past the treeline soon. Carla turned up the heating in the car and switched on the side lights.

Julia could still feel the presence of the power in her body. She sat in the back, watching the passing scenery. Everything seemed so sharp, so vibrant with colour. The paramo, the Kogi said, was the heart of the world, the abode of the great Mother. They said if one saw the reflected light of the sun in a lagoon from the paramo, one would die. Perhaps it was true.

Julia hadn't seen such wilderness since she had left South America. That had been a noisy landscape, rich and colourful; here, with the severe monochrome of conifers and unmarked grey sky above them, she sensed that if they stopped and listened, the only sound to reach them would be the occasional caw of a crow. There was an overawing mystery here, a presence in the shaded corridors between the trees, the ground carpeted with pine needles. 'What's going to happen when we meet him?' she said softly.

'I don't know,' William said at last. 'Are you scared?'

'No. You?'

'Not any more.'

'We're getting cold.'

'Do you want me to turn the heating up?' Carla asked. They both laughed.

'Cold to our emotions,' Julia explained. They were, she could sense it.

They tried Harry's number, but the line was dead. They had the telephone company check it out, and they were told the phone had been disconnected.

'How can we find him now?'

'Tulkina is a village – we'll find him.'

Julia could hardly believe it. She was so close. After four years of looking, she was on the author's doorstep. This was the air he was breathing, this the light he saw from his window.

'Look out!' William pointed, but Carla saw the moose too late. She jerked the wheel away from the animal but it sprang towards the car and they caught it a glancing blow on the rump. The car spun in the gravel, completing a ninety-degree turn until it came to rest, pointing towards the moose. Their harnesses had held them, and they were unhurt, but the animal was in pain. They watched it struggling to push its back legs up, but it kept collapsing. It was an old bull, bellowing into the sky, its long neck stretched straight out. They could see that its back legs were broken.

The engine was idling over, and Carla pressed the gas, but its rear wheels were in the ditch and spun without gripping the road. William reached for the ignition button and switched the engine off.

'We can't just leave it,' he said.

Carla was wide eyed, her hands gripping the steering wheel. 'What are we going to do?' she asked at last.

William got out but the women stayed behind the wheel, watching him as he approached the animal. Julia realised she had seen all this before. This was how her parents' book had begun: her mother had run over a sheep, Michael whom she was later to marry, coming to rescue her. She mouthed the three words which began the story – *imagine this scene*.

28 ∫

William and Julia and Carla are moving too fast – forgive me if I slow them down a bit, give them the obstacle of the moose to surmount. The story might peak too soon, and they might arrive on my doorstep before I'm ready for them. What readiness looks like, however, I don't know.

I *do* know that these last few days have been the closest to happiness I can remember. Unlike William and Julia, there are no obstacles in my way any more. Now that Harry has gone, I find myself committed. There is no longer any point holding onto the lip of the well (an image my subconscious threw up which I haven't yet shared: I am holding on by my fingertips to the jagged edges of a deep well. My imagination tells me that if I let go, dreadful things will happen. The sky will fall on my head. I will fall into the open mouth of a monster. That kind of stuff. My intellect tells me that, yes, this is an image my subconscious threw up, that abandoning control may not be so dangerous after all.)

While the kettle boils for coffee, I prise the lid off the can of paint. This will do just fine: curtains would just collect dust. If I paint the windows over, I'll have twenty-four hour shade. And nuclear reflectors thrown in for free.

I don't know whether to paint all the windows, or leave a row clear at the bottom. I debate the matter aloud, and then decide to go ahead and do it. What do I want to see outside for when I can always open a window? I put on my mask and paint the whole lot.

It seems to take all day. I work slowly, stroke by stroke whiting out the view. Sometimes I stop to rest, or just gaze out at the melting landscape. My eyes are playing tricks on me: the paint is like snow, like sky, like white bed sheets. I'm not aware of the gathering gloom until I'm on the last window. It's not evening – I have painted myself into a corner. I turn round to view my handiwork. The diffused white light makes the room into an elongated igloo. I paint in the remaining few panes, turning twilight to dusk.

The skin on my hands has become increasingly itchy, and I see that I have developed an allergic rash to the paint splashes. I rub them on my trousers, but it only makes them itch more. Without warning, my belly convulses and before I can take a step towards the bucket, I vomit. Nothing but a stream of yellow-brown liquid issues from within me, but my stomach continues to heave, three, four times, a hollow retching which hurts my throat.

My mouth is stinging with acid, so I fill the kettle with melt water to make some coffee. I wait a few minutes before I realise no sound is coming from the kettle. I bang the plug into place and shake the kettle, but it makes no difference. It's hard to see in the half light and I switch the lamp on. That, too, is broken.

'Ah.' I hear my voice in the gloaming as though it's somebody else. That's it, the generator has run dry.

I stand in the quiet, listing my supplies. No candles. No heat. No hot food. Two cans of rice pudding and a can opener. Luckily the typewriter is mechanical.

And then I realise. The elevator. I hadn't bothered to think what would happen when the gas ran out. Walking the length of the factory, I know that when I push the red button to activate the elevator, it won't work. I'm right, of course.

I feel my way along the wall to the fire escape and open the door. The light is blinding and I stand in the draught for a minute with my eyes shut. I can feel the twenty-five foot drop below me.

Opening my eyes, I estimate the distance from the doorway to the cast-iron stairs of the fire escape. It sways in the wind, but it never reaches closer than ten feet away.

So, this it is. Trapped in an igloo at the end of the world. Once I start, I can't stop – I slam the door shut and lean against it, laughing.

It's a shade darker inside my plastic tent, but I need no light to continue with my plait. I work for hours until my fingers are stiff and my eyes are stinging. The string is now a rope as thick as my wrist. I trace my fingers over its surface in the dark; plaits within plaits within plaits.

Just one more chapter to go, and that will be it. Somehow I have to deal with William and Julia and Carla, put them to rest if nothing else.

The rice pudding tastes better than I thought. The combination of milk and sugar will probably give me diarrhoea, but the honey bag was changed this morning, and anyway, I have let go the sides of the well.

I wander round in the gloom, eating straight from the can. The ache in my stomach eases after a while. One of those moments: being aware of standing on the surface of the planet, my head in space, one of the human poles below which everything else revolves. I am the hub of a turning wheel. It's so quiet that I find myself whispering. There is nothing, not even the sound of wind. This is the post nuclear winter my generation were all afraid of. The end of the world comes in silence, and in the silence you can hear voices on the wind. Can you? What would they say? I'm talking to myself.

Our generation knew our cleverness would be our undoing, but we thought the end would come quickly, apocalyptically. We were wrong. It was our children, born into the twenty-first century, who could truly see it was not a bullet to our heads that would kill us, but the seeping of poison into our bloodstreams. It is too late now. We have almost killed the Mother, just as the Kogi foresaw. We are killing her with our ignorance and ugliness, just as we killed the Kogi.

I use a wooden pole for a walking stick and wander round the factory, flicking the beam of a flashlight over the contents as though I am a burglar.

I come across what looks like a water stain on the wall. There is something familiar about the shape, and I study it closely. Suddenly, I realise what it is. I struggle out of my jacket and shirt and hold my right arm to the wall. The stain is the exact size and shape of the birthmark on my arm.

'Okay, God,' I say. 'What's going on? First I get the bone on the back of the head. Then every time I go into Harry's, the TV talks to me. Now this. Explain, please.'

I'm so dizzy I have to sit on the floor. My nausea is returning. 'And another thing.' It takes too much effort to speak, so I have to think my sentences instead. It's never occurred to me till now, but what is a twine factory doing in the Arctic circle? Hemp, or whatever they use to make rope, doesn't grow within a thousand miles of here, and why locate a factory in the middle of nowhere? Am I being invented just as surely as I am inventing William and Julia?

'Well?' I say. I wait for an answer, but I know one won't come.

One more chapter, and that's it. Things have been timed well – even with no heat, I can surely survive another twelve hours. I don't suppose it helps having painted the windows a reflective white. Now even sunlight can't do its job. But I'm pleased with the way the factory looks. I have created a perpetual dawn, enough light to see, but not so much to hurt my eyes.

It's a lot colder now the heating has gone off. When I dab my fingers against my face, the skin feels frozen and lifeless. I'm living inside a dead man's body.

I try typing with my gloves on, but I get a flurry of typos, so I cut the end off my gloves, exposing half an inch of fingertip. After a couple of minutes I can feel my skin burning with the cold of the keys and so I rest between sentences with my fingertips in my mouth.

The story so far: Julia and William and Carla are on their way to Tulkina. They have run over a moose, and are at this very moment arguing about what to do. They think they are real. They think I am real. They are still not sure about their families. *I'm* still not sure about their families.

Even if they could ask all their questions of me, how could I answer them? I don't know. Presumably the expectation is that, as their author, I should be the omniscient one. But it seems they have a partner in confusion.

Do their parents exist? What shall I say? Kate and Michael O'Brien, James Morrison and Connie – the fictional progenitors of the likewise fictional William and Julia, do any of them exist?

Clearly they don't walk and talk in the consensual world, but in *aluna*, in the world of ideas? I sometimes think of my characters as inadvertently squashed mosquitoes between the yellowing pages of my novels. Once upon a time, they buzzed around the air, but now they just show themselves as bloody spots on the page, memories of hot summer evenings.

If, in some sense, they *are* real, what would happen when creator (for if they have a creator, I am surely he) and creature come face to face? Are the Hindu pundits right? Would it be the end of the game of hide and seek, *atman* and *brahman* recognising each other with a whoop of joy and happily home for tea? Mother and child only separated by the illusion of sensory perception, and when our eyes open, two becomes one becomes all. Maybe all that is needed is a clarifying of vision.

I made the error of assuming there was some connection between *aluna* and virtuality. I sensed there was a parallel somewhere, but they have nothing to do with each other. *Aluna* is what some physicists laughingly call 'deep' reality, while the computer generated illusion is neither virtual nor reality. It is a hoax. No less than our physical senses. Ladies and gentlemen, we carry around our own face sucker without realising it.

Meanwhile, my dear creations are stuck in a ditch while a bloodied moose bellows into the sky. I feel sorry for them, hapless puppets that they are. The scene is just a pencil sketch at the moment. I could colour it in, spend a day or two on the details, working the illusion for all it is worth, but that would just be putting the moment off. And this is decision time.

The fingernails that peep through my gloves are leeched of blood and as pale as blanched almonds. Wrapping myself in the sleeping bag makes no difference. I can feel the chill right down to my bones. If I had the strength I would do some exercises. Instead I have to imagine running on the spot, flapping my arms in the air.

Why did I do this to them? They were an hour away from rescuing me, taking me back home. The truth is, I miss Carla. But though I want to go home, I still can't bring myself to manufacture the words to make it happen. It looks as though this manuscript is all that will remain – my suicide note.

I am so cold I can't stop shivering. I guess I'm slipping into hypothermia. Time to get some heat before my brain gives out on me. I find a metal waste-paper basket and punch holes in it with a screwdriver. Then I collect as much paper and scraps of wood and cardboard spools as I can. I ball a sheet of paper up, light it and drop it into the bin. Within a minute I have a little blaze going. I assumed the smoke alarm wouldn't work, but it must be battery-powered, for it starts its screeching. With a knife I scrape two small pellets from my rat-gnawed bar of hypoallergenic soap, and mould them into ear plugs. Once jammed into my ears, the screeching, though still audible, is bearable. I crouch over the brazier, hands almost in the flames, Ulysses, deaf to the sirens.

What to do with William and Julia and Carla? Alone on a deserted road, night – albeit a bright one – drawing in. I can have them phone for a tow truck, be rescued and continue their quest. How credible is that, considering how far they are from Inuvik? Or shall I have William be gored to death by an enraged moose? A certain satisfaction for me in that scenario; to tell the truth I still don't really like William. Julia could somehow return to England and her family, Carla to Vancouver, and the mystery of the author remain unsolved. That would avoid delving into the metaphysical complications of meeting me face to face. Another option is to have them somehow get the car out of the ditch by their own efforts (slipping and sliding, grazed knees, spinning wheels etc.) and then continue with their journey. Or perhaps they can be forced to spend the night in the car, the battery runs low and they freeze to death. I don't mind doing that to William and Julia but I can't bring myself to kill Carla. She's still my wife, after all.

Or I could just leave them, withdraw the word from them and leave the book unfinished to face the complaints of readers.

I put the last of the scrap paper into the fire. The heat uncurls the sheet on top and I see the first line I wrote on the typewriter: *To be or not to be, that is the qwsetion.*

Give me one good reason why I shouldn't leave William and Julia in *aluna*? One good reason why I shouldn't allow myself to be marooned and leave the rest of the world to its own devices?

I can hear Harry Homme's response to that: give me one good reason why you *should*. But Harry, that's not good enough.

I can feel the glue that keeps my feet to this planet unsticking by the moment. I wish the parrot was here, and we could talk it through.

'What are we going to do, Toto?'

'Fuck the bastards!'

I have a dream of coming home. When I was younger, the dream was tangible. It was a home of bricks and fireplaces, children, dogs. But something happened, for as soon as I had these things, it ceased to be a home any more, and was just a house. These children, taller and broader than me now, were rarely my sons. Mostly they were people I recognised no better than well-known television actors. Over the years as the yearning intensified, so the focus dissipated, until it was clear I was longing for something with no form. It made no difference what I tried: from alcohol to fame, nothing made the difference. Carla's patience was tested sometimes to breaking: I had everything a happy man should have. What was the problem? How could I explain that the home I was seeking was that of selflessness, my boundaries magically erased? I wanted to not exist. Not to kill myself, but to lose my individuality. *Samadhi*, I suppose it's called, the experience of unity. I call it home because it seems I had it when I was a child. I belonged, I was related. I tried to give William and Julia an echo of this experience, a sense of unity, being at home in the world, because the world *is* you. The back to your front. And in that single-pointedness nature becomes sacred, and the unfolding life is a sacrament.

William's question, my question: who am I? No surprise that this is why we are killing the Mother, why we find no home in the world – because we don't even guess the answer. We think we are particles, immune, autonomous, a bag of bones with an eighty-year lifetime. Perhaps if we allowed ourselves to be as confused as William, something might happen, but fear and greed are the nuclear force of the ego, and these are just too strong for fission.

The only thing left to burn is the manuscript. I tamp the pages into shape and sit with it on my lap as though it is a child. Would it be murder to burn my creation? Would it make any difference if William and Julia went up in smoke just so I could have a few moments of warmth? I flick through the pages, pausing to read the occasional sentence, and then select the top ten pages and drop them into the brazier. As I watch the paper curl, then brown, then pop into flames I have no sense of regret. It was all an illusion, masks and paint and costume all created by myself. I drop the pages wad by wad into the flames until there are none left.

I am about to add the blank paper to the blaze when I change my mind: I haven't finished with William and Julia yet. One more chapter and that will be it.

When the fire burns down to nothing, I coil my braided rope into a lasso and throw it over a metal beam above me. I am pleased with my handiwork. The rope is thick and strong, and after I use some of the soap to grease it, the noose slides easily. I take a look round the factory. Layers of brown smoke hang in the air, my plastic tent is spattered with streaks of bird shit. The alarm beeps to itself. Carla's unread letters are still pinned to the wall. A bit of a mess, I admit.

They saw a blue truck coming towards them from the direction of Tulkina. William stood in the middle of the road and flagged it down. The truck stopped in a cloud of dust and the driver got out. He was an Inuit, an old man with a lined face and a battered cowboy hat. He ignored William and went up to the moose. The animal had collapsed, its legs peddling the air. It seemed not to see Harry when he laid his hand between its antlers as though to feel its temperature. He turned to William.

'Get my gun from the cab.'

William did as he said. The man loaded the rifle and handed it back to William. 'You started it, you finish it.'

William looked back at the car. Julia was watching him, Carla had averted her gaze. He levelled the rifle until it was between the eyes of the animal, almost touching the wiry fur. Harry was making clucking noises to soothe the moose.

The barrel was cold against his skin and he wanted to loosen his grip. His finger closed on the trigger and the rifle leapt in his hands. The moose slumped, one leg twitching for a moment. Before the echo of the gun shot had reached them from the distant hills, it lay still.

Harry took the rifle from William and went back to the pickup. William stared at the animal. A trickle of blood ran between its open eyes, dripping from its snout onto the road. He had never seen a dead animal this close. Harry backed the truck up and William had to move out of the way. He watched Harry take a length of rope from the cab and then let down the tailgate. He looped the rope round its antlers.

'Give me a hand here.'

Together they dragged the carcass until it was half in the truck, then Harry climbed in and pulled while William pushed from underneath. It was warm and heavy and the stink of wet fur was in William's nostrils.

Carla watched them through the dusty windscreen, her hands tight on the steering wheel. The two men walked back to the camper. William's face was white. Carla put her window down, realising who Harry was.

'Where are you headed?' the man asked.

'You're Harry Homme, aren't you?'

He neither confirmed nor denied her statement. A bead of snot hung on the end of his nose and he wiped it with the sleeve of his jacket.

'We're going to Tulkina.'

'You'll be the only folks there.'

The disappointment was like a physical blow. 'Are we too late?'

'For what?'

'Isn't my husband still there?'

'The writer? I guess so.'

'In the string factory?'

The old man nodded almost imperceptibly.

Julia leant forward from the back seat. 'Can you tell us how to find him?'

'You'll find him.'

Julia recognised him now, the glint in his black eyes. Mama Francisco, Jarnier, Harry Homme, they all had the same look. The cold from the open window was tightening the skin on her face. She looked up at Harry, wanting to tell him the truth, but she couldn't get her mouth to work.

Harry threw the coiled rope to William. 'Let's get you out of this ditch.'

They hitched up the rope between them and towed the camper back onto the road without difficulty. The man untied the rope and tossed it into the back of his truck and then returned to the cab, disappearing from sight. The engine roared and the truck pulled away.

'Hey!' Carla scrambled to get the car started, but William laid his hand on hers.

'We can find him on our own.'

They watched the blue truck until it was out of sight. Then they turned round and drove into Tulkina, the midnight sky a pale ink wash above them.

So, what am I going to do – allow them to find me? Harry was a surprise, turning up like that. But he *has* gone, hasn't he? Even if I decide to go back, I've no way of doing so.

They were in the town within an hour and parked in the main street in front of the school house. They hadn't thought to buy warm clothes in Vancouver, so they wrapped themselves up as best they could before getting out of the car. William wanted to split up and take a street each, but Julia insisted they stay together. She was unnerved by the quiet of the place, the shuttered windows and silent streets.

They walked together to the end of the street, the two women linking arms.

'Listen,' William said, catching Julia's sleeve.

I stoke the fire, and drop the last of the paper into it. The smoke is making my eyes stream, and I can't get close enough to feel any of the heat. I check the rope, tugging on it and then letting it take my entire weight. The beam bows above my head, but it will be strong enough to hold my body for long enough.

I take the pole I use as a walking stick, and make a final tour of the factory. I linger at the travel poster. If that was a door, I *would* step through, but it's too late now.

I unpin the three letters from the wall. There is nothing to stop me reading them now, so I open the first:

> Darling,
> Jack told me where you are. I phoned the man at the store, but he said you didn't want to talk to me. Please come home. I love you.

> I love you, too.

At first Carla could hear nothing except her breath. And then it came to her gusting on the wind: the high-pitched beep of a smoke alarm. Like bloodhounds sniffing the air, the three of them followed the trail until they found themselves outside the white sugarcube factory. They knew they had found what they were looking for. The sound was coming from the second floor. They looked up. The windows had been painted in.

William saw the elevator and called them over. 'This must be the way up.' He pressed the button to call the elevator, but nothing happened. He tried opening and closing the trellis door, but it made no difference. 'It's dead.' He flicked a light switch. 'The power is off.'

They returned to the street and looked up at the windows. One of them was smashed, a burlap bag hung clumsily over the hole.

'Hello!' Julia called.

They waited, but the only sound was that of the smoke alarm. She searched her pockets for something to throw at the window, and then stooped to pick a handful of grit from the road. It rattled loudly against the window when she threw it, but still there was no response.

The second letter reads:

> Darling,
> Did you get my note? Please contact me. The network won't give me time to fly to find you. Don't be a bastard. Please.

The sound of an engine made them turn and look down the street. The blue pickup was coming towards them. They didn't move until it stopped and Harry got out.

'You'll need a ladder,' he said, indicating for them to join him at the back of the truck. He let down the tailgate and told William to jump inside. The legs of the moose had already stiffened and its eyes were glassy as though it were a stuffed trophy. William stepped over it and disentangled the extension ladder from the rest of the stuff, and together they got it onto the street. At first it didn't look as though it would be long enough to reach but, extended to its full length, the ladder rested just under the windowsill.

'Who's it to be?' the old man asked.

Carla gestured for one of them to go up. William and Julia exchanged glances and then both looked up at the window. The smoke alarm had stopped. Whatever had set it off wasn't a fire.

The third letter:

I don't know what to do. My heart is breaking. I can't bear the thought of never seeing you again. I don't care if you're infected. I don't care if I catch it. I just want to see you again. Please don't die alone.

I sit on the floor to think about this. She would sacrifice her life to be with me? Am I so stupid that I never saw this? I thought I was sparing Carla something, not denying her. I read the letter again through my tears.

But how can I get back to her? It's too late. Harry has gone. There is nobody for nearly two hundred miles. The halftrack is empty, there is no gasoline.

Julia told William to go up. The rungs were so cold they burnt his hands. He stopped half way up to look around and blow on his fingers. The ladder was bending in the middle, but Harry was standing on the bottom rung to hold it in place. A crow shuffled and then launched itself off a neighbouring roof. From here William could see the whole settlement. It was an oasis town, houses clustering together for warmth, holding the Arctic cold at bay.

William had never seen anything as beautiful. The midnight light was sharp and dramatic, the landscape seeming to vibrate around him, the colours shimmering. It was as though he could sense the minute vibration of every molecule. Everything was alive: the ladder, the buildings, the road signs. He felt light, as though the pull of gravity had suddenly lessened. He had never felt so alive.

William climbed the last few rungs and rapped on the window. The pane was opaque, painted white on the inside. He waited a few seconds and then knocked again. No reply. He was about to bring his elbow back to smash the glass when he heard the sound of movement from inside the factory. William watched the window open and

The window is sticking in its frame and I have to bang to free it. When I swing it open I almost expect someone to be there on the other side, William at the top of a ladder. I look down to the sidewalk, the patches of grass pushing through concrete, and then down the street. Nobody. The village is as quiet as it has always been. I remove my mask and take a deep breath. I can smell salt water on the air. A pair of seagulls swoop over something washed up on the shore, noisily squabbling over it.

My fingers are too cold to work properly and it takes me some minutes to untie the rope from the beam. I coil it into a lasso and then open the fire escape. The fire ladder is about ten feet away, the sun directly behind it. It takes me five throws before I manage to hook the end of it. The sun shines in my face as I pull the ladder towards me, so I shut my eyes. I secure the rope to the wall and with some difficulty climb down to street level.

I'm unsteady on my feet and I consider going back for my walking-stick, but the climb would be too difficult. I realise I only have one shoe on. My left sock is stretched into clown-like proportions. I guess my toes should be cold, but I can't feel them. I hobble to the end of the street, walking back the way I had come on the first day.

They have all gone now. Everybody. Just me and the seagulls and the polar bears. I like the quiet, and this is my home as much as anywhere, but I want to see Carla again. I want a miracle to happen.

And then I see it in front of me – the enormity. It has been there all along – just one more step and I'll be over the edge. I can resist it no more. I can feel myself falling. Falling into happiness. Head over heels I go, my thin old body swaying with the effort of staying upright. A pebble is under the arch of my bare foot, but I don't resist it any more. I let the ground take my weight, the sharp edge of the stone passing through pain into something else, something I can allow.

I look up and let the view flood into my eyes – the weather-beaten clapboards, the empty windows, the gravel-strewn road, all vibrating with happiness. I breathe as deep as I can, the cold air rattling my lungs. The sound in my ears is the sound of the sea.

There is a last letter from Carla in my back pocket. My fingers won't bend and I have to pull it out with the heels of my hands. I struggle to unfold it. It's a sheet of ComSat paper, but there is no typed message, just a handwritten scrawl in blue crayon. I have trouble focusing on it, and I have to squint to make out the words. My whole body is buzzing with joy. I realise it's from Harry. So he *can* write:

> I filled the engine. Im in Inuvik with Carla. William and Julia too. Well be glad if you join us.

The wind snatches the paper from my hand but I make no attempt to catch it. I watch it dancing away from me, head over heels, head over heels.